Praise for Ellie Alexander's *Meet Your Baker*

"Alexander weaves a tasty tale of deceit, family ties, delicious pastries, and murder against a backdrop of Shakespeare and Oregon aflame. *Meet Your Baker* starts off a promising new series."
—Edith Maxwell, author of *A Tine to Live,*
A Tine to Die on *Meet Your Baker*

"With its likable characters, tightly plotted storyline, and innovative culinary tips, *Meet Your Baker* is sure to satisfy both dedicated foodies and ardent mystery lovers alike." —Jessie Crockett, author of
Drizzled with Death on *Meet Your Baker*

"This debut culinary mystery is a light soufflé of a book (with recipes) that makes a perfect mix for fans of Jenna McKinley, Leslie Budewitz, or Jessica Beck." —*Library Journal*

"Marvelous . . . All the elements I love in a cozy mystery are there—a warm and inviting atmosphere, friendly and likable main characters, and a nasty murder mystery to solve . . . I highly recommend *Meet Your Baker* and look forward to reading the next book in this new series!"
—*Fresh Fiction*

"With plenty of quirky characters, a twisty, turny plot, and recipes to make your stomach growl, *Meet Your Baker* is a great start to an intriguing new series, but what sets this book apart and above other cozy mystery series is the locale. Ashland comes alive under Alexander's skilled hand. The picturesque town is _____ ribed in vivid terms, so that _____ book than just a backdrop t _____ _ader

"*Meet Your Baker* is t_____ xander, which will delight _____ hts."
_____ ight Owl

"A delecta _____ eshop mystery is a re_____ n the series, just as tas_____ ook Review

St. Martin's Paperbacks titles by Ellie Alexander

Meet Your Baker
A Batter of Life and Death

A Batter of Life and Death

Ellie Alexander

St. Martin's Paperbacks

This is a work of fiction. All of the characters, organizations, and events portrayed in this novel are either products of the author's imagination or are used fictitiously.

A BATTER OF LIFE AND DEATH

Copyright © 2015 by Kate Dyer-Seeley.
Excerpt from *On Thin Icing* copyright © 2015 by Kate Dyer-Seeley.

For information address St. Martin's Press, 175 Fifth Avenue, New York, NY 10010.

ISBN: 978-1-250-05424-1

Printed in the United States of America

St. Martin's Paperbacks edition / July 2015

St. Martin's Paperbacks are published by St. Martin's Press, 175 Fifth Avenue, New York, NY 10010.

10 9 8 7 6 5 4 3 2 1

Torte may not be a real place, but it lives in my head as a happy mash-up of childhood memories in our family kitchen. This book is dedicated to my parents. To my dad, who quoted Shakespeare while creating magnificent layered tortes, many thanks for your red editing pen and drool-worthy recipes. To my mom, who ignited my passion for reading and baking, everything I touch contains a trace of you.

Acknowledgments

I write in isolation. It's only with the help of these incredible people that my mangled thoughts become a book. To my first set of eyes, Erin, Beth, Judy, Erica, Elaine, and Arnie. To my editor, Hannah, who makes my work so much stronger and is always up for talking pastry. To the marketing team of Shailyn and Cara who help get the book in readers' hands. To Erika my event planner who knows how to throw a killer party. To my agent, John, "the king of the cozy." To my family, who cheer me on, taste endless recipes (good and bad) and who make Torte come to life every day, my deepest thanks.

Chapter One

They say that time heals a broken heart. I've noticed that no one mentions exactly how *much* time it takes, though. A week? A month? A year? Having a solid number might have made me feel better, since my heart was mending slowly.

While I waited for the heartache to subside, I busied myself with building a new life in my sweet hometown of Ashland, Oregon. Never would I have imagined that I'd be saying that, when I left the ship and my husband last summer. Returning to Ashland was supposed to be a temporary stop until I figured out what I was going to do next.

Mom had advised me to take things slow. "One day at a time, Jules. You don't need to figure everything out this minute."

She was right. Her words stuck, and so did I.

The summer breezed by in a whirlwind of activity. Ashland is home to the world-famous Oregon Shakespeare Festival and a playground for outdoor enthusiasts with sunny mountains and rivers. During the summer months, our little town bursts at the seams with tourists, actors, playwrights, backpackers, and whitewater guides. Torte, our family bakeshop, sits right in the middle of downtown.

Mom's been serving up a selection of sweet and savory pastries with a side of love for nearly three decades. She and my dad purchased the cheery space that houses the bakery when I was a kid. Most of my early memories are of sitting on a bar stool next to the butcher-block island while the two of them kneaded bread dough and chatted with customers. Dad would quote Shakespeare sonnets and engage out-of-town visitors in lively discussions about OSF's latest plays. Mom would press tart crust into tins and act as a sounding board for locals who came to the shop for more than just a warm cup of coffee.

Their love affair wasn't fancy. It was quiet and easy. Maybe that was part of my problem. I wanted what they had. The other part of my problem could have been that my name set me up to be a romantic. Really, Juliet Montague Capshaw? I didn't have a chance. Ill-fated romance is literally my namesake.

My parents thought naming their only child after one of literature's greatest heroines would ensure a life of passion. I'm not sure they thought it all the way through, though.

When I left for culinary school after Dad died, I shortened my name to Jules. It fits. I'm pretty laid-back and casual for the most part. The one exception is in the kitchen. There I run a tight ship. It's a good thing because after being home for a few weeks I realized that Torte needed me as much as I needed it. Mom's a genius in the kitchen and when it comes to caring for our customers, but running the bakeshop on her own had really taken its toll. I was glad to be able to help lighten her load.

Torte needed updating and a serious influx of cash. The steady throng of tourists in and out the front door this summer had helped. We'd been so slammed for the last few months that I was actually looking forward to the off-season so that we could spend some time mapping out a long-term plan for Torte's future.

That's what we'll focus on today, I thought as I laced up my tennis shoes and grabbed a jacket off the hook hanging by my front door. The October sun greeted me as I headed down the stairs from my apartment and out onto the main square. Downtown Ashland is like a little village with a collection of shops, restaurants, and the famed OSF theater complex an easy walk up the hill. Lithia Park, the jewel of town, flanks one end of the downtown. Its meandering pathways, ancient trees, and natural streams make it one of my favorite places on the planet, which is saying a lot. A decade of working on a cruise ship allowed me to visit ports of call all over the world. Other places might be more exotic or boast a more happening night life scene, but Ashland's sophisticated charm and quaint beauty was unparalleled.

I smiled and waved as I passed Elevation's front door. My apartment is above the outdoor store and I've gotten to know the owners. They keep promising to take me climbing once things slow down. From the look of the store this morning, climbing would have to wait. A group of tourists were bunched near the front of the store, waiting for a turn on the indoor climbing wall.

Sulfur fountains bubbled in the square. Visitors drink the fizzy mineral water, pumped in from Lithia Springs, for good health and good luck. I stopped and watched as a teenager, eager to impress two young girls, drank a mouthful of the water and then quickly proceeded to spit it out all over himself. It's definitely an acquired taste.

I continued on toward Torte. Its bright red and teal awning swayed in the slight midday breeze. Flower boxes with clematis cascading down the side hung below the windows. I greeted customers enjoying their pastries at the bistro tables on the sidewalk, and checked to make sure their coffee was fresh before heading inside.

Usually I arrive at the bakeshop much, much earlier than

this, but last night I had stayed late to have dinner with a producer who was in town from California. Mom told me to sleep in. Things were starting to slow down as we eased into the off-season.

I felt surprisingly excited to share my news from last night's dinner with everyone. As I swung open the front door, the familiar smell of rising yeast and espresso made me pause and take in a deep breath. Torte is the kind of place that lifts your mood. The space is inviting, with corrugated metal siding, royal teal and red accent colors, and concrete floors. A giant chalkboard menu with rotating daily specials fills the far wall. Each table and the booths along the windows had been polished and held bright fall bouquets. A preschooler noshed on a cookie the size of his head while he scribbled on the bottom of the chalkboard—a space Mom reserves exclusively for our youngest customers. In the far corner, a writer tapped on her laptop while downing a latte. Tourists ogled the glass pastry cases at the front counter.

Yep, this is the place for me, I thought as I snagged an apron with our Torte logo from the wall and wrapped it around my waist.

I passed the chalkboard on my way to the open kitchen in the back. It read, "They Are All but Stomachs, and We Are All but Food."

"Nice quote, Mom." I walked up behind her and pinched her on the waist.

She jumped, sending flour flying in the air. "Jules. You startled me."

"You need hearing aids, Mom."

"I'm much too young for hearing aids, honey." She brushed flour from her apron and studied me. "You look refreshed. How was the dinner?"

I glanced toward the front of the shop where Andy, our

resident coffee geek and college student, stood at the espresso machine, pulling shots. His boyish good looks and easygoing attitude charmed a customer waiting for her drinks. Quite an impressive feat. I've found that people tend to be chatty and polite *after* they've consumed a cup of our delicious brew, but Andy has mastered the art of coffee talk. He's also mastered coffee art. I watched as he poured the shot into a mug and designed a foam leaf on top.

Sterling, our newest employee, manned the cash register and pastry case. Mom and I sort of adopted him earlier this summer. He'd showed up in Ashland the same time I did, and while our paths were different, we were kindred spirits in our nomadic lifestyles and search for home. Sterling, like Andy, had a natural rapport with customers—although his approach couldn't be more different.

Andy typically talks sports with customers, and likes to get their input on his latest coffee creations. He keeps a spiral-bound notebook under the counter and whips it out whenever he has time to mix a new drink. His signature concoctions have become legendary around town and with tourists, who keep coming back to Torte for more. Lately, he'd been experimenting with fall flavors—amaretto, caramel, and an organic pumpkin pie latte made with real pumpkin purée.

Sterling's dark hair, tattoos, and startlingly blue eyes tend to captivate our customers, especially the female ones. He has just the right balance of an edge with a kind heart. The girls swoon over his sultry looks, but it's a wasted effort. He only has eyes for Stephanie, the somewhat sullen, alternative college student who's been apprenticing under Mom and me for the past couple months.

Stephanie used to work the counter, but it turned out that customer service wasn't exactly her strong suit. I've been pleasantly surprised at the progress she's making in the kitchen. She has innate skill and "the touch," as Mom likes to say, when it comes to pastry. If I could only soften her up a little, it would make things so much easier.

Mom flicked me with a dish towel. "Jules, you with me? How was dinner?"

I returned my attention to her. "Sorry. It was good. Really good. I want to tell everyone about it, though. How about if we try to call a team meeting once this mid-morning rush dies down?"

Mom brushed a tray of pies with an egg wash and sprinkled the crusts with crystalized sugar. "You want to throw these in the oven?"

I took the tray of pies and opened the oven door. We used to have two industrial ovens, but one had been on the fritz since July. We'd been getting by with one, but Mom and I were pinching pennies to upgrade. If we were going to take Torte to the next level, it was going to cost a chunk of cash.

Autumn aromas permeated the bakeshop. Mom chopped apples and pears for individual fruit crisps that we'd serve warm in ramekins with a scoop of vanilla ice cream. Stephanie mixed snickerdoodle cookie dough.

"Hey, be sure to keep your hair tied back," I cautioned as she twisted off the beater. "You don't want to get hair in that dough."

She nodded and readjusted the black headband that secured her ebony hair streaked with purple. "Do you wanna taste this before I scoop it?"

I have a strict rule that everything must be tasted before it gets baked. The same rule applies after baking, too, but it's much easier to taste the product before it goes in the oven. I took a pinch of Stephanie's cookie batter and popped it in my mouth. "Needs just a little more cream of tartar."

Stephanie reached for the leavening agent. "Like what— a teaspoon?"

"Yeah, probably about that. I usually base it on flavor. Did you taste it?" I motioned toward the metal mixing bowl.

She shook her head.

"Try it. It's too sweet. The cream of tartar will give it a nice bite."

Stephanie followed my instructions and then began placing round balls of cookie dough onto trays with an ice-cream scoop.

I pulled my hair back into a ponytail, catching my reflection in the window. I've always worn it long, but I keep thinking maybe I'll do something drastic, like chop it all off into a cute bob or something—a fresh start. Then I look in the mirror. I'm not sure short hair would work with my angled jawline and long neck. When I was growing up I used to think I looked like a giraffe. Mom promised me that being graced with a lean frame and ash-blond hair was a blessing, but sometimes it felt more like a curse.

"I'll start on a soup," I said, grabbing a handful of vegetables from a cardboard box on the counter. We get local produce delivered from nearby farms every morning. With the return of cool crisp mornings and the changing leaves outside, customers have been eager for soup and fresh bread at lunchtime.

Today I opted for a butternut squash and apple purée that I'd serve with a splash of olive oil and crème fraîche. I diced onions and sautéed them in butter. The smell momentarily overpowered the scent of baking pies and bread. Despite my late night, I quickly found my rhythm. The kitchen always energizes me somehow.

A little after eleven, things began to quiet down in the front. Andy restocked his espresso and Sterling wiped down the tables. In the summer, we rarely get any sort of lull, but now that the season was winding down things tended to ease before lunch.

I finished my soup and left it to simmer on the stove.

"Can everyone come back here for a second? I've got some news to share."

As the team gathered, I noticed that Stephanie stood on the opposite side of the island from Sterling. I couldn't figure out what was going on between those two. It was evident from the way I'd catch them glancing at each other when they thought that no one was looking, that they had a mutual attraction. I wondered if they were trying to conceal their attraction, or if they'd had a fight.

"Stop stalling, young lady." Mom interrupted my thought. "Tell us what happened last night." The laugh lines at the corners of her eyes and lips creased as she looked at me with anticipation.

Andy balanced four mugs brimming with creamy coffee in his hands.

"Well." I paused for effect.

She bumped my hip and pointed at Andy. "Don't let her have one of those until she spills the beans about last night."

"Good one, Mrs. C." Andy passed out samples to everyone except me. "Try these, you guys. It's a pumpkin-cream latte. Tell me if it's too much. I tried to go real easy on the sugar."

The coffee smelled divine, as usual, but even more compelling was its color. The combination of milk, espresso, and pumpkin gave it a warm amber color. I tried to reach for a mug, but Mom held out her hand to stop me.

"I said talk, young lady. It's not every day we have a major television producer on our doorstep."

"Okay, okay. Just let me have one sip and then I'll dish." She handed me the mug.

I took a sip of Andy's invention. It tasted even better than it looked. The spice mixed with the milky espresso paired nicely and the pumpkin purée gave it an interesting texture.

Mom tapped her fingernails on the butcher block. "Juliet."

"Yes, I know." I rested my mug on the island. "This is great, Andy. Add it to the menu."

Mom cleared her throat.

"As you all know, I met with Philip Higgins, a producer for the Pastry Channel, last night. They want to film the show *Take the Cake* here in Ashland. Have any of you guys seen it?"

Stephanie twisted a strand of purple hair around her finger. "That's the one where pastry chefs compete against each other, right?"

Sterling looked surprised. "You watch the Pastry Channel?"

She shrugged. "Research."

Impressive. Stephanie acted aloof most of the time. She must be taking her apprenticeship seriously if she was watching the Pastry Channel in her free time.

"Stephanie's right." I took another sip of the pumpkin-cream latte. "According to Philip, *Take the Cake* is one of the network's top shows. Five pastry chefs from all over the country will be competing against each other. The winner takes home twenty-five thousand dollars and a contract for their own show. I guess it's a pretty big deal."

"Why are they coming to Ashland?" Andy asked. He'd obviously had his fair share of summer sun. His cheeks had erupted with freckles and matched the color of the pumpkin coffee.

"Good question. I asked Philip the same thing. He said this is the third season of the show. They filmed the first season in New York and last year in Austin, Texas. His goal is to rotate it all around the country."

"How did we make the list?" Mom asked.

"Philip is friends with Lance. I guess they worked together in the theater years ago, before Lance became the artistic director for OSF. Philip is planning to feature the theater complex and actors in the show. He thinks that the richness of Shakespeare and OSF's stages will add a layer of drama to the show. In fact, they're planning to film the entire show at the Black Swan Theater."

"Cool." Andy elbowed Sterling. "Maybe we'll get a shot at being on TV."

I warmed my hands on the mug. "Actually, that's part of my news. They also want to use Torte."

Mom let out a little yelp of delight and clapped her hands together. "They want to film here?"

"Don't get too excited," I cautioned. "They want to *pay* us to use Torte's kitchen for one of the contestants. They might film some little clips of the contestant prepping here, but it's not like they'll film the whole show here or anything like that."

"It doesn't matter. What great exposure for the shop! And they want to pay us?" Mom's cheeks turned pink with excitement.

"Yeah. Like a couple thousand bucks."

Mom raced around the island and threw her arms around me. "Good work. You know what this means? One step closer to new ovens!"

I didn't want to burst her bubble. New ovens were still a bit out of reach for us, but a payment from the Pastry Channel, especially during our slow season, would definitely put us closer.

"This is the best news all week!" Mom beamed. "When do they come?"

"Two weeks." I pointed at Andy and Sterling. "We're going to need to do some rearranging before they arrive. Things are going to get tight. Philip plans to have the competitors using our space after hours for the most part, but depending on their filming schedule we might have 'guests' in the kitchen during regular hours."

Mom straightened her apron. "That should be fine.

Things are already slowing down, and by November they'll be dead."

"That's pretty much what I said to Philip. He's going to be using the kitchen at the Merry Windsor and OSF too."

"Richard Lord will eat that up." Andy rolled his eyes.

Richard Lord, owner of the Merry Windsor Inn across the plaza from Torte, is the town's self-proclaimed king. The Merry Windsor lacks quality in their offerings both in food and customer service, but that hasn't stopped Richard from touting his newly remodeled restaurant and coffee counter as the "Best Shakespearean Pastry Palace in Town." That's literally what the sign hanging on his forest-green awning says. He might fool out-of-towners with his marketing gimmicks, but locals know that Torte is the *only* bakeshop in town where they can find authentic hand-crafted pastries.

"Don't worry about Richard," I said to Andy. "We have bigger and better things to concentrate on."

Never could I have imagined that bigger things were indeed coming, and most of them weren't better.

Chapter Two

The next two weeks passed quickly, despite the fact that downtown Ashland looked like a ghost town just in time for Halloween. OSF "goes dark" as they say in the theater business the first weekend in November, which means our little village does too. Things pick up a bit when the ski runs open on Mount Ashland, but otherwise Main Street would be quiet until February, when the actors in the company return to the stage.

News that the Pastry Channel production crew was arriving had locals buzzing with excitement. Not only would our little town gain national recognition, but the production crew and contestants would spend money in our shops and restaurants. *Take the Cake* was exactly what Ashland needed.

I reminded Andy, Sterling, and Stephanie as much while we put the finishing touches on Torte's quick revamp.

Stephanie climbed down from a ladder and wiped paint from her fingers. "What do you think?" she asked me as she stepped back to admire her work.

I studied Stephanie's design. She'd suggested that we stencil Torte's logo on the kitchen wall. That way when viewers watched at home, Torte would be prominently displayed. Since she'd actually watched every episode of *Take the Cake,* I gladly welcomed her input.

"It's perfect." I said to Stephanie. Then I turned and took in all of our hard work. "Everything looks great, guys." We'd managed to rotate the island in order to make room for a temporary cutting block on casters that would serve as a workspace for the contestant who would be baking with us for the next few weeks. Sterling had reorganized the hooks on the far wall to make room for the contestant's utensils and pot holders. The ovens and walk-in fridge were stationary, but Andy had cleared a section in the fridge so that our guest chef could have a reserved spot.

Things were definitely going to be tight, but I was used to working in cramped quarters. After I'd spent ten years in a cruise-ship kitchen, Torte seemed expansive, even with our makeshift remodel. At least we didn't have to stock extra supplies this time of year.

"I think this is going to work." I frowned. "It better work."

"It'll work, boss." Andy elbowed Sterling in the rib. "If it doesn't, blame him, though."

"Right." I laughed as Sterling captured Andy in a headlock and rubbed his red hair, which had naturally lightened in the sun over the summer. "Philip, the contestants, and film crew should be here soon." I glanced at the clock on the far wall. "Sterling, once you release Andy, will you go change the sign on the front door to CLOSED?"

Sterling released Andy from his grasp. "On it."

"Stephanie, can you help arrange the pastries? Andy, you can start prepping coffees, okay? I want everyone to feel welcome when they arrive."

As they finished setting up the bakeshop for the arrival of our special guests, I took one last look over the contract that Mom and I had signed with the Pastry Channel. Everything seemed straightforward, but I hoped I wasn't missing something important.

I *was* missing Mom. She and the Professor, as we call him, were on a wine-tasting tour of the Willamette Valley. The Professor's real name is Doug, but he looks a lot like a professor with his tweed jackets and wire-framed glasses. He's the town's official chief of police and our unofficial Shakespeare aficionado. Mom and the Professor have a budding romance. When she told me he was taking her on three-day tour of wine country, I wondered if things were starting to get serious.

She deserves happiness—and a break—more than anyone I know. Until I'd returned to Ashland, she'd been managing Torte by herself for nearly two decades. Normally, running the busy bakeshop without her for a few days wouldn't be a problem, but I had to admit that managing the details of a production contract had me a little nervous. I knew baking and how to run a kitchen, but when it came to television, I was clueless. I didn't even own a TV.

Part of me wondered if the timing of her getaway was intentional. She'd been encouraging me to take a more active role in the shop, which I had. I took over doing the books, and mapping out a plan for Torte's expansion, but with Mom gone the responsibility of prepping the bakeshop to look good on TV fell to me.

I hope we're ready, I thought as I flipped through the paperwork one last time. Philip had sent over the contestant bios and an outline of the schedule. Everything seemed self-explanatory, at least to my untrained eyes.

We'd be hosting Chef Marco from New York. I was familiar with the name. Chef Marco owned two high-end patisseries in Manhattan where he worked as executive chef. The waiting list to get into one of his eateries was months long, thanks in part to the fact that he was a pastry chef to the stars. Hollywood celebs and Broadway stars graced magazine covers as they walked the red carpet in front of his restaurants to nosh on delicate sweets. His client list read like a who's who of Hollywood.

The list of requirements Marco sent over for his work-station was the size of a small book. I knew we couldn't accommodate most of his requests due to space, so I'd just have to keep my fingers crossed that the chef would be okay with only getting a chunk of our kitchen.

Philip would be camping out at the Black Swan Theater along with Elliot Cool, the host of the show, and the rest of the production crew. The other contestants were being put up in various commercial kitchens around town. I pitied whoever was stuck with Richard Lord.

My stomach fluttered with nerves and excitement as the bell on Torte's front door jingled. "Showtime," I called to Andy, Stephanie, and Sterling. "Tighten your aprons, everyone."

Sterling welcomed everyone inside as Stephanie greeted them with a tray of pastries and a shy smile. Andy offered carafes of coffee.

I smoothed my hair and hurried to the front.

"Jules." Philip greeted me with a kiss on both cheeks. His graying scruff scratched my face. "Lovely to see you again. We were just discussing on the drive over from the airport what a charming, charming little town you have here."

I smiled and motioned for everyone to take a seat. "The space is all yours for the afternoon. Take as long as you need. Andy, our head barista, will be happy to make any-one a specialty coffee, and Stephanie is going to bring around some snacks. Help yourself to anything, and wel-come to Ashland."

Philip typed with both his thumbs on his smartphone. Without looking up he mumbled, "What's that?" He wore expensive jeans and a tight purple T-shirt with a black sports jacket over it.

When I'd had dinner with him to discuss the idea of using Torte, his phone had been like an extra person at the table with us. Most of our conversation that night involved me repeating details, because he was only half paying attention. We have a strict policy at Torte that cell phones get stored in the office during working hours. Mom built the business by really listening to our clients. One of her biggest pet peeves is when tourists don't even bothering looking up from their phones when placing an order. I had a feeling that Philip was going to test her patience.

I repeated my welcome to Philip.

He looked up from his phone, turned and clapped a portly man with a white chef's coat on the back. The chef clutched a notebook under his arm. "What did I tell you, Marco, isn't she lovely? This is Jules Capshaw, owner of Torte. You'll be working here with her and her mother, Helen."

I could feel my cheeks warm. "Please make yourself at home. We'll try to stay out of your way. Just holler if you need anything."

Philip grabbed my arm. "Actually, I'm hoping you can join us. We've had a slight change of plans, and I have a proposition for you."

A proposition? I didn't like the sound of that. Philip's demanding personality put me on guard.

Stephanie circulated with a tray of sweet and savory offerings. Philip picked an almond croissant from the tray, broke it in half and took a bite. "Perfection. Absolute perfection." He handed Marco the other half. "Try this, chef. I think she'll do quite nicely."

Marco's rounded cheeks didn't give any hint of whether he enjoyed the croissant as he slowly chewed it. Philip waited with anticipation.

What was going on? What would I do quite nicely on?

After Marco finally swallowed, he appraised me. I had to stifle a little laugh because the rotund chef stood about shoulder high to me. His stern, scrunched face was a sign that he was trying to intimidate me, but it was difficult to feel fear when the Pillsbury Dough Boy was scowling at me.

He shrugged. "It is okay. Just okay." He tapped a sausage-sized finger to his lips and stared me down. "She'll do."

Philip clapped him on the back again. "Yes. She's perfect."

Marco grabbed a pastry and waddled over to a table.

Scrolling on his phone with one thumb, Philip wrapped his free arm around my shoulder and escorted me to a table. He smelled like expensive aftershave. I'd peg him to be about Mom's age, maybe mid-fifties. Unlike Mom, who was aging naturally, allowing her chestnut-brown hair to streak with gray, Philip definitely fit the part of a Hollywood television producer. The skin around his eyes had been stretched and smoothed. His entire face looked tight and slightly shiny. It reminded me of the Saran Wrap we stretch over cookie dough while it chills.

He placed his phone on the table. "Jules, this is your lucky day."

I raised an eyebrow. "How so?" I'd met plenty of charmers like Philip during my time on the ship and growing up in a community centered around the stage. It was going to take more than a dazzling smile for me to trust his motives. A warning voice sounded in my head. Proceed with caution, Jules.

His phone buzzed. He reached down to silence it. "I'll let that go. You, my dear, are my top priority at the moment."

I could feel my muscles tense. Whenever people are overtly complimentary I get suspicious.

"We had a last-minute scheduling glitch," Philip said, with his hand covering his phone. I wondered if this was to stop himself from looking at it. "One of our *Take the Cake* contestants had to drop out. I believe you know him—Jed Cellars."

Jed Cellars was the head pastry chef at the Ashlander, the nicest hotel in town. However, it was currently operating without anyone in its dining room. Not because of the dwindling tourists, but because they'd had a huge kitchen fire last week, and the restaurant was currently shut down.

"Of course I know Jed."

"Then you heard about the fire?"

I nodded.

"We need someone to take his place. He's too involved in getting his kitchen up and running again."

I felt terrible for Jed. Recovering from a total kitchen demolition was no small task.

Phillip continued. "This is a boutique show, and I need a boutique chef like you. We're not a major production like some of the other junk the network likes to put out."

"A boutique chef?" I raised my brow. "I'm not sure what that means."

He removed his hand from his phone and began gesturing as he spoke. "The network likes to put on these competitions with glorified home bakers as the contestants. You know, a 'chef' who owns a drive-through coffee shop. *Please.*" He rolled his eyes.

"They let twelve, maybe twenty people compete. Most of them can't even boil water. *Take the Cake* is filmed on location, in a stunning town, with only the crème de la crème of pastry chefs. It's an expensive production, which means we handpick five of the best chefs in the country. Each week one person will get voted out by the judges, until we come to the final episode where we'll crown a new winner."

"Okay." I'm sure I sounded skeptical.

Philip didn't seem to notice. He studied me. "How tall are you?"

"Five eight. Why?"

He knocked on the table. "That's what I thought." Sneaking a look at his phone, he shook his head and turned it upside down. "Jules, has anyone ever told you that you have the look for television?"

"No." I wrinkled my nose. Wow, he was really laying it on thick.

"Oh, but you do." He reached over and turned my face to the side. "Those cheekbones are to die for. Do you know how many actresses would kill for your bone structure?"

I stepped away from him, and shook my head. Praising my appearance wasn't going to help his cause, nor was invading my personal space. I wished he would just get to his pitch, and stop trying to butter me up.

Philip stared at my hair. "Is that color natural? It's so blond."

I nodded. *Where is this going?*

"I can see that you're unsure. Hear me out." He steadied his gaze on me. "I want *you,* Juliet Capshaw, to be a contestant on the show. It's perfect. In the biz we call it a synchronistic opportunity. This was meant to be. You'll win viewers over the moment they see you, and you can bake!" Philip practically bounced in his seat. "Plus there's a twenty-five-thousand-dollar prize and major network contract for the winner—we're talking your own show, cookbooks, magazines, and appearances on morning talk shows. You could be a real star, Jules."

"Uh, let's slow down here. TV's not really my thing."

His phone buzzed again. "Listen, I have to take this call. You wait right here. But you should know that I'm used to getting my way and *you* are going to be on this show."

I tried to protest, but he waved me off and hurried outside to take his phone call. Synchronistic opportunity.

That sounded like Hollywood jargon to me. Having sailed all over the world on the cruise ship, I'd learned that the word "opportunity" actually gets its roots from the sea. It's derived from the phrase "Ob Portu" which Carlos, my currently estranged husband, told me means waiting for the tide. A ship can't leave port at low tide, so in days past sailors would wait for the tide to change by hauling cargo on board. Once the tide came in, they would set sail.

In some ways that's what I'd been doing in Ashland—waiting for the tide to change, for the sea to rise and send me in a new direction. Was this my opportunity? I'd never had visions of becoming a television star, but twenty-five thousand dollars was a lot of cash. The prize money could help us take Torte to the next level. As I waited for Philip to return, I tried to imagine myself on TV. How would I come across? Stiff? Too serious? On the other hand, I absolutely love baking. The idea of sharing that love through the airwaves with viewers all over the country sent a shiver of excitement up my spine. Maybe this was my "synchronistic opportunity" after all. If I didn't jump on board now, the ship might sail without me.

Chapter Three

When Philip returned, he was followed in by Richard Lord and Lance, OSF's artistic director. The contrast between the two of them was striking. Richard looked like he'd personally sampled every pastry in town. His orange plaid golf pants stretched over his round belly, reminding me of the pumpkin from Andy's latte. If Richard was a pumpkin, then Lance was the vine. He moved like a cat with his long, thin frame.

Lance joined me at a table and greeted me with air kisses. "Darling, Philip just told me the great news." He gushed. "Our little starlet is going to be on TV."

"I haven't said yes yet, Lance." I poured him a cup of coffee. Of course Lance was *in the know*. In addition to directing the vision of OSF and its large company of actors, Lance served as the resident village gossip.

"Darling, but of course you will." He darted his eyes in Richard's direction. "Just think if you don't take this, Philip will be forced to scrape the bottom of the mixing bowl, so to speak, and ask someone like Richard Lord."

"Good point." I grinned. "Twist my arm. I'll do it."

Lance clapped his hands together. "That's our girl. You'll love Philip. He and I go way, way back."

Richard lumbered over, and without asking, he pulled out a chair, intentionally scraping it on the floor. "What are you two conspiring about?"

"Us? Nothing. Richard, you're so paranoid." Lance rubbed his goatee and winked.

Richard gave him a dirty look. "Hardly. You two are probably trying to work me out of this deal."

"What deal?" I asked.

"This television show deal."

"You're going to be on the show too?" If Richard was a contestant, too, forget opportunity, I was out.

"What are you talking about, Juliet?"

"*Take the Cake.* Are you going to be a contestant?"

"No, but the show's going to pay me to use our newly renovated kitchen, and I don't want the two of you scheming to work me out of the deal."

"Us?" Lance batted his eyes and fanned his hand in front of his face. "Richard, I'm injured. How could you think that Jules and I would do something like that?"

Richard scowled. "Don't put on your theater drama with me."

Lance smiled broadly at Richard and muttered under his breath to me. "Why didn't we think of trying to cut Richard out?"

I kicked him under the table. Philip called us to attention, before Richard could complain any more.

"Welcome, welcome, everyone." Philip's phone was still in his hand. "For those of you who are joining us from Ashland, I want to tell you what an adorably charming little town you have here. Our viewers are going to fall in love with it.

"If I could have our contestants stand, I'd like to introduce you all."

Four people stood, including Chef Marco. Philip took a moment to introduce each of them. He started with Marco.

"I'm sure you're all familiar with the celebrity chef. We're thrilled that he's signed on to do this year's show."

Marco gave a little bow as Philip went through a lengthy list of his accolades. I noticed Marco decline Andy's offer of coffee. He kept one pudgy hand on his notebook and glared at Andy like he was trying to steal it or something.

Andy refilled mugs around the room as Philip spoke. After he'd refreshed everyone's drink he stopped at my table and knelt down.

"Hey, boss, Chef Marco is asking for something stronger. What do you want me to do?"

"Stronger—as in a drink?"

"Yeah, I think so."

I glanced at the clock on the wall—it read 2 P.M. I guess it was happy hour somewhere, as the saying goes. "You could open a bottle of that Oregon pinot in the back. Do you know how, or should I come do it?"

"Sterling knows how."

"You might as well offer everyone else wine too."

Andy got to his feet, saluted me, and returned to the counter.

Philip continued to tout Chef Marco's experience. He spent an inordinate amount of time name-dropping all the celebrities who were fans.

"Linda, give us a little wave, please," Philip said to a woman sitting in a booth by the window. She looked to be about his age and wore a bright pink bedazzled suit jacket and skirt with matching heels and a jeweled scarf, an outfit that was distinctly not Ashland. We're pretty laid-back in this corner of the world. People tend to wear casual clothing, geared for the outdoors. Hiking trails start in Lithia Park and wind up into the foothills, making it easy to take off for a quick midday hike. The other trend around town is bohemian chic. Since this is a community of artists, people's wardrobes often end up reflecting their work.

"Linda Belle is the owner of Luscious Linda's. She's joining us from Georgia and I'm sure you'll all enjoy her Southern confections."

Linda waved with her fingers. "Hi, y'all. I'm just thrilled to be here with y'all in Or-y-gone."

She butchered pronouncing "Oregon" the way most people from other states do—it's *"gun,"* not "gone."

Philip next introduced Nina Perry, a vegan chef from Los Angeles. She was probably close to my age and looked like she could easily mix in with the hippie crowd here in Ashland. She wore her hair in a long braid down her back and a flowing skirt and sandals.

"Nina's the owner of Garden of Vegan, one of my favorite shops in L.A. She's the first vegan chef we've had on the show and I'm excited for her to show you the magic she can do without using butter."

The last contestant, Sebastian Le Goude, scowled as Philip introduced him. He wore black from head to toe. A long unlit cigarette hung from the corner of his mouth.

"Sebastian is head pastry chef at Nourriture, a French bakery in Portland, Oregon. I'm sure many of you have already heard his name being thrown around. Nourriture was named best new bakery by *Cuisine* magazine last month. He trained with top chefs in New York and Paris before opening Nourriture in Portland, right, Sebastian?"

Sebastian gave him a disinterested look. Andy returned with a bottle of wine and a tray of glasses. He poured a glass for Chef Marco, who urged him to fill his glass to the top.

When Andy offered a glass to Sebastian, he scoffed. "Non, non, it is not ze time for drinking yet."

Marco stared at Sebastian, as if trying to decide how anyone could claim it was too early for a drink. Sebastian rolled his unlit cigarette in his fingers and gave Marco a look of disgust.

Sebastian's sentiment was shared by the rest of the room. Marco seemed pleased by this fact and instructed Andy to leave him the bottle.

Andy caught my eye. I shrugged, so Andy left the bottle with Marco who had already polished off his first glass.

"Jules, would you stand, please?" Philip extended his hand in my direction.

Heat burned on my cheeks as I pushed back my chair and rose.

"Jules Capshaw, owner of this adorable shop, Treat, has graciously agreed to take a recently vacated spot."

"It's *Torte*," I said.

"Right. Right. Torte. She'll be our final contestant this season. I know you all have been sampling her products, and I'm sure you'll agree she'll be a great addition to the show. She might need her own show. A pastry chef who looks even better than her sweets—whew, that could bring up our male demographic."

I caught Richard Lord's eye. His face looked as red as mine felt. Lance sat back with his arms folded, grinning ear to ear, and my team all gathered behind the counter looked wide-eyed. Andy gave me a thumbs-up. What had I got myself into? Maybe I should have trusted my initial instinct.

Sebastian cleared his throat and addressed Philip like I wasn't in the room. "She is not a professional chef, non? She is a home baker."

"I assure you, she's a professionally trained chef. She went to culinary school in New York and rose to fame on a world-class cruise ship before returning here to her hometown of Ashland." He turned to me. "Did I get that right, Jules?"

"Pretty much." I sat down.

Lance leaned in. "What's with the uptight Frenchie?"

"No idea." I could feel Sebastian's eyes on me.

"He must have tried one of your croissants and is sweating it." Lance nudged my waist.

"Right." I laughed. "That's definitely it."

Philip scanned his phone. "One last intro. Where's Elliot?"

A young guy, who I'd peg to be in his mid-twenties, with a flashy Hollywood smile and perfectly spiked hair, made to look tousled, jumped to his feet. "Hey, hey, Ashland, happy to be here." He made a clicking sound and shot imaginary guns with both hands.

"You all know the Pastry Channel's golden boy, Elliot Cool," Philip said with a pained smile. "We're thrilled to have Elliot on board as this season's host. He's got his own lineup of shows. The network had to pull some strings to get him here."

Elliot gave Philip another click of his finger gun. "That's right. I'm happy to be here. Happy to sign autographs, take photos." He passed around glossy headshots and brochures to each table. "Check out my Pastry Pop-Ups online. We're doing cra-zie things with pastry, man."

I glanced at a brochure. Elliot's shops had a disco vibe with neon-colored cupcake displays, strobe lights, and desserts constructed in funky geometric shapes.

Behind the counter I watched Stephanie flush as Elliot wound his way in her direction. She handed Andy her phone so that she could pose with Elliot. While Andy clicked shots of her and the Pastry Channel star, Sterling looked less than pleased and busied himself wiping down the already spotless counter.

"I love your shows." Stephanie twisted her hair around her finger. "I've been watching them to get some ideas for working here."

"Nice. That's awesome. We should hang out while I'm in town. I can give you some tips and stuff."

"Sure." Stephanie tried to act nonchalant.

Marco polished off the bottle of wine and began to sway slightly as Philip explained how the production schedule would work, kitchen assignments, and how the first challenge was to create a custom layer cake for the first round of judging, which would start tomorrow.

"We'll be shooting the introduction on set, so I need you to deliver your cakes directly to the theater. After tomorrow, my camera crew will be following you all over town, and getting footage of you at work in each of your respective kitchens," Philip said.

Nina and Sebastian would both be sharing the Merry Windsor's kitchen—it was bigger than ours, since Richard's staff serves full meals in the hotel's dining room in addition to serving coffee and pastries at the newly added espresso bar. Not that anyone actually bakes in that kitchen. Richard's idea of morning treats are dry, store-bought muffins with little to no flavor. Not that I'm biased or anything.

Linda would be working at OSF with Lance. That left us stuck with the inebriated Chef Marco. How was this guy in any shape to bake?

Lance offered words of consolation as he looped arms with Linda and escorted her outside. Richard Lord snarled, "Good luck with the drunk, darling," and left with Sebastian and Nina on his heels.

Philip asked me to wait for a moment and went over to Marco's table. I couldn't hear what he said, but his body language made it evident that he was not happy with the chef.

While I waited for Philip, I told the rest of the staff to call it an afternoon. They'd managed to clean all the trays and dishes, and the workspace in the back gleamed. Stephanie chatted with Elliot and offered to show him around town. Sterling zipped up his hoodie and took off with his skateboard under his arm.

"Is everything okay with him?" I asked Andy as he positioned a Southern Oregon football cap on his head and plugged headphones into his phone.

"He's cool. Jealous, but cool."

"I didn't know Stephanie had such a crush."

Andy tucked the headphones around his neck. "Maybe she doesn't. You know what my mom says—absence makes the heart grow fonder." He stuck the headphones into his ears. "Catch ya tomorrow, boss."

I thought about his words as I watched him walk across the plaza. His analogy didn't quite work since Stephanie wasn't actually absent.

I knew something about absence. It had been almost four months since I'd last seen Carlos. In some ways it felt like yesterday. If I tried, I could smell his musky aftershave and the scent of garlic and onions on his skin and hear his Spanish accent whispering my name. Usually I don't try. When I returned home, we made a deal that we wouldn't talk until the new year. I was sticking to my end of that deal. He'd broken my heart, but I wasn't broken anymore. I needed this time in Ashland to cocoon myself and figure out what was next. If I kept running the loop of our relationship in my head, I'd never be able to move on.

Moving on was what I needed to do now. I hoped I hadn't taken on too much by agreeing to be a contestant. Philip promised to return first thing in the morning with a new contract for me to sign. He dragged Marco to his hotel room at the Merry Windsor to sleep it off.

Time for me to start baking.

Chapter Four

I may have taken on too much, I thought the next morning as I glanced around Torte. The dining room was packed with locals who had come in for news about *Take the Cake*. I'd spent most of the night working on my entry for the competition—a triple-layer Bavarian chocolate cake.

Marco arrived looking disheveled sometime after noon. He looked like he'd slept in his chef's coat. The little hair he had was matted to his forehead and he reeked of booze.

Andy asked me if he was still drunk. If I had to wager a guess, I'd say yes. He kept taking swigs from a half-full bottle of absinthe that he unsuccessfully tried to disguise under a dish towel.

We were due at the Black Swan Theater in two hours to start shooting the first segment of the show. Philip had explained that all of the judging would be done on the set, but since this was a "boutique" show part of the appeal was giving viewers at home an insider's look into a busy professional kitchen. Opening Torte to Philip's camera crew was fine with me, but having Marco share our space was a disaster. He'd been ordering my staff around, demanding they help him with his entry. That wasn't part of the deal.

Regardless of whether I was a contestant on the show

or not, our contract with the Pastry Channel spelled out that we were to provide the visiting chefs a functional workspace and nothing more.

I reminded Marco of this fact more than once, and had to jump in when he started berating Stephanie for not bringing him the proper flour. He clutched his worn notebook like it contained the arm code for a nuclear weapon.

"This could be a long week, guys." I huddled the team together when Marco stepped outside for a break, which was probably code for pulling out the bottle of liquor. "I know he's being demanding. Trust me, I'm used to working with chefs like this. If he bothers you, come get me. I'll step in. Just try to focus on your tasks for Torte as much as you can."

Sterling craned his neck toward the windows to steal a look at the chef. "That dude is a celebrity chef? Right. Only if he met his celebrity clients in rehab."

Everyone chuckled. "Once you get to his level, he probably has a whole team of sous-chefs doing all the work for him," I said.

"I'd say your odds of winning this thing are looking better by the minute, boss," Andy chimed in. "He's not even gonna be upright by the time you start rolling. Plus, have you seen that mess of a cake he's working on—disaster."

Stephanie twirled a strand of purple hair around her finger. "Total disaster. I wonder what Elliot's going to think."

Sterling's jaw stiffened. "I better get back to the front. I see a couple OSF people heading this way."

"Just remember, let me be the bad guy, okay?"

Everyone agreed and returned to their stations. I tried to placate Marco as much as I could. Andy was right. Marco was already in bad shape. He slurred his words and nearly fell over twice. His cake looked like something a first-grader put together. The tiers were uneven, the frosting looked way too thick, and the piping work was a joke.

Comparing our entries side by side I knew mine would win in an instant. My four-layer cake sat perfectly round and level. I'd frosted it in a dark chocolate icing and piped it with white French buttercream. Each layer showcased a different style of piping. I was pleased with the final result. As to how it would stack up against the other competitors I wasn't sure, but Chef Marco's cake wouldn't win at a grade-school bake-off.

We packed up our cakes late in the afternoon to trek up the hill to the Black Swan Theater. Andy stayed behind to close up shop. I was worried that neither Marco nor his cake would make it up Pioneer Street to "the bricks." That's what we call the large courtyard in front of the theaters.

Somehow Marco managed to stumble up the steep sidewalk to the Black Swan. The smallest theater in the OSF complex, it's used by the company for workshops and classes and as a space for writers and actors to test new material. Philip's crew had transformed the space for the show.

Huge banners reading TAKE THE CAKE hung from the ceiling, and lighting and screens were angled toward the set, a temporary kitchen complete with appliances—none of which actually worked. Thanks to the magic of television, viewers at home would never know.

Elliot Cool paced back and forth, speaking into a lapel mic. He spotted us and flashed me a toothy smile. His smile evaporated as Marco wobbled in behind me, nearly knocking me and my cake off my feet.

He stormed over to Marco. "Man, no! You are not messed up again. This is ridic. Where's Philip?"

Marco's response ran together in one long unintelligible sentence.

Elliot tapped his foot and scanned the room. He yelled to the lighting and sound crew. "Where's Philip? Someone needs to get him now."

Marco rocked unsteadily from side to side, his sloppy

cake tilting with him. It reminded me of trying to move during heavy seas on the cruise ship.

"Can I put this down somewhere?" I asked Elliot, nodding toward my cake.

Elliot glared at Marco. "You stay right there. Jules, follow me."

I readjusted my cake and tagged behind Elliot, who showed me where to place my cake for filming.

"He's wasted." Elliot's over-the-top smile disappeared. "I told Philip this would happen."

"What do you mean?" I had to shield my eyes from the lights positioned on the kitchen.

Elliot pulled me away from the glare. "He's messed up all the time. Philip knows it but for some idiotic reason won't cut him."

"Why would Philip want to keep Marco on the show if he knows that Marco's a drunk?"

Elliot shrugged. "Ask Philip." He waved to a woman with a makeup bag slung over her shoulder. "You ready for me?"

She shook her head and pointed at me. "Nope. Her. You're Jules, right?"

"Right." I looked at Elliot.

"Makeup."

"I need makeup?"

"This is show biz. Everyone needs makeup. I'm gonna go find Philip. Catch ya later."

He breezed behind the black curtains that hid the stage. The makeup artist took me to a chair set up in the corner of the room where she proceeded to cake heavy, thick makeup on my face. I'm not a makeup kind of girl. I appreciate dusting my cheeks and eyelids with powder, but that's usually the extent of my morning routine. Working in the heat of the kitchen doesn't lend itself to foundation.

The makeup artist lined my eyebrows and curled my lashes. "You have great skin," she said as she ran a berry-colored tube of gloss over my lips. "Philip's right. The camera is going to love you." She leaned closer. "I hear he thinks you're going to win this whole thing—have your own show. Now I see why he's lobbying for that. Foodies usually have a face for radio, if you know what I mean."

The gloss tasted slightly bitter. "I don't think he's lobbying for that. He just needed someone to take the place of one of the contestants who dropped out."

"That's not what I've heard," she responded, holding up a hand mirror. "Take a peek. Let me know what you think."

I almost didn't recognize myself. She'd used blush to highlight my cheekbones and a mix of gold and green eye shadow that brought out the yellow and brown flecks in my eyes. It was way too much makeup for my taste, but I had to give her credit for making me look like I belonged on television. I wore my hair straight and parted straight down the middle.

She handed me a chocolate-brown apron with *Take the Cake* embroidered in white. "Here's your costume. Better head up to the kitchen. It looks like Philip's getting ready to get started."

I laughed internally at her referring to the apron as my "costume." Most of my time is spent with an apron on, which doesn't give much opportunity to showcase my style. Not that it matters anyway; my wardrobe tends to be pretty simple. Like my cooking, I prefer my clothes to feel effortless, clean and elegant. My closet consists of tailored pants, well-cut skirts, and plenty of everyday T-shirts and casual dress shirts. With winter fast approaching, I was going to have to do some shopping for sweaters and warmer clothes. I'm sure Mom would gladly join me on a shopping excursion. She loves to shop as much as I love to bake. Passing a sales rack at a boutique without stopping would be torture for her.

I thanked the makeup artist and headed to meet my fellow contestants. Lining the black granite countertop were four incredible cakes. Linda presented a two-layer butter pecan cake with caramel ganache. Nina had baked a vegan carrot cake with a rum-raisin sauce served warm on the side, and Sebastian offered an almond cake with marzipan flowers hand created on the top. My Bavarian double chocolate cake and Marco's mess of a cake rounded out the competition. Aside from Marco's, everyone's cakes looked show-ready. I was impressed.

Linda and Nina were summoned to the makeup chair, leaving me alone with Sebastian. Marco, Elliot, and Philip stood near the door. Actually, Philip stood near the door, holding Marco upright. Elliot's voice could be heard above the chatter of the lighting and sound crew walking through their final preparations before we started filming.

My stomach felt fluttery. I'd never appeared on TV before, and I have a tendency to stiffen when I get nervous.

Sebastian examined each cake on display, muttering under his breath in French. I couldn't understand a word he said. My nose picked up the scent of stale cigarettes on his clothing. In culinary school at least half of the chefs smoked. I have a sensitive nose, so I was probably biased, but I wouldn't want cigarette smoke anywhere near my pastries.

Marco broke free from Philip's grasp and stumbled toward the set with the now almost empty bottle of absinthe under his arm.

"Thief!" Sebastian shouted. "Zat is mine. It is very expensive—not to be wasted on a big, fat chef. I've been looking everywhere for it."

I thought Marco might collapse at my feet as he attempted to fling the bottle at Sebastian's head. Instead he fell forward, toward Sebastian's cake. I gasped and held my breath. Philip caught him from behind at the last second before he nearly destroyed the delicate marzipan work.

"You're done, Marco." Philip handed the bottle to Sebastian.

Sebastian gave them both a look of disdain. "What am I to do with dis? Dis is not enough for my next creation." He twisted off the cap and stuck his nose in the bottle. With an exaggerated look of disgust he walked over to the sink and dumped the remaining liquor down the drain. Then he turned and focused his dark eyes on Chef Marco. "Dis is sabotage. You will pay."

Linda and Nina, their faces equally coated in a thick layer of pancake makeup, came over to see what the commotion was all about.

Marco lunged at Sebastian. Philip held him back. "I know things," the drunk chef blurted out.

Philip cleared his throat and tightened his grasp around Marco. "Listen, everyone, we're going to need to postpone production until the morning. Your cakes look stunning and I see that some of you are already in makeup so I'm going to switch a few things around a little. If you're in makeup we'll shoot a little vignette about your background tonight. Then let's meet back here at eight A.M. sharp, and finish this, okay?"

Elliot, who'd returned from backstage, tore his lapel mic off and threw it on the counter. "This is so lame. A waste of time for one wasted chef. Philip, you better get this production together or I'm out."

Philip watched him go, and then turned toward us. "Listen, I know this seems a bit disorganized, but I promise you, I know television. I've built Pastry Channel stars from nothing to worldwide fame. That's my vision for the show."

He squeezed Marco again, whose eyes were barely slits. "I'm going to help sober my buddy up and we'll be ready to roll tomorrow."

Linda reached over and patted his arm. Her wrist full of bracelets clinked. "Sugar, don't you give it a thought. We'll sit tight tonight, right, y'all?"

Nina sighed. "I guess I can go back to the hotel and look over some recipes."

"Disaster." Sebastian twisted a leaf on one of his marzipan flowers and walked away.

Philip ushered Marco to a bench while the rest of us waited to film our one-on-one background spots. He began to snore. Drool pooled in the corners of his open mouth. I couldn't wrap my head around the idea that he was a celebrity chef.

After I answered a few questions about my background and Torte, the production crew told me I was free to leave. I had to admit that I was surprised at how natural I felt once I started talking about baking. Philip stopped me on the way out.

"Jules, so sorry about this—this mess." He paused and snuck a glance at Marco passed out on the bench. "We'll right this ship tomorrow, don't worry. Can you come by closer to seven? I have the new contracts for you to sign, and I want to make sure we have time to go over them in case you have any questions."

I agreed, but as I walked down Pioneer Street toward my apartment, I wondered if I'd made a huge mistake involving myself in the show at all. I had to side with Sebastian. *Take the Cake* felt like a sinking ship.

Chapter Five

The next morning I rose to the sound of birds outside my window. Like me, they were awake before the sun. Pulling on a pair of jeans and a T-shirt, I gave my face an extra scrub. I'd removed most of the makeup last night, but my pores felt clogged and dry. After downing a quick cup of coffee, I twisted my hair into a ponytail and headed outside. I took off at a steady clip toward the park. On the ship I used to walk laps on the upper deck before dawn. This morning I found myself missing that release.

A group of deer grazed on the lush fall grasses near the entrance to the park. They didn't bother to look up from their breakfast as I passed by.

I remember whenever we'd hang out in the park when I was a kid, Dad would wander off to examine a fallen twig or sit and watch the ducks circle on the pond. He used to say, "One touch of nature makes all the world kin." At the time I didn't understand the meaning of Shakespeare's words. As an adult they resonated deeply. The deer, the trees, the river, we were all connected. I paused for a moment to soak in the natural beauty around me. That was definitely something I didn't experience on the ship.

The walking path led me past the children's play

structure, and deeper into the woods. I looped through the musty, tree-covered trail and around to the other side of the river. My body temperature rose as I walked briskly along the path. This is the way you need to start every morning, Jules, I told myself as I loosened the zipper on my jacket and turned toward Torte. The quick, refreshing walk had helped to bring me back to center.

Every morning, long before the rest of the sleepy village is awake, we follow a daily ritual at Torte: stir, mix, roll, knead—bake. Repeat. A little before six, Andy arrives and weighs the beans, adjusts his ratio as needed, and tastes shots. It's these details and touches that matter and keep our customers coming back for more.

I prepped for the morning rush and made sure Andy, Stephanie, and Sterling had the pastry cases stocked and the coffee brewing before I left to meet Philip. He'd asked us to bring all the ingredients we used in our cakes. I packed a grocery sack with chocolate, baker's flour, eggs, butter, and sugar.

As I pushed open the front door to the bakeshop, I ran straight into someone waiting outside and spilled the contents of my bag on the ground.

"Thomas! Sorry. I didn't see you," I said, bending down to survey the mess. Thomas is Ashland's detective-in-training and also happens to be my high school boyfriend. He hasn't changed much since our early years. With his boyish face and mischievous smile he could pass for someone much younger. Only his police uniform and sandy stubble gave away the fact that he wasn't a teenager anymore.

Thomas propped the door open with his foot and knelt to help me gather my things. Fortunately everything was still intact.

"Are you taking Torte on the road, or something, Jules?" Thomas laughed and handed me a bar of dark chocolate.

"No. Believe it or not, I'm going to be on TV."

"So I heard. Well, I always knew you were destined for fame and fortune."

Some of the flour had spilled on the sidewalk. I refolded the bag and tucked it in with everything else. "Right. That's me." I brushed flour from my hands.

"Don't sell yourself short." He got to his feet and gave me a serious look. "But don't forget about us little guys when Hollywood comes calling."

"Trust me, Hollywood is not going to come calling, and even if they did I'm quite happy right here."

"That's what I like to hear." Thomas grinned. His entire face lights up when he smiles. It's one of the things I loved best about him when we dated back in high school. His attitude is contagious. I could feel my spirits lift.

"Are you covering for the Professor?" I asked, tapping the badge pinned to his chest.

"I'm it until he comes back. It's what I do—keep the streets of Ashland safe for the likes of you, miss." He saluted me.

"You know I hate to be called 'miss,' and I don't think there's much to keep safe around here right now." I motioned to the empty sidewalks. "Everyone's gone home."

Thomas pointed his index finger and gave me a stern look. "Don't you jinx this week for me. I was just about to go grab a coffee and read the morning paper." He flashed his iPad. "I've been enjoying a little downtime after the crazy summer we had."

"I'm with you. Quiet is good." Thomas and I had reconnected when I discovered a body at Torte last summer. I shivered at the memory.

"Before you go, Jules, a bunch of us are going to get together this weekend—casual, have some beers—maybe grill, if this weather holds. I know everyone would love to see you."

I'd been so consumed with Torte since being back that

I hadn't ventured much farther than the square. Maybe it was time to change that. Seeing old high school friends sounded like fun. "Sure," I said to Thomas as I started toward Pioneer Street. "Just let me know when."

"Great!" Thomas called after me. "It's a date. I mean—no—it's not. I'll call you."

I didn't turn around to see him, but I could tell he was probably bright red. His light skin tends to flare at the slightest sign of stress. I chuckled to myself as I trekked up the hill. Making him squirm was too easy.

Once I reached the Black Swan Theater, I peered inside. I was surprised to see that it was plunged in darkness. I must have beaten Philip here, I thought as I fumbled on the wall near the door to try and find a light switch. I found one and flipped on the overhead lights.

Something felt off. I couldn't exactly describe why, but the hairs on my arm stood and goose bumps started to form.

You're probably cold, Jules. It's a like a freezer in here, I told myself as I walked toward the kitchen.

I rubbed my forearm, trying to keep warm. Maybe there was a thermostat somewhere close by. If I could find it, I could crank the heat up.

First I wanted to drop off my baking supplies in the kitchen, then I'd go hunt for the thermostat. As I entered the fake kitchen, I did indeed drop my baking supplies—all over the floor. Flour and sugar exploded in the air. Eggs cracked on the floor. I was about to follow them. My body went limp at the sight of what looked to be Chef Marco facedown in a vat of frosting.

I blinked several times and tried to brush dust from my face. My eyes must be deceiving me, I thought as I inched closer. Was it some weird prop for the show?

Nope. That was Marco, in the flesh.

"Chef Marco, are you okay?" My voice sounded like it was coming from someone else's body.

"Chef—are you okay?" I moved another inch closer.

There was no response. I had a sinking feeling I knew why, but the only way to confirm it was to touch him.

I grabbed a spatula from the counter and poked Chef Marco with it.

"Chef?" I tried one more time.

The portly chef didn't budge. He'd been buried in buttercream.

Chapter Six

I dug through the mangled bag of ingredients for my cell phone and punched in Thomas's number.

He answered on the first ring. "Jules, you miss me already?"

"Thomas, you have to get up here now."

"Easy there. Slow down. Remember, this is the off-season—there's no need to rush."

"Thomas!" I cut him off. "Get up here now. Chef Marco is dead!"

"What? Jules, our connection must be bad. I thought you said someone's dead?"

"I did! Chef Marcos, one of the contestants for *Take the Cake,* is dead." I glanced toward Marco's body and took a step backward. "Thomas, please come quick."

"On my way. Don't touch anything."

The room felt even colder than when I'd first walked in. I hugged myself and ran my hands up and down my arms to try and keep warm. I wasn't sure if it was actually freezing in the old theater, or if I was reacting to the sight of a dead body.

What could have happened to the chef? My mind became hyperfocused. Could he have been so drunk that he passed out in the frosting? My eyes scanned the room and landed on the countertop. All of the cakes had been destroyed. Sebastian's delicate flowers looked like they'd been plucked from the top of his cake and scattered on the floor. His cake was smashed and smeared all over the counter. My Bavarian chocolate buttercream had finger marks swiped all over the sides and top. Linda's and Nina's cakes both had chunks missing from them, like someone had grabbed fistfuls of the desserts.

Marco must have gone on some sort of drunken rampage—ruining all of our entries.

The door flew open and Thomas raced in.

"Jules! Are you okay?" He stopped at my feet and assessed me from head to toe.

"I'm okay," I lied.

He pulled me away from the kitchen. "Come on, you need to sit."

I looked down for the first time. I was a mess. My jeans were coated in flour. Egg had splattered on my tennis shoes, and I couldn't stop shaking.

"Jules, you're freezing." He grabbed a folding chair and pushed me into it. "Wait here. I'll be right back."

He disappeared behind the stage. I wondered where Philip was. How much time had passed? He was supposed to meet me here at seven. It had to be long past that now.

Thomas returned with a cape. "Put this on." He wrapped it around my shoulders.

"A cape?"

"It's the best I could do." He sat down next to me. "I want you to take some slow and steady breaths, okay?"

I tightened the cape around me. "Okay." I inhaled through my nose.

"Good," Thomas reassured me. "That's it, keep breathing." He placed his hand on my knee. It felt warm and comforting. "I need to go survey the scene. Are you going to be okay if I leave you here for a few minutes? I don't want you passing out on me."

I huddled under the cape and gave him a half laugh. "I'm not going to pass out, I promise. Go."

He looked unsure, but got to his feet and pulled on a pair of latex gloves. "Just keep breathing. Keep wrapped up. I'll be right back."

I nodded.

At that moment the front door opened and Philip breezed in. His cell phone was glued to his ear. "No way. We already talked about this. There's no out clause." He noticed me and held his hand over the phone. "Be right with ya. Just have to finish this call."

Before I could respond, he stepped back outside. I could hear him arguing with whoever was on the other end of the phone.

Thomas surveyed the kitchen. Fortunately, from my vantage point at the front of the theater, I couldn't see Marco's body with the way the lights had been positioned. Every once in a while I caught a glimpse of Thomas making a note on his iPad, or crouching down to get a better angle.

Philip's voice became agitated outside. "That's it. No more negotiating. I'm done." He must have hung up on whoever he was talking to, because he stepped inside and greeted me with a broad smile. "Jules, I'm so sorry to have kept you waiting."

He stuffed his phone in the front pocket of the suit jacket he wore over a basic white T-shirt. "Business. You know how that goes." Reaching into the laptop bag that hung on his shoulder, he removed a file folder and started to hand it to me. For the first time he took notice of me. "You don't strike me as the cape type, Jules."

I took the file from him with quivering fingers, and

motioned for him to sit. "Philip, this is serious. Really serious."

"Uh-oh." He rested his laptop bag on the floor and sat in the folding chair. His jeans had holes that looked like they'd been intentionally sliced in them. I knew this trend was hot with twenty-somethings, but Philip was at least Mom's age. I'd look ridiculous in ripped jeans, but somehow it worked on Philip. "That doesn't sound good. You're not backing out on me, are you?"

I shook my head. "No." I took a deep breath. "It's Chef Marco."

His knee bounced. "Jules, you're not auditioning for a part here. Stop dragging out whatever you have to tell me. My nerves are already frayed."

"Mine too." I pointed to the kitchen. For some reason I couldn't make my mouth form the words that Marco was dead.

Philip sighed and rubbed his temples. "What has he done now?"

I inhaled again, making eye contact with Philip. "He's dead." My voice cracked a little.

Philip threw his head back and started cracking up. "Good one, Jules."

"I'm serious." I motioned toward Thomas. "The police are here now. Marco is dead."

"What?" Philip jumped to his feet. "That's impossible."

"I wish it was. I found him here this morning."

"What? No, that can't be true." He glanced around the theater like he was looking for something. "I took him back to the hotel last night."

I shrugged. "Maybe he came back up here?"

Philip shook his head. "No way. He couldn't even stand." He moved toward the kitchen.

Thomas came up behind him and held out an arm. "I

need you to stop right there, sir. No one can come in here. I'm securing the perimeter. This is a crime scene."

Philip stopped in mid-stride. He swiveled his head in my direction. His eyes were twice their normal size.

A crime scene? Not again.

Chapter Seven

Philip stayed just outside the kitchen, watching Thomas's every move. When Thomas completed his initial observation, he placed two folding chairs across the entrance to the galley kitchen in order to block anyone from entering. Then he called for backup.

I removed the cape. My temperature was climbing, probably in rhythm with my heart rate. Did Thomas really think that Chef Marco had been murdered?

He escorted Philip over to me. "I'm going to need to talk to both of you independently, and get a list of everyone who has access to this building."

"Do you think it was really murder?" I blurted out.

Thomas gave me a hard look and turned to Philip and extended his hand. "I'm sorry, I didn't get your name?"

"Philip Higgins, producer of *Take the Cake*." Philip shook Thomas's hand. "Listen, I've got a ton of money riding on this show. Is this going to take a while?"

"It's going to take as long as it takes." Thomas must have gotten that phrase from the Professor. "You're in charge around here?" Thomas asked.

Philip rubbed his temples again. I thought he might end up with deep purple bruises on the side of his face from rubbing them so hard. "Yep. Listen, if I can't shoot today it's going to throw the entire production schedule off. I need to make a couple calls."

"You can step right outside, but don't go far. I'll take Jules's statement first, but then I'm going to need to talk to you." His rigid stance made it clear he was in police mode. Thomas escorted Philip to the front of the theater and held the door open for him.

Philip walked outside. I could tell that he wasn't used to taking orders from anyone, especially someone much younger than him. He adjusted the collar on his jacket and hunched his shoulders back as he exited.

"Do you really think someone killed Chef Marco?" I asked, folding the cape on the back of the chair. "He was really drunk last night. I just figured he passed out."

Thomas scowled. "It doesn't look that way, Jules. We'll know as soon as the coroner arrives, but I have to follow procedure and protect the scene." He looked toward the window where Philip paced outside. "What do you know about him?"

"Philip? Not much. He's a big-time producer. He seemed to be the only person who could control Chef Marco. He said he took Marco back to the hotel last night. We had to cancel the show because Marco was so drunk."

"One sec." Thomas sprinted to the front, grabbed his iPad and clicked it on. "I need to get this all down. I don't want to miss a single detail, especially since this is my first time securing a crime scene on my own." He looked at the iPad. "The county sheriff is on his way. I hope he gets here soon."

"You keep saying crime scene—why?"

"Jules, first of all the odds of someone passing out in a mixer filled with frosting are pretty slim, don't you think?"

I agreed.

"Second, Marco has a large contusion on the back of his

head. I'm not a doctor, but I'd bet money that's the cause of death. The coroner will be able to confirm that."

I felt like I might be sick.

"Jules, you okay?" Thomas grabbed my arm. "Maybe you should sit back down."

"It's fine. I just can't believe I'm involved in another murder." My hands trembled.

Thomas kept his hand on my arm. "I was going to say the same thing. Anything you want to tell me? You didn't really go to culinary school, did you? I'm guessing you've led a secret life as a special agent on the seas." He winked. I could tell he was trying to put me at ease.

I gave him a half smile.

"That's more like it." He motioned to the chair. "Sit, I have a few questions."

He typed on his iPad while I filled him in on everything I could remember from last night. I explained Marco's drunken behavior and how I wondered if he'd sabotaged all the cakes. When I left last night, Marco and Philip were the only two left. Philip claimed to have taken Marco back to the hotel. Maybe he hadn't? Could he have hit Marco and left him to die? Was there any way the inebriated chef could have trekked back up the hill last night if Philip did indeed leave him at his hotel?

Thomas held up his index finger. "Jules, you're not getting involved in this case. I made a big mistake this summer asking for your help. Leave the questions to me. There is no way I'm taking a chance on you getting hurt again."

My hand reflexively went to my right shoulder.

Thomas noticed. His voice softened. "Does it still hurt?"

I rubbed the scar. "No, not really." The scar was a physical reminder of the danger I'd been in a few months ago, and how lucky I was to be alive.

He leaned closer. I could smell a hint of lavender and lilies on him. His family owns A Rose by Any Other Name, the flower shop two doors down from Torte. Thomas helps out in the shop when he's not on duty. "Jules, if this is murder—and I think it is—I don't want you involved. Got it?"

"Got it." I traced the small scar on the palm of my hand. Helping Thomas with a murder investigation last summer had definitely left its mark. I understood why he was being so serious, yet there was part of me that felt shut out.

Sirens wailed outside. The county sheriff and coroner arrived. Thomas told me to head back to Torte as he directed the coroner and sheriff to Marco's body. "I'll come find you at Torte later," he whispered, walking me to the door.

My eyes had to adjust to the sunlight outside. The flashing strobe lights on the county sheriff's vehicle made it more difficult. I wondered how much time had passed. The sun had risen overhead, casting a cheery glow on the bricks. I felt anything but cheery.

Philip grabbed my arm and startled me. "What did you tell the cop?"

"What do you mean?" I pulled away.

"What did you tell him about the show and Marco?" He had to shout over the sound of a siren on yet another police car arriving at the scene.

"The truth."

"Which is?"

I shrugged. "That Marco was drunk last night and that I thought he may have intentionally destroyed our cakes."

"Oh, yeah. That's exactly what I was going to say too." He clicked his phone on. "Listen, I've gotta make a few important calls here. This is going to put a big-time crimp in my production schedule. I'll let you know as soon as the cop tells me when we can start filming again." He scrolled on his screen. "And I've got to find another replacement contestant. Damn. Maybe we should have stayed in L.A."

He didn't notice as I continued down the hill and was out of earshot. I knew that Thomas told me I had to stay out of his investigation, but it struck me as strange that Philip was so preoccupied with the show. Shouldn't he be concerned that a contestant—someone he seemed to have known well—had just been murdered?

Chapter Eight

"Boss, are you okay?" Andy greeted me at Torte with his backpack slung across his shoulder.

He held the door open for me. "I'm taking off for my morning class, but maybe I should stay. You don't look so good."

"No, no. Go. I don't want you to miss your class." Was my mouth forming words? My voice sounded distant, like it didn't belong to me.

Andy waited while I stepped inside.

"I promise. I'm fine." I waved him on. Andy and Stephanie both attend Southern Oregon University. We arrange their work schedules around their classes. Since the university is a short distance from Torte, they both come early to help open and, depending on their class schedule, they can leave and come back.

He tugged his backpack up his shoulder and wrinkled his forehead. "Okay. Catch you after class."

Sterling was boxing up pastries at the counter. He paused when he saw me. "Hey, Jules. You're back early. Did you have a run-in with a mixer?" he asked, noting my flour-coated jeans.

"You don't even want to know."

Stephanie came from the kitchen with a tray of red velvet mini Bundt cakes, glazed with a cream cheese frosting.

Sterling pretended not to notice her. He counted each pastry in the boxes he'd assembled on the top of the case—twice.

Stephanie cleared her throat. "A little help?" She nodded to the glass case.

He looked up from the boxes. "Huh?"

"Help," she snapped.

I wondered what my role in their bickering was. I don't get involved in the personal issues of my staff. Mom probably would know what to do, but not me. I learned early on from one of the head pastry chefs I apprenticed under on the cruise ship that personal issues have no place in the kitchen.

"Juliet, there's no place for arguing in the kitchen. The tension comes out in the food."

This same sentiment was repeated often, by Carlos. Of course his Spanish accent and less than perfect grasp of English made the idea seem much more romantic. "Julieta, *mi querida,* if you hold your shoulders so tight, like this, when you are baking, that tension it will come through in the pastry. You must relax."

Relaxing wasn't on my agenda at the moment. Stephanie thrust the tray of red velvet cakes at Sterling and turned and stormed back to the kitchen. He looked injured. "Women." He rolled his eyes. "What is it with you guys?"

"Me?" I asked. "Don't rope me into this." The room felt like it was slightly spinning. Keep it together, Jules, I told myself, reaching for the countertop for support.

He placed the cakes in the display case. "Sorry. I just don't get why she's mad at *me.* She's the one acting all into Elliot. The dude looks like he's been dipped in Hollywood. I don't get it. He's not her type."

I couldn't help but chuckle at his description of Elliot.

That was better. Maybe I was feeling more normal after all. "She's probably just a little star-struck. Don't worry about it. She'll come around."

Sterling shrugged.

"Listen, I need to run home and change. Are you going to be okay without me for a few?"

Sterling studied my appearance again. "What happened?" He looked concerned.

"You're not going to believe it." I sighed. "Chef Marco is dead."

"Let me guess, alcohol poisoning." Sterling frowned. He'd spent some time on the streets before arriving in Ashland and did a stint in rehab. I was impressed that he'd been able to make positive changes at such a young age. It's not the typical way stories like that usually end.

"No, he was murdered." I felt my voice catch.

"Seriously? Oh, man, that's insane."

"It gets worse. I found him."

"Jules, you're going to get a reputation. That's two murders in how many months?"

I picked up a cake from the tray and pinched off a piece. "Yeah, that's pretty much exactly what Thomas said."

"I thought Ashland was supposed to be a quaint town. I've seen more murder here than I did living on the streets in So Cal."

The moist cake melted in my mouth. I'd have to tell Stephanie that she'd done a great job on these. The cream cheese glaze added just a touch of tang without being overly sweet. The sugar rushed straight to my head. I took another bite. It was exactly what I needed.

"Do you need anything?" Sterling asked as I popped another bite into my mouth.

"Nope. I'm good. I think this is doing the trick. You're sure you're good here?" My body gave an involuntary shudder. "I want out of these clothes."

Sterling handed me a paper napkin. "We got this. Go."
I hesitated.

"Jules, you're always worrying about everyone else. Weren't you just lecturing your mom about taking care of herself a few days ago?" He paused and gave me a hard look. "You should follow your own advice."

I polished off the rest of the cake and wiped my hands on the napkin. "Okay. I'll be quick. I promise," I told him as I left. "If Thomas comes down, tell him I'll be right back."

Sterling pushed me out the door. "It's cool. Go change. Like I said, we got this."

I smiled as I walked to my apartment. Mom and I really had an amazing staff, especially given that all of them were in their early twenties.

The combination of chocolate and sugar from the cake gave my stride an extra little kick. Either that or it was the adrenaline rush from finding a dead body. I gave my head a quick shake. This couldn't be happening again.

I took the stairs to my apartment two at a time. I wanted out of these clothes this instant. Not that a little flour on my jeans would usually bother me, but this morning it was a visual reminder that I'd just witnessed a murder. In addition to changing, I knew there was another important thing I needed to do—call Mom.

After a quick shower and change of clothes I hit Mom's number on my phone. She picked up on the third ring. I almost hung up. This was the first vacation she'd taken in years, but we made a pact upon my return that we wouldn't keep secrets from one another. I knew if I didn't at least fill her on what had happened, she'd feel betrayed. Plus I figured Thomas had probably already called the Professor.

Her voice sounded light when she answered. "Juliet, I'm so glad it's you. I was just planning to call you."

"How's the wine tasting, Mom?"

"Wonderful. We've had the best time, and I have some

great new wines that we can add to our line at Torte. You should see how many cases we're bringing back. Doug's truck is packed."

"I'm so glad you've had a good time, Mom."

"What's wrong? I can hear it in your voice. Is it the shop?"

"Has the Professor talked to Thomas yet?"

She paused. "I don't think so, why? What's going on? Honey, are you okay? Is it Thomas?"

"No, nothing like that."

"Juliet, stop stalling. What's going on?"

"There's been another murder, Mom."

"What? At Torte? Who?"

"One of the contestants on *Take the Cake*. Not here, up at the Black Swan."

"Oh, thank goodness." She let out a sigh. "I mean, of course it's terrible that someone's been killed, but I'm so relieved you're not in the middle of it this time."

"Well."

"Juliet?"

"I kind of found the body."

"Oh, no." I could hear the concern in her voice.

"Yeah. Thomas should be calling the Professor. I just wanted to make sure you heard it from me first."

"We'll leave now."

"Mom, no. Don't cut your trip short on my account. Everything's under control."

It sounded like she covered up the mouthpiece. I could hear her talking to someone—probably the Professor.

"Mom, please don't leave early because of me. I promise I'm fine. Thomas is watching out for me and the crew at Torte is helping out a ton. Really, I just wanted you to know."

She sounded unsure. "We were planning to be home to-night anyway. You take care of yourself. I'll be there soon."

Chapter Nine

I returned to Torte to find Nina, Sebastian, and Linda huddled together in a booth. They caught sight of me. Linda waved me over.

"Sugar, we heard the news. Can you believe it?" She dabbed her eyes with a monogramed peach handkerchief.

Sebastian scoffed and peered out the window. "He was an idiot."

Linda frowned. "Where I come from, we don't speak ill of the dead."

Sebastian ignored her attempt to chastise him.

Nina scooted over in the booth to make room for me. "Can I ask you a favor?" she asked as I took a seat.

"What's that?"

"Now that Marco is—well—you know, not going to be part of the show. I was hoping I could use his workspace here? I can't stand Richard Lord. He's about as far from vegan as it gets."

I was with her on that. "Do we even know that the show's going to continue?"

Linda sniffed and neatly folded her handkerchief on the table. "Philip says it will."

"Doesn't it seem a little morbid to go on under the circumstances?" I asked.

Sebastian huffed. He tapped a package of cigarettes on the table. "Non. Chef Marco destroyed my marzipan. He drank my special imported absinthe. I think he deserved what comes to him."

I raised my eyes. "You can't mean that. He's *dead*."

Sebastian scowled and looked out the window. His black attire matched his attitude.

Nina twisted a hemp bracelet on her wrist and nodded in agreement. "I agree with both of you. It's horrible that he's dead, but he did destroy everyone's cakes. I think he actually put *butter* in my vegan batter."

Linda leaned across the table and patted Nina's hand. Her nails, painted in pink, each had a diamond stud glued on the tips. How did she bake with those?

"Sugar, I wouldn't put it past him. He was desperate to win. Imagine destroying our beautiful creations. I think he stole my great-grandma's secret banana cream pudding recipe. I can't find it anywhere."

I wasn't sure their assessment of Marco matched mine. While I agreed he most likely ruined our cakes, I wasn't sure it was intentional or sabotage. More like a drunken stupor.

"So is it okay if I move in here?" Nina asked again.

"Sure, it's fine by me, but I'm really not convinced this show is going to continue. We only have four contestants now."

Linda offered me a syrupy smile. "Sugar, we are in very capable hands. Philip is a pro. He'll whisk this little problem right under the rug, and we'll be back on camera in no time."

Being back on camera wasn't my top priority at the moment, but I met her smile and excused myself to the kitchen. Baking might help take my mind off the morning's gruesome event. Nina followed after me, her long flowing skirt skimming the floor.

"Where do you want me?" she asked. I wondered why she was so eager.

Stephanie whisked egg whites in the industrial mixer. She caught my eye and stared at Nina.

"I'll need to clear off Marco's workstation." I motioned to the messy space. "But I don't think I should do anything until the police have a look."

Nina took a step back. "The police? Why would the police need to look here?"

"Because he was *murdered*." I was starting to wonder why all my fellow contestants seemed so unfazed by Chef Marco's death.

Stephanie laughed. I shot her a look.

"Sorry, I know. But you think that they'll look here?" Nina repeated.

"I'm sure they will."

"Oh, oh well, yeah, that's fine. I need to go get my things together at the Merry Windsor anyway. I'll check back later." She backed out of the kitchen and scooted to the front door.

"What's with the hippie?" Stephanie asked, testing the firmness of the egg-white peaks with her finger.

"She wants Marco's spot."

"That's cold." Stephanie began folding the airy egg whites into her cake batter.

"I agree." I watched Nina scurry across the plaza. "But she is stuck with Richard Lord so I can't exactly blame her." I grabbed an apron from a hook and wrapped it around my waist. I needed to bake.

I opted for one of my favorite fall cookies—I call them amaretto dreams. I discovered them while at port in a tiny bakeshop in London, and I craved them so much that I recreated the recipe. It took me a couple tries to perfect, but when I succeeded I felt quite proud of myself. Their flavor and texture is the perfect accompaniment for fall.

Stephanie and I worked in silence. I creamed together butter and sugar for the dough base while she poured cake batter into eight-inch round pans. After the butter and sugar had blended together in a creamy consistency I added eggs, almond extract, amaretto liqueur, and a tiny splash of anise. It smelled divine.

"What are you making?" Stephanie asked as she slid cake tins into the oven. "That smells really good."

"Amaretto dreams." I smiled, wishing this was some terrible dream that I could wake up from.

She picked up the bottle of anise and twisted it open. "Whoa." She waved her hand in front of her nose. "That's wicked."

"I know." I twisted the cap back on. "A little goes a long, long way with this."

"Got it." She watched as I chopped chunks of dark chocolate and sliced almonds. Her alternative look and aloof attitude sometimes made me forget she was just a kid. She leaned on her elbows as I stirred the chocolate and almonds into my dough. "Why aren't you using the mixer for that?"

"I like the arm workout." I flexed my arm with the wooden spoon in my hand. "When I'm incorporating chocolate and nuts like this into the dough I like to do it by hand, especially since I'm not making a huge batch. If we were in the middle of summer rush and going through a few dozen of these every hour it would be different." I scooped a spoonful of dough and handed it to her. "See how the chocolate is really chunky? That's what I want for this cookie. Sometimes the mixer chops it up too much."

She studied the dough.

"Taste it." I nudged her.

I smiled as she used her pinky finger to scoop a taste off the spoon. She was a quick study.

"It's good. I like the flavor. It's unusual."

"Exactly. That's what sets us apart here at Torte."

The bell on the front door jingled and Elliot Cool breezed in. Stephanie handed back the spoon and brushed a strand of purple hair from her face. She ran her tongue over her teeth. "Do I have anything on my teeth?"

"You're fine," I assured her.

She pulled a cookie sheet from the rack. "I'll help with these." She tried to look intent on scooping perfectly round balls of dough onto the sheet, but she kept trying to catch Elliot's eye.

If he noticed Stephanie in the back, he didn't give anything away. He made a beeline to the booth where Linda sat nursing a cup of iced coffee. Sebastian had followed Nina out, leaving Linda alone.

I couldn't tell what they were talking about, but Elliot didn't look happy. Linda kept reaching out with her jeweled arms, trying to pacify him. He brushed her off and pointed his index finger at her.

She glanced around the room and leaned closer to him, like she was trying to say something that she didn't want anyone else to hear.

Elliot threw his head back in a half laugh and shot her a nasty look. He pushed to his feet and left Linda looking slightly stunned.

On his way out the door he took notice of Stephanie and me in the kitchen. His posture shifted, as he strolled to us and gave us both a toothy smile.

"Ladies, how goes it?"

Stephanie visibly blushed. That was a first.

"So this is where the magic happens?" He reached into the mixing bowl and snagged a taste of the cookie batter.

Working the batter around in his mouth, he nodded. "Hmm. Interesting flavor combination. I taste amaretto, right?"

Stephanie wrapped a strand of hair around her finger. "Yeah. How'd you know?"

"Years in the biz." He turned to me. "This isn't extract, though; I'm thinking you used the real thing, right?"

I had to admit even I was a little impressed. I mean, I guess I've always been under the impression that most television hosts are hired for their looks and personality and less so for their culinary prowess. I had to give Elliot credit for having a good palate to accompany his good looks.

Before I could answer, Stephanie handed him the bottle of liqueur. He appraised it and placed it on the counter. "Good stuff. Nice. That's the way we do things at my pop-up pastry shops. Nothing but the best. Baking should be sexy, you know."

I thought Stephanie might actually swoon. Not that I've ever seen anyone swoon, but she fit the description. Elliot responded by layering on the charm. I understood why Sterling was irritated, and I was more than a little surprised that Stephanie of all people was gaga for the food star. There was something about his blinding smile that I didn't trust.

"Not that I'm surprised to see such sexy baking from such lovely ladies. My money's on your chocolate cake," he said to me. "It was the star of the show last night for sure."

"But you didn't even taste it."

Elliot caught Stephanie's eye. "She doesn't get sexy, does she?"

Stephanie twirled her hair and shook her head in agreement.

"Your cake looked the best." Elliot spoke to me like he was addressing a child. "That's baking sexy and all that matters when it comes to the show."

He scooped another taste of the cookie dough. "You

heard the news, right? About Chef Marco? Dude, total bummer. Now Philip has me running all around. Not in my contract, but hey, I'm the kind of guy who jumps in wherever I'm needed." He snapped his fingers together. "I gotta run, but let's hang later. I want to see more of your little town."

Stephanie nodded. I figured this was because she didn't trust herself to speak. Elliot left, completely aware that all eyes followed him out the door. One set of those eyes belonged to Linda Belle, who maintained her window seat. Her Southern smile had evaporated from her face, replaced by pursed lips. She hardened her eyes and watched Elliot leave.

Our eyes met across the room. She looked frazzled for a moment, but quickly returned to her usual demeanor, waved with her fingers and shot me a sugary grin. Then she picked up her handkerchief and hurried off in the same direction as Elliot.

I wasn't sure what was going on with her and Elliot, but I couldn't help but wonder if it had something to do with Marco's murder.

Chapter Ten

The scent of my amaretto dream cookies baking in the oven filled the space. It was almost time for the lunch crowd to start funneling in, and I hadn't started on specialty sandwiches yet. In the fall and winter locals flock to Torte and all the other restaurants in town during the lunch hour. When OSF is in full swing most locals avoid being anywhere near the theater between eleven and two, as it's usually a mob of tourists trying to grab a bite to eat before catching the matinee.

I'd enjoyed reconnecting with people from town the last few weeks. Torte's a great spot to linger over a cup of coffee and a croissant sandwich when it's not buzzing with tourists. We make all of our soups and sandwiches fresh every day. Our standard menu includes an old-fashioned PBJ with homemade jams. I love mine grilled on the panini maker with our rustic French bread. We offer a cranberry-walnut chicken salad and basil egg salad. Our deli case is stocked with locally sourced meats and cheeses so that our customers can create their own sandwich. To finish off any order, we box up sandwiches with a cookie and drink for a quick lunch on the go.

With fall on my mind, I thought I'd try an apple-inspired

sandwich for today's special. I chopped organic Rogue Valley apples and shredded a pork loin that I had chilling in the fridge. I tossed them in apple cider vinegar, salt and pepper, and a splash of olive oil. Pork and apples tend to pair well together. I'd serve it in a baguette with arugula and Fontina cheese.

Thomas beat the lunch crowd in. He waited for me to finish assembling the sandwiches, taking a cup of coffee that Sterling offered him while standing at the counter. I still hadn't gotten quite used to seeing him in his uniform. In high school he'd been a goofy football player who liked to make us all laugh. I'd witnessed his serious side and dedication to following leads without jumping to conclusions when we worked together on Ashland's last murder, yet watching him size up Torte in his blue police uniform made me stifle a giggle.

"What's the latest?" I asked, bringing him an apple and pork baguette on a plate with two amaretto dream cookies.

"Is this for me?" He ran his fingers through his sandy hair.

"I figured you might want lunch."

"You are a mind reader, Jules." He took the plate and directed me toward a table in the far corner. "Let's go sit."

Andy should be back from his morning class soon. I checked with Sterling to make sure he had the front under control before joining Thomas.

"You're not going to eat?" He ripped off a chunk of the sandwich with his teeth.

"Not if you're going to devour my food like that." I feigned disgust.

That only encouraged him. He yanked another bite and chewed from one side of his mouth. "This is so good; you can't expect me to eat it like a civilized gentleman. This sandwich was made to be eaten like a man." He thumped his chest.

I rolled my eyes. "It does make me happy to know that some things—*or people*—never change."

"What? How can you say that, Jules? I've changed. Look at me." He patted his taut stomach.

"Right." I smirked. "Can we talk about Chef Marco?"

Thomas rested the remaining portion of his sandwich on his plate and glanced around the room. "What do you want to talk about? I thought I made it clear that I don't want you messed up in this."

I folded my hands on the table. "I already am, Thomas. I found him."

He sighed. "I know. Are you doing okay?"

"Why does everyone keep asking me that?" I snapped.

"Maybe because we care about you." He looked at his sandwich.

"Sorry. I guess I'm a little on edge."

"Jules, it's okay. Someone was murdered. Even in this line of work it's not exactly something you ever get used to, you know."

"Did the coroner confirm that?"

"He as much as did. Said he'd have more info this afternoon, but that it looked like blunt force trauma to the head."

I swallowed hard. "Have you talked to the Professor?"

Thomas plucked a piece of arugula from his sandwich and nodded. "He should be back later. I think we have everything under control, but I know the Professor won't be able to rest until he sees the scene. Speaking of the crime scene, are any of Chef Marco's personal items here? I'm going to need to go through them."

"His workstation is full of his stuff." I nodded. "I'll take you back there after you finish your lunch. Did you talk to Philip? The rest of the contestants seem to think that the show is going to keep filming."

"I don't know about that." Thomas polished off his sandwich and bit into an amaretto dream. "I made it clear that he can't use the space today. We'll have to see how things progress. The guy is really demanding, though. I think he's used to getting his way." He munched the cookie. "Man, this is awesome. What is it?"

"Amaretto."

Thomas laughed. "Now I know your secret. You keep your customers coming back by hopping them up on booze. Juliet, you little sneak. Who knew?"

I kicked him in the shin.

"Ouch." He keeled over. "I forgot what a wicked kick you have. Mercy, mercy."

"You want to go see Marco's stuff?"

He popped the last half of cookie in his mouth, grabbed the empty plate and stood. I'm used to being one of the tallest people in a room. When I was younger it made me self-conscious. I used to intentionally slump my shoulders, especially when cute guys were around. Thomas is a couple inches taller than me. I liked having to look up slightly to meet his eyes.

As we walked to the kitchen the chime on the door rang. Andy, Nina, and a handful of locals on lunch break filed in. Without missing a beat, Andy dropped his backpack by the office, washed his hands, tied on a clean apron, and was pulling espresso shots before Thomas even had time to rest his plate in the sink.

Nina floated over to us. Her toes stuck out from underneath her long peasant skirt. They were painted green. I'm a stickler for safety. It's probably due to my training in culinary school and working in the rigorous environment of a ship's kitchen. Nina's open-toed sandals were a no-go at Torte. Not only do open-toed shoes give customers the wrong perception on cleanliness, but they're not safe.

Kitchen accidents happen all the time. A rolling pin could drop and break a toe, or she could scald them with any of the hot sauces we usually have reducing on the stove.

She fluffed her skirt and stood with arms at her sides, almost like in some sort of strange yoga pose. "Jules, is this the police officer I need to speak to?"

I introduced them. Nina clutched Thomas's arm, and spoke in an affected voice. "I don't know if Jules has mentioned this yet, but I really need to move my workstation here. They placed me at the Merry Windsor, and I'm a vegan chef."

"Okay?" Thomas waited for her to continue.

"Are you familiar with the vegan lifestyle?"

Lifestyle? I moved away from them and flipped through Mom's recipe book until I found what I was looking for—a butter pound cake.

Nina touted the benefits of living the vegan lifestyle. I chopped butter by the pound. The irony wasn't lost on me.

Thomas listened politely, with Nina hanging on his arm the entire time. Once she finished her dissertation on veganism he removed himself from her clutches. "I'll have to try one of your pastries. They sound interesting."

They walked into the kitchen. "Jules, is this Marco's workstation?" Thomas asked.

Nina started and gasped as Thomas picked up a spatula from Marco's mess.

"Are you okay?" He put the spatula down and came closer to Nina.

She regained her composure and pointed to me. "It's all that butter. I'm not used to being around this much butter."

I held the butter up. "*This* is making you jumpy?"

She grabbed Thomas's arm again.

I gave him an incredulous look. He gave me a warning for my face.

Nina giggled. "No. I think I'm just jumpy from Marco's murder."

Her reaction was strange to say the very least.

She fluffed her skirt again. "I'd love to make this work. Even though I'm not a fan of butter, I'm glad to see you're using natural products here. Everything at the Merry Windsor is processed." She shuddered. "We've got to be sure that that butter doesn't contaminate any of my baking, though."

"Not a problem." I plopped the butter in my hand into the mixing bowl and tried to catch Thomas's eye.

Thomas stepped toward Marco's things and Nina scurried away. Calling over her shoulder, she said, "I'll be back with my things, and I'll be ready to bake something special just for you."

"What was that about?" I said as I attached the bowl to the mixer and clicked it on low.

"What?"

I could feel my top lip curl. "Uh, Nina. Her weird reaction to butter."

"She's just upset about the murder. Trust me, everyone reacts differently to stress. I've seen it again and again. You never know how it's going to affect someone. Like with you this morning, I was mentally going through my 'what to do if someone goes into shock' checklist."

"I wasn't going into shock."

Thomas scowled, reached into his pocket and pulled out a pair of gloves. He stretched them on his hands and began to sort through Marco's things.

"Don't you think that it's a bit strange that Nina freaked out, though?"

He didn't seem to be listening. "What's that?" He held a bottle of vanilla extract in the air and sniffed it.

"Nina. She jumped at the sight of *butter*?"

"Jules, you're funny." He set the bottle back on the counter, ignoring my comment. "Can I store all this in your office? I need to keep everything secure until the Professor gets back."

"Fine."

"Is that going to be a problem? You sound mad."

"No, it's no problem. But are you seriously going to blow off how weird that just was with Nina?"

"Am I blowing it off?"

"She freaked out, about *butter*." I raised my eyebrow.

Thomas wheeled the cart toward the office. "I think she's really passionate about being vegan. That's all."

I squeezed between him and the counter to open the office door. "Maybe."

Thomas parked the cart next to the filing cabinet in our tiny office. Not that it mattered. Mom and I mainly use it to do the books and place vendor orders. "This isn't going to give you much room in here, are you sure it's not a problem?"

"Positive. Don't sweat it. Let me tell you what the problem is going to be."

Thomas held the door for me as we exited. "Butter?"

"Exactly." I punched him in the shoulder. "Nina is really not going to like it when she realizes she has to share our workspace. She thought she was getting Chef Marco's. We might taint her vegan products with deadly items like butter or eggs."

Thomas gave me a thoughtful look. "If it would help, I can bag everything up and take it into the evidence room. The Professor likes to examine evidence 'in the real world.' That's the only reason for keeping Chef Marco's things here. If it would make things easier for you and Nina, I can bag it, tag it, and take it with me."

He emphasized "Nina." I assured him that she and I would work something out. He left to check in with the coroner. I returned to my butter pound cake. What was wrong with me? Thomas was a friend, nothing more. I'd made it clear that I wasn't in the space to think about anything other than a friendship right now. Then why was I so irritated that he was showing interest in Nina?

Chapter Eleven

Lunchtime brought a packed house to Torte. Not only because locals were eager to reclaim their town, but because word had spread about Marco's murder. The pork and apple sandwiches and amaretto cookies were sold out before we were halfway through the rush. Andy's pumpkin cream lattes were a huge hit. The line at the espresso bar held steady despite the fact that he was cranking out coffees at record pace.

The four of us worked in rhythm. Stephanie started new batches of cookies and muffins—anything we could turn around fast. Sterling rang up customers and dished out pastries. I delivered lunch orders to each table, and kept my comments on Chef Marco's death brief.

After about an hour the crowd began to thin. Lance strolled in with two young starlets from the company on either arm. He carried himself like someone familiar with the stage, with an upright stance and touch of drama in his deliberate walk. Plus he was the only person in the room wearing a suit and ascot.

He escorted his leading ladies to a table and caught my attention. I wiped my hands on my apron and carried a tray of assorted pastries, cookies, and individual cakes to the front.

"Ah, the lovely Juliet. As lovely as your dainty sweets. What do you have there?" Lance stroked his goatee.

I held out the tray. "What's your pleasure?"

"Oooh, they all look delish, but I'm not here for pastry. We need to have a tête-à-tête about my soiree."

Lance hosts a bash at his house at the end of every season. He invites the entire company (at least those still in town) over for a celebratory dinner served al fresco in his large backyard garden. In the past, Mom has provided all the desserts for the party, but this year Lance hired us to cater the entire event. It will be Torte's first official catering client. If all goes well hopefully we can expand that side of the business and start doing more private events.

I handed the tray to Sterling.

"Shall we step outside?" Lance asked.

Doing a quick check of the dining room, I decided I could sneak out for a few minutes. The line at the coffee bar had vanished and there were only three tables in use. Sterling and Andy could handle those.

"For sure."

Lance ordered coffee and pastries for his actresses and held the door open for me.

The mid-afternoon fall sun filtered through the trees. A group of actors gathered near the fountains in the town plaza acting out an impromptu scene. Lance gave them a nod of approval.

"End of the season. We've only got two shows left, and then it's a wrap. They don't know what to do with all the extra time they have on their hands."

"No more matinees?"

"Nope, those are done. We have *Othello* tonight and one final performance of *The Shrew* tomorrow. Then we tear it down and go dark." His eyes misted. "I always get a touch of nostalgia at the end of the season." He fiddled with his ascot and drew in a breath. "But that's not your worry. I hear we have another murder."

I waited for him to say more. Lance and I had become friends—well, at least acquaintances—over the last few months. I liked him, but I was never quite sure of his motives. That's probably due in part to his constant effort to persuade me to audition for the company.

"Philip came and told me what happened right away." He grimaced. "Buried in buttercream. That's a stageworthy way to go if I've ever heard of one."

"Lance, a man is dead."

"Juliet, I kid. But even you must admit it's a *theatrical* death to say the least." He tugged on his ascot.

I scanned the plaza. Lance was completely overdressed in his suit. Everyone around us wore jeans, but Lance didn't look out of place. "Are you hinting at something?" I leaned closer.

"It sounds staged to me."

"And?"

He shook his head. "Darling, for someone so intelligent, you really can be thick."

"I get what you're saying. I just don't understand the significance, or why you're talking to me about this. If you have a theory on who killed Marco you should tell Thomas."

"No theory, darling. An observation perhaps."

"Lance, what are you trying to say?"

"I know the theater and I think whoever killed Marco has a penchant for dramatic flair."

"Who?"

Lance looked incredulous. "How would I know?"

"Isn't Philip your friend?"

"What does Philip have to do with this?"

"Lance." I couldn't keep the frustration out of my voice.

"You're the one hinting that someone with a theatrical connection killed Marco. Philip is the most obvious suspect in my eyes. He has a background in the theater, is consumed with making *Take the Cake* a top-performing show, and he was the last one at the Black Swan last night. He had motive—not wanting the drunk chef to tank his show—and opportunity."

"Ha!" He held his index finger in the air. "I knew it."

"Knew what?"

"You are sleuthing."

My cheeks felt warm.

"I see you blushing, darling. Don't try to hide it. I knew I could ferret it out of you." He brushed his hands together. "Success. We should really team up, you know."

"Lance, what are you talking about?" I lowered my voice as an elderly couple with a Torte box passed by us. "I'm not sleuthing."

He moved closer to me and put his arm around my shoulder. He squeezed it tight and then pointed to the group of actors in the plaza. "I know acting. You cannot fool me. You're going to help Thomas with this case and I want in."

I pulled away. "Want in? What does that even mean?"

"It means the show is closing, and let's face it, things are going to get slow in our sleepy little town. I don't start my school tour program for another couple weeks. Let's have a little fun and team up together. We can be like a modern-day Nancy Drew—and that other boy detective. What's his name?"

"You're asking me? I don't know."

Lance frowned and furrowed his brow. "I watched what you did this summer. People trust you. I think it's those pale blue eyes and that to-die-for naturally blond hair. You're like our own Sherlock, only much, much more lovely. What do you say?"

"Seriously, I'm not investigating anything. In fact it's

quite the opposite. Thomas made it crystal-clear that I'm not allowed anywhere near Marco's murder."

"Tsk-Tsk." Lance waved his finger from side to side. "We all know he didn't mean it. I've seen the way he looks at you. He most certainly wants you by his side."

"Lance. Stop." I hit him in the shoulder.

"You'll have to do better than that." He narrowed his ebony eyes. "If Thomas told you to stay out of this murder business I have a feeling that's only going to make you more determined, *Juliet.*"

I let my mouth hang open.

He tapped it shut. "That's not a good look on you. Remember, cheekbones. Don't pretend to be shocked. You and I have a lot more in common than you think."

Sterling tapped on the window. "I have to get back to work, Lance. I promise. I'm not having anything to do with Marco's murder."

"So I guess that means you're not interested in what I know."

I paused. "What do you know?"'

"Really, you are so transparent, darling." He pointed to Sterling. "It looks like you're needed inside. You better run along. Come by the theater and we'll chat about my party. Ta-ta." He blew air kisses on both my cheeks and waltzed to the plaza.

I turned to go back inside. Was Lance right? Was I that obvious? As much as I hated to admit it, there was something about solving a murder that drew me in. Maybe it was also an easy escape from worrying about my real-life problems, like Carlos halfway across the world. More than anything, I couldn't stop thinking about what Lance might know. He might be right—I was already deep in the investigation, and I didn't want out.

Chapter Twelve

Sterling handed me the phone as I stepped inside. "It's that producer."

"Jules, glad to get you live. *Take the Cake* is shooting tomorrow. I don't care what the police say. I want you at the theater. Nine A.M.—sharp! Be ready for hair and makeup."

Before I could respond, he hung up.

I stood staring at the phone.

"Everything cool?" Sterling asked. He pulled on a white hoodie with bright geometric shapes and a colorful skull. When I'd met him this summer his wardrobe consisted of one black hoodie. I was glad he was at least adding some color to his rotation of hoodies.

"It's cool. I guess as they say, 'the show must go on.' "

"My shift is done. I was gonna go skate, but I can stay if you need me." His skateboard was tucked under his arm, like an extra appendage.

"No. I'll be fine. You go. See you tomorrow."

Sterling pulled his hood over his head. He glanced to the back where Stephanie was washing cookie sheets. I thought he might say something, but he didn't. He spun the wheels on his board and walked away.

Stephanie and Andy helped clean up. They both had

evening classes so I'd be on my own for the last hour or two. We usually close late in the afternoon, but during the slow months it just depends on whether or not we have any customers. I don't mind customers hanging out at one of the bistro tables if I'm working on the next day's prep, even if it's technically after "closing."

I went to work on another Bavarian chocolate cake. Was Sebastian right? Had Marco intentionally destroyed our cakes? Maybe. Although he was so drunk, it was also likely that he had a late-night craving and decided to swipe whatever was nearby.

The doorbell jingled. I thought it was a customer, but instead it was Nina. She carted in mixing bowls, pastry knives, and two large hemp bags of her vegan ingredients.

"Where do you want me?" she asked, resting the bags by the espresso machine.

"We're going to have to share the island."

"What? I thought I was getting Marco's station. Where's his stuff?"

I nodded to the office since my hands were coated in chocolate. I was going to try a new technique for drizzling a melted ganache on the top. To practice, I poured it over waxed paper. "The police asked us to move his things. Come on back. I'd help, but as you can see I'm sort of a mess."

Nina brought her bags to the island and began unloading her baking supplies. She removed waxed paper from a glass bowl and began stirring a creamy substance that looked like butter.

"I thought you didn't use butter?"

"This isn't butter. It's futter."

"I'm sorry, what?"

"Futter. It's a vegan butter substitute."

I appreciated that she was passionate about her lifestyle, but really, futter? It took everything in me not to laugh.

"You know, you should really explore incorporating

more vegan options into your menu. Veganism is growing rapidly. I tried to tell Richard Lord the same thing but he laughed at me."

I swallowed hard. I was just as bad as Richard Lord. Nina was right. Veganism had been gaining popularity, especially among celebrities. In an alternative town like Ashland, I'm sure many of our clients would appreciate having more vegan items on the menu. I decided it was time for an attitude shift. Instead of being a food snob, which I'm usually not, I could take this opportunity to learn some new recipes and techniques from Nina.

"So tell me how it works? I know vegans don't eat meat, but you also don't eat any animal byproducts, is that right?"

She lined up a row of organic spices. "That's right. We don't eat eggs, dairy, or any other products derived from animals. The diet has tremendous health benefits, but as I was saying earlier it's also about ethics. Do you know how they treat animals in the big commercial farms?" She pointed to the eggshells in front of me. "You wouldn't believe the life those poor baby chicks had to lead."

"Hold up." Chocolate dripped from my fingers and splattered onto the waxed paper. "We source all of our products locally. All of our eggs come from free-range chickens from a nearby farm."

"That's what they all say."

I thought about responding with a snarky comment, but decided that if Nina and I were going to work in the same space together I should probably let it be.

"You want to try some futter? You'll never know the difference." She offered me a spoonful.

"Sure." I took the spoon and tasted the creamy mixture. "Nice—a light and airy texture. Am I tasting coconut?"

She took the spoon back. "Yeah. I use a mixture of coconut and olive oils. I can teach you how to make it."

"That would be great." I smiled. Baking without butter

was like painting without a canvas in my opinion, but her faux butter had a smooth texture and interesting flavor. I didn't think it compared to the gorgeous, rich original, but I was definitely up for experimenting with it.

"Thanks for letting me hang here." She whipped the futter. "I don't know how you can put up with Richard Lord. He's such a jerk, and his kitchen is stocked with nothing but processed food."

"He's something, that's for sure. But Ashland is a small town so Mom and I do our best to put our differences with Richard aside."

"I heard you used to be an actress. They're saying you're going to get your own show. You must be good."

"No. No. I did a few plays when I was younger, that's all. Trust me, I've never been an actress." I poured the last of the melted chocolate onto the waxed paper.

"If you can put on a nice face to Richard Lord then you're an actress in my book." We made eye contact across the island. She grimaced. "Hey, what do you know about Sebastian?"

"Nothing. Why?" I walked to the sink to wash the chocolate off my hands.

"I'm not sure. I can't put my finger on it, but there's something weird about him."

"You mean other than being a snotty French chef?"

She shook a combination of spices and sugar into her futter. "My bakery is in L.A. I'm used to dealing with high-end clientele every once in a while. It's not that." She paused. "I don't know. It's probably nothing."

I dried my hands on a towel and reached up to the open shelves along the wall for a cake stand. "Did he do something?"

"No. Forget it. It's me."

The front door opened before I could push her for more. I looked up to see Mom walk in.

Chapter Thirteen

"Mom. You're back!" I hurried to the front and embraced her.

She set her canvas bag on the floor and hugged me back. "We had to come, honey. There's no way Doug would have enjoyed another minute of our trip knowing that there was a murder investigation going on."

I took a step back and held both her hands. "You look great. You're so tan."

"Juliet, I've only been gone a few days."

"It looks like you've been somewhere tropical."

Her cheeks were bronzed and her eyes glowed. I hadn't seen her this relaxed in a long time.

"We sort of were. This weather has been amazing, and the wineries were stunning. We spent most afternoons sharing a bottle of Oregon pinot in the sun."

"You need to go on vacation more often, Mom. You look like a new woman." I squeezed her hands.

"Well, if I get a welcome like this every time, I'll do it." She dropped my hands and picked up the canvas bag. "Come on, I can't wait to tell you all about it." Her face turned serious. "And hear how you're doing."

"I'm fine, Mom."

She frowned.

"Really." I gave her a look to warn that we weren't alone and waved her toward the kitchen. "Mom, this is Nina. Nina is a vegan chef from L.A. who's here for the show. She's going to be baking here with us."

Mom rested her bag on the counter and extended a hand to Nina. "I'm pleased to meet you. If you need anything, feel free to let us know."

Nina thanked her and covered her mixture. "I want to bake this in the morning, before we tape. Is there a place in the refrigerator I should store it?"

"Of course, let me show you," Mom said, and led her to the walk-in fridge.

With her vegan futter creation cooling, Nina stacked dishes on her section of the island. "I'm going to the play this evening. What time do you arrive in the morning?"

"Early," Mom and I replied in unison.

Nina laughed. "Okay, I'll see you in the morning."

After she left, Mom unpacked her bag. She placed two bottles of wine, a jar of hazelnut and chocolate sauce, rosemary olive oil, and a lavender-infused honey on the island. "Doug and I had some incredible food at the wineries. I brought back a few of my favorites for you to taste. I know you want to expand and do some dinners during the slow season. I have a feeling that you can create something spectacular with these." She found the corkscrew and uncorked a bottle of Willamette Valley pinot noir.

She poured two glasses of wine and sliced a loaf of our nine-grain bread.

"Hand me that tray, would you?" she asked as she opened the honey.

I passed her the tray. She arranged slices of bread, honey, olive oil, hazelnut spread, and spoons for tasting. Handing me the glasses of wine, she said. "Let's go sit."

She carried the tray and I followed with the wine. We sat at our favorite booth next to the window. A handful of people were gathered in the plaza. They looked like they were dressed for tonight's performance of *Othello*.

We clinked our glasses together in a toast. "To you taking more vacations," I said.

She smiled and swirled her wine. "It was nice to get away. I just wish we didn't have to come back to such terrible news."

I scooped a spoonful of chocolate hazelnut sauce onto a slice of bread and bit in.

"Your face says it all." Mom grinned. "Isn't that delicious? They were harvesting hazelnuts while we were there. It's quite a process to watch. I fell in love with that spread."

The hazelnuts had been ground into melted milk chocolate for the sauce. In my opinion there's not a much better pairing than the two. I helped myself to another scoop. "I love it."

"I knew you would." Mom dished herself a slice of bread drizzled with olive oil. "Now, are you ready to talk about this murder?"

I licked chocolate from my lips. "I don't know where to start. So much has happened in such a short amount of time. I haven't even told you that *I'm* a contestant now."

Mom's eyes widened. "You're a contestant? How did that happen?"

I filled her in on how Philip convinced me to participate. Then I gave her a brief rundown of Marco and how he'd angered all the contestants in his drunken fit. When I got to the part about discovering his body I watched her brow furrow. Was that really just this morning? I felt like I'd been awake for days.

When I finished, Mom considered everything I'd said

and took a sip of wine. "I'm so sorry you have to go through this again. What can I do to help? Do you want to pull out of the show? Is it getting too stressful for you?"

"I thought about it, but if I was to win, think of the money, Mom. We could actually get Torte outfitted with everything we need."

She gave me "the mom look" as I call it. "Stop right there, young lady. We are doing just fine, thanks in large part to you. No amount of money is worth your stress."

"I know, but—."

"No buts."

"Okay, okay." I threw my hands up in surrender. "I promise I'm not going to do it just for the money. I'm already in this far. I finished my entry for the first round of the show tomorrow so I figure I'd at least give it a shot. If I end up feeling stressed, I'll tell Philip I'm out. Deal?"

Mom poured another splash of wine in our glasses. "Deal, but I know you, Juliet Capshaw, and I'm going to be watching you. If I decide it's too much, I get to pull the plug too."

"Fair enough."

We finished sampling Mom's foodie souvenirs. She gushed as she shared details about her romantic road trip with the Professor. Her face lit up as she told me about meeting the vintners, strolling through the grapevines, and how they got lost multiple times on the back roads of Oregon's wine country. Apparently the Professor learned what a terrible navigator she is. She can't read a map to save her life.

Her voice got a little shaky as she reached across the table and held my hand. "I hope I'm not making you uncomfortable."

"No, why?"

"It's been a long time since your dad died. I still miss him every day. I don't think that dull ache in my heart will ever heal, but it's been really nice to have someone like

Doug to do things like this with. I didn't realize how much I'd missed having companionship."

I dropped her hand, stood, and scooted next to her in the booth. "Mom, I love that you have someone to hang out with." My eyes began to mist. I leaned my head onto her shoulder. "Dad would want this for you too."

Tears welled in her eyes. She kissed my head and wrapped her arm around me. "What would I do without you?"

Our moment was broken by a knock on the door. Mom wiped her eyes and sat up. I blinked mine and went to see who was outside.

Philip stood on the other side of the door with his cell phone attached to his ear. When he saw me he tapped on the door. "Jules, you're here. Great. Can I come in?"

I unlocked the door.

Philip rushed in. "Glad I caught ya." He looked at his phone. I could hear someone on the other end calling his name. "Sorry. One sec." He spoke into the phone with one hand covering it.

All I heard was him repeating, "Yeah, yeah, yeah, on it." He shut the phone off and took notice of Mom who had brought our tasting tray to the front counter. "Who is this vision of beauty?" Philip brushed past me and walked straight to Mom. When he reached her he kissed both of her cheeks.

"Mom, this is Philip. He's the producer of *Take the Cake*."

Philip looked from Mom to me and back again. "I see the genetic resemblance." He moved his hands like he was framing Mom. "Imagine—a mother/daughter baking duo. Ladies, we should talk."

The sound of the door jingling made us all turn around. The Professor stood in the doorway, wearing a tweed jacket and carrying a day bag on his shoulder. "You forgot this in my car, Helen," he said, coming inside.

Mom scooted from her chair and went over to get her bag from the Professor. "Thanks, Doug. That's so sweet. I didn't need that tonight."

The Professor took notice of Philip. His demeanor stiffened ever so slightly. I'm sure to someone who didn't know him it would have gone unnoticed. He strolled over to Philip and extended his hand. "I don't think we've met."

Philip returned the handshake. "I'm in town producing a reality baking show. You may have heard of it, *Take the Cake*."

"Ah. Yes." The Professor nodded. "My crime scene."

"Your crime scene?" Philip looked at Mom for clarification.

Mom jumped in. "Sorry, Philip. Doug is our lead detective here in Ashland."

Philip's eyes lit up. "Good. Glad to hear it. Maybe you can help me. I need to roll film first thing in the morning, and the young detective up at the theater isn't cooperating."

The Professor was quiet for a moment. "A man has been murdered. Protecting the integrity of the crime scene is vital. I'm glad to hear that Thomas is following protocol."

"I get that." Philip started pacing around the table. "I hope you can also understand how imperative it is to stay on schedule. This is an expensive undertaking to shoot on location like this. Can I get a guarantee that the set will be mine by tomorrow?"

"A guarantee?" The Professor ran his fingers through his ginger beard that was starting to fleck with gray. "I'm afraid I can't do that, but I'm on my way to the theater now to take a look at how the investigation is proceeding."

Philip didn't look pleased with the response. "I'll come up there in a while. I've got to keep this production on track."

"Suit yourself." The Professor bid us all good night and left for the Black Swan.

A timid knock on the door sounded a minute later. I

figured the Professor must have forgotten something, but Linda Belle stood outside in a hot-pink dress with a sequined shawl around her shoulders.

"Oh, hi, y'all." She greeted us with the drawl. "Philip, what a surprise to see you here."

An awkward look passed between them.

I stepped aside. "Did you want to come in, Linda?"

She smiled broadly. "Actually, since Philip is here, I was wondering if I might borrow him for a minute."

"I was just about to convince these two beautiful ladies that we need to sit down and talk about a mother/daughter show. I can see it now—*The Baker's Daughter*. The camera will fall in love with both of you." Philip reached down and kissed Mom's hand. "But I can tear myself away for a few minutes."

Linda's face turned as pink as her shawl. "Thanks, sugar."

Philip started after Linda.

"Hey, Philip," I called. "Was there something you needed to talk to me about?"

His cell phone buzzed. He slid it on without looking. "What's that?"

"You said you needed to talk to me?"

He texted with one thumb as he left. "No, it can wait. See you bright and early."

Mom picked up the tray and headed to the kitchen. "That was interesting."

"Interesting?"

"He's a bit over the top."

"What do you expect, he's friends with Lance." I grabbed our wine glasses and rinsed them in the sink.

"Can you imagine Ashland without Lance?" Mom secured lids on the sauces.

"So true." I dried the wine glasses and hung them on the wall. "Speaking of Lance, he stopped by this afternoon."

Mom wiped off the cutting board. "Did he want to go over details for his end-of-season party? We should probably finalize the menu with him soon."

"I sketched out some ideas. You should take a look and let me know what you think." I pointed to the dry erase board that was mounted on the wall behind her. "That's not the only reason that he came by, though. He said he had some news about Philip, but he wouldn't tell me what it was."

"Did you tell him to talk to Doug?"

"Of course." I didn't mention anything about Lance wanting to partner up to try and help solve Marco's murder. I didn't think she'd approve.

"Bolognese sauce—that sounds perfect." Mom studied the whiteboard. "Hearty, rich, and easy to expand the recipe. Do we know how many people are coming yet?"

I shook my head. "I'll head up to the bricks. I'm sure Lance will be around. I can ask him about numbers and finalize the menu. If you think the Bolognese will work, I thought we could do bruschetta appetizers on his grill with a variety of toppings, and then for the main course serve the pasta, fresh baguettes, and Italian salads with a sun-dried tomato and basil vinaigrette."

"My mouth is watering. I think it's time for dinner." Mom grinned. "Any thoughts on dessert?"

"I hadn't gotten that far yet. Lance wants an Italian theme this year to celebrate all the critical acclaim OSF received for *The Merchant of Venice*."

"We could make your dad's Italian cream cake, and maybe poach pears in a red wine for starters."

"Look at us. We're so good." I untied my apron and threw it in the hamper next to the sink. "I'll run it by Lance and then I'll start playing around with the sauce. I have a recipe from the ship that I want to tweak a little."

Cooking for me is a sensory experience. When I have

time, I love to experiment with recipes, allowing the scent and flavor of a simmering sauce to direct my palate on what to add next. Carlos says cooking is a sensual experience. He sure made it look that way when he worked in the kitchen. He'd blast salsa music and move his hips to the beat while dicing vegetables or filleting beef. A bunch of the waitresses used to gather in the hallway to get a glimpse of him at work. I couldn't blame them. I used to do the same.

"Juliet, you're a million miles away." Mom's voice shook me free from the memory.

"Sorry. Just thinking about the party." What I didn't say aloud is that I was also thinking about Carlos, and Marco's murder. I was surprised by how little disruption there had been with Marco's death. Working on the menu for Lance's party felt equally weird and reassuring. Maybe that was normal after such a traumatic event.

Mom looked skeptical, but packed the olive oil, wine, and chocolate sauce in a grocery bag and handed it to me without saying anything more. "These are for you."

I took the bag and followed her to the front of the shop.

She paused at the front door. "Are you sure you're up for talking to Lance tonight? It's been a tough day, honey. I'm worried about you."

"I'm fine. You know me, I need a distraction. If I can't find Lance, I'll come back and work on the pasta sauce for a while."

She stood on her tiptoes and kissed my cheek. "Okay, but don't work too hard. I've got to go get unpacked from the trip. I'll see you in the morning."

I waved as she walked down Main Street. I couldn't tell her that my motivation to see Lance tonight had less to do with the menu and more to do with murder.

Chapter Fourteen

Dusky evening light greeted me outside after I sketched out our proposed menu for Lance and locked the shop up for the night. I crossed the plaza toward the Merry Windsor Inn. Richard stood on the sidewalk smoking a cigar. He was immersed in a conversation with two other older men, all smoking. I scooted past before he noticed me.

Walking is one of my favorite pastimes, especially when it's quiet. Ashland was quiet tonight with only a handful of diners seated at patio tables outside as I passed restaurants on my way up the hill to the theater complex.

The bright red and yellow Shakespearean banners attached to lampposts blended in the with the brilliant fall foliage on the trees. The evening light cast a sepia glow on the trees and the empty sidewalks. I took a deep breath in through my nose and let out a little sigh.

Once I made it up the hill, the bricks sat empty. Everyone was inside for the show. I crossed the street to the box office and checked in with the girl at the counter.

"I'm here to see Lance. Is he in his office?" I asked.

She glanced at her watch. "Probably. The show's already started, so he's finished with his intro."

As the artistic director, Lance introduces each show. The

audience—theater groupies as we sometimes call them—loves to feel like they're getting an insider's glimpse into the show from his perspective.

"Do you want me to call down there?" the girl asked.

"No, that's fine. I know the way. I'll go check."

The box office is next to the Black Swan and located across the street from the Bowmer and Elizabethan theaters. I crossed the street and entered the modern indoor theater. I knew my way around the complex from my time spent there as a kid and from delivering cakes and pastries to the theater. OSF is by far our biggest client.

Lance's office door was slightly open. I knocked lightly and peeked my head in.

"Juliet!" Lance removed his black hipster glasses and motioned me in. "To what do I owe this pleasure?"

I sat on his black leather couch and handed him our proposed menu. "I wanted to get this to you for approval so we can order from our suppliers."

Lance tapped his fingers on his goatee and ignored the paper I offered him. "And that's the only reason you trekked up here, at what?" He paused and glanced at the clock on the wall. "Eight-Fifteen."

"The party's in a few days." I pushed the menu closer.

He snatched it from my hand and turned it upside down on his desk. "This can wait." He stood and came over and sat on the couch next to me. "Why don't we talk about why you're really here, first?"

I could feel heat rising in my cheeks. One of the major drawbacks of having fair skin is that I blush easily.

Lance noticed. "Aha! I see those fine cheekbones glowing." He clapped his bony fingers together. "Enough with the act, Jules. You like the game of cat and mouse as much as I do. Admit it, and let's have a little fun. Otherwise I'll have to stalk you, and make your life positively miserable." His eyes twinkled with devilish delight.

A smile broke on my face. Lance had me pegged. "Am I that transparent?"

He reached over and stroked my arm. "Are we talking about your skin?"

I slapped his hand away.

"Play nice," he cautioned.

"What were you trying to hint at earlier with Philip?"

Lance clicked his tongue on his teeth. "Not so fast. Do we have a deal?"

"What kind of deal?"

"We're going to partner up as a little team, right?"

"I guess, but I really don't know anything. Honestly."

He tapped my knee. "That's why you need me."

"So dish. What do you know?"

Lance kicked the door shut with his foot and scooted closer on the couch. "I know that Philip couldn't have murdered that fat French chef last night."

He looked quite pleased with himself as he sat back and waited for my response with wide eyes.

"How do you know that?"

"Because, darling, he and his little tryst were with me last night."

"Tryst?"

Lance practically beamed. "I knew you'd love that." He reached into the breast pocket of his suit jacket and pulled out a tin of mints. He popped one in his mouth and offered the tin to me. "Mint?"

"No. Tell me about this tryst."

Lance slowly slid the mint tin closed and returned it to his pocket. "Patience. Patience."

I rolled my eyes.

He chuckled. "You can't blame me for wanting to build a little drama into my big reveal. It's what I do."

I hardened my eyes.

"Okay, okay." He lowered his voice. "Philip and his paramour were dining with me at Puck's Pub last night."

"You told Thomas about this, right?"

"Juliet, you're no fun. Of course I told the authorities. Philip's a friend and I know that that detective of yours would like nothing more than to pin this murder on Philip and close the case."

"Thomas is not *my* detective and, really, stop with the whole theater act. You know as well as I do that neither he nor the Professor are like that."

Lance cut me off. "We digress. What I didn't mention was that our dinner wasn't exclusively business."

"Go on."

"When Philip contacted me last year about doing the show in Ashland we talked about ways we could loop OSF in, make it mutually beneficial, you know."

I nodded. "Shocking."

"Business is business, darling."

"Believe me, I know. I feel like I'm selling a little piece of my soul by doing this show."

Lance dropped his jaw in mock surprise. "Say it isn't so." He turned serious for a moment, completely losing his affected tone. "Jules, you could never sell your soul. You and your mom are a different kind of breed."

I was taken aback by his serious shift. "Wow, thanks."

He gave me a devilish grin. "We'll never speak of it again. Now back to this *murder* business. As I was saying, Philip and I have some plans to cross-promote each other's shows. We met last night to discuss it and he brought along a lady friend."

"Who?"

"I believe you know her as Luscious Linda."

"Linda? The Southern belle? But Philip's been totally over the top flirting with me, Mom, everyone."

"Exactly. Throw suspicion away from his real fling."

"Wait, did you tell Thomas that Linda was with you? I don't understand."

"Oh, I told him she was with us for a while, which she was. Only she claimed she had a headache once Philip and I started talking shop and she ducked out early. For all I know that Southern charmer could be our killer."

"I don't understand. What didn't you tell him, then?"

"That Linda and Philip are having a smoking-hot love affair."

"Okay?" I gave him a questioning look. "What's the big deal?"

"First off, Linda's in the process of a nasty divorce back home in Georgia. She doesn't want word to get out. Philip's not exactly eager to share the news either. It's a conflict of interest for him to be involved with one of the contestants."

"I'll say." There went my chances of winning the twenty-five grand. "Did they just hook up in town, or have they known each other for a while?"

"Philip told me they had instant chemistry when he flew out to Georgia to interview her for the show. They've been at it like rabbits ever since."

"I did not need to know that. Thanks."

Lance chuckled.

"When did Linda leave?" I wished I knew the timeline for Marco's murder. "How long were you and Philip at Puck's Pub? That must be the window of time that Thomas thinks Marco was killed in?"

"Easy. Easy." He tapped his fingers on his goatee. "There's one way to find out. Don't you have a box of pastries or something to deliver to the police?" He gave me a knowing wink. A buzzer chimed on Lance's desk. He looped his fingers together and stretched. "That's my cue."

"Wait, before you go. What about the menu?" I pointed to the list on his desk.

Lance held the door open for me. "I'm sure it's perfect. Whatever you and you mother bake is a gift to the palate."

"What about numbers? Do you have a head count?"

He smoothed his goatee. "Details, darling. I'll send over a note tomorrow. Don't worry about it. You just focus those fine cheekbones on our little project. Ta-ta." He blew me a kiss and strolled down the hallway.

My mind spun as I walked down a dark and deserted Pioneer Street to my apartment. The air felt slightly damp and smelled of composting leaves. So Philip and Linda were an item. What was their connection to Marco and his murder? Could one of them have killed him to keep their affair secret? If Philip was at dinner with Lance when Marco was killed then he had an alibi. That made Linda the most likely suspect.

I was ready to be home and for this day to end. Then a new thought hit me. Lance was so eager to help me "investigate." Could he have an ulterior motive? Was there a chance he was lying to try to protect his friend?

Think about it tomorrow, Jules, I told myself as I kicked off my shoes and fell onto the couch.

Chapter Fifteen

Surprisingly, I slept through the night. When I awoke the next morning, my neck was stiff and my knees cracked. I'd crashed on the couch. Ouch.

I spent a few minutes stretching before I started my morning ritual—coffee. Brewing the perfect cup of coffee is nirvana for me. I can't do a thing until I hear the beans grinding, feel them vibrating into a fine powder in my hands and let the scent of their rich, earthy aroma hit my nose. Then, and only then, can I officially wake up. It's less about the caffeine for me than the process. I mean, a little caffeine boost certainly helps kick-start my day, but more than anything I get wrapped up in the ritual and art of brewing my ideal cup of coffee.

Vendors send us samples of their products all the time hoping that we might serve their beans at Torte. I brought home a bag of locally roasted beans from a small roaster in nearby Medford. When I opened the bag, a robust, dark flavor filled the room. The beans were coated in fine oil, an excellent sign of freshness. Going on looks and smell alone, I was pretty sure I had a winner in my hands. But I'd have to wait for it to brew before I could give it my final seal of approval. Sometimes beans can look and smell aromatic and fresh, but then once brewed end up with a bitter aftertaste. That's always a killer.

While I waited for my coffee to perk, I gave my face a quick rinse, brushed my hair into a high ponytail, and threw on a pair of jeans and a charcoal gray V-neck long-sleeved shirt. The crisp fall air required layering. By later in the day the temperature would warm into the mid-sixties or seventies, but mornings were cool. I didn't bother applying any makeup. If we were going to film this morning, the Pastry Channel makeup artists wanted a blank canvas to work with. It was easy to oblige. My normal skin-care routine is pretty simple—rinse, moisturize, and apply some lip gloss and mascara, and I'm out the door.

My coffee was ready by the time I'd dressed. I added just a touch of real cream and stirred. Holding the warm mug in my hands, I held it just under my nose and took a deep breath in. Smell is equally important to the flavor of coffee, or any other food for that matter. In culinary school, one of my instructors made us plug our noses while tasting different espressos. It's amazing how much smell informs taste. This coffee smelled ripe and aromatic.

I took a sip. Perfection. The coffee held a bold flavor, with a hint of chocolate and berries. It had a smooth finish without a hint of bitterness. I'd have to share this with Mom and Andy. It might be a contender for the bakeshop. We'd been discussing having a rotating local artisan blend "on tap" each month. Andy had approached me about hosting a coffee cupping session where customers would get an opportunity to sample a variety of blends and vote on which one they wanted in the shop. This was definitely going to get added to our list.

After I finished my coffee, I laced up my shoes and headed out into the still dark morning. I'm used to rising before the sun. I like it. I almost feel like the empty, early mornings and I share some sort of secret that the rest of the world is missing out on.

Dew coated the grass, and a slight mist hung in the air. I stuffed my hands into my jeans pockets to warm up as I took a long loop around the circular plaza before going to Torte. The shop windows were backlit, and I paused looking at elaborate fall displays. At the bookstore, the shopkeeper had erected a giant paper oak tree. Books in bright orange, greens, reds and yellows, hung from each branch and were piled like fallen leaves on the windowsill below. The kid's clothing shop had an assortment of umbrellas, rain boots, and raincoats on display. I smiled as I passed by, pleased that my fellow business owners took such pride in creating inviting and artistic displays for customers.

When I turned the handle to Torte, the door was unlocked. Mom must have beaten me in.

"Morning!" I called out, closing the door behind me.

A chorus of "Good mornings" greeted me in return.

I stored my purse in the office and headed for the kitchen where Mom, Nina, and Linda were all gathered around the island.

"Wow. It's a party in here this morning," I said, grabbing an apron from the hook and turning on the water in the sink to wash my hands.

Nina unwrapped her cake tins. Mom had stacks of butter warming and our Torte recipe book open in front of her. Linda had plastic tubs of baking supplies and ingredients taking up the middle space.

"I hope you don't mind, sugar, but your mama said it would be okay for me to work here with you ladies too." She removed tubs of glittered sugar and pearl cake embellishments from the tub. "I've got to get this finished for the competition this morning, and the theater is having a big old cast breakfast this morning. There was simply no space for me."

I caught Mom's eye. She shrugged. "Uh, I guess. We don't have a lot of space either, though."

"That's okay, y'all. I'm almost done with my cake. Just need to add some glitzy finishing touches. I'll stay out of your way. I just couldn't stand the thought of having to work with that rude French chef, Sebastian. Where I come from I'm used to being treated the way a lady should. That man is no gentleman."

Nina rolled her eyes. "Where I come from women like to be treated as equals." She shot a look at Linda's neon-colored tubes of frosting. "And we like our food natural."

Linda pretended not to hear her.

"Has anyone heard if we're even going to shoot?"

"The show is going on, as they say," Linda said. "I knew Philip would pull it off."

Mom made a big production of starting the oven, explaining to both of them that we were down an oven and would have to share. "Why don't I start coffee. Any takers?" Mom grinned through tight lips.

"I'd love a cup." Linda set a plastic Tupperware on the counter and removed the lid. She scooped gobs of white frosting onto her cake.

"Is it organic fair trade?" Nina asked.

"We use Stumptown beans," I chimed in.

Nina placed her cake in the warming oven. "I guess that'll do."

"That's not up to temp yet," I said, pointing to the oven.

"It's fine." Nina shut the oven and followed Mom to the front.

I started cubing the butter for the first round of morning pastries. Linda reached her manicured hand toward me. "You know what I don't understand about these hippie types these days is that they're so uptight and serious. It used to be that hippies were mellow and fun-loving."

That seemed like a broad overgeneralization, but I didn't

want to get in a debate with Linda over it. I'd classify Nina as New Age and health conscious, not a hippie.

I decided to change the subject and see if I could get anything out of her about where she was last night instead. "How was the play?"

Linda's fluffy frosting spread in mounds on her cake. I prefer frosting to complement the cake, not compete with it. She was being generous with the frosting to say the least.

"What play?" She stuck her index finger in the tub of frosting and took a taste. "Just like mama used to make it. Wanna try some, sugar?"

I took a taste of the frosting she offered. The texture was lighter than I expected it to be, but tasted like she used margarine instead of butter. A fireable offense at Torte. "What do you use as the base?" I asked, sliding the tub back to her.

"It's my mama's secret recipe, but I'll share it with you." She leaned closer. I could smell her peach-scented perfume. Another bakeshop no-no in my book. No one wants perfume-infused baked goods.

"What's that?"

"Crisco."

"Ah. Of course." I scooped the cubed butter into a mixing bowl. What was it with my competitors? Did they have some sort of antibutter conspiracy going on? "How was *Othello*?" I asked again.

"Oh, that play." She stuck her pastry spatula into the frosting. "It was quite charming."

Othello, charming? She had to be kidding. *Othello* is one of Shakespeare's most famous tragedies.

"I've never heard anyone call *Othello* charming."

"It was a riot. We just don't have theater like y'all do down South."

Linda tapped gold dust over her frosting. A riot? She was most certainly lying. I'd heard *Othello* described in many ways, but charming and a riot—never.

I added sugar, vanilla, and eggs to the butter and turned the mixer on low. Linda embellished her cake with gold and silver edible pearls. It wasn't exactly my style, I'm a fan of clean lines and simplicity, but if she was going for a sparkly showstopper, her cake certainly shined.

"What do you know about Philip?" I tried a less direct tactic.

Linda pasted on her signature smile, but I noticed her hand trembled as she tried to twist the cap back onto the gold dust. "Philip? Not much. He's a big Hollywood producer. That's about all I know."

"Do you think he could have anything to do with Marco's death?" I decided to try a direct approach.

She fumbled with the gold dust. It fell onto the butcher block and knocked over two other bottles of crystal sugars. "Now, why would you say that?" She didn't meet my eyes as she gathered her decorating supplies.

I alternated adding buttermilk and flour to my batter. "He and Marco were last seen together. Plus he seemed pretty worked up that Marco was trashed the other night. I get the impression that he's pretty intense about the show. If he thought Marco was going to ruin it, maybe he snapped."

Linda tried to regain her composure. She stacked her supplies on a shelf near the sink and brushed gold dust off her neon-pink apron. I'm not sure why, the dust blended in with her outfit. She batted her eyes and gave me a little wave with all her fingers. "I better head up the hill and deliver this. I have an early appointment for my makeup. Don't worry your pretty little head about this nasty murder business. I'm sure the police will figure it out. I can't imagine that Philip could have anything to do with it." Her voice sounded breathless.

I glanced at the clock. It wasn't even five-thirty. I couldn't imagine that the makeup team would be at the theater this early, but she didn't give me a chance to ask. Without another word, she picked up her cake and clicked on her high heels to the front door.

The oven dinged. Nina scurried to remove her cake. Today her hair fell in soft waves to her shoulders. I'm envious of anyone with natural curls. My hair is as straight as a pastry knife. No amount of product or attempt at curling it works—it just falls flat. My first bunkmate on the cruise ship had mounds of frizzy curls. She was jealous of my baby-fine straight locks and would spend hours trying to flatten her curls. I guess we always want what we don't have.

Nina's cake had baked to a honey color with a lovely golden top. She set it on the counter to cool and began mixing honey and futter together. Her slightly tan face, dotted with freckles, made her look like an advertisement for natural eating. Maybe there was something to this vegan thing after all.

I finished my muffin batter and scooped it into paperlined tins. Mom kneaded dough for sweet rolls and scored loaves of rising bread before sliding them into the oven. Managing three of us in the same space was doable, but when Stephanie arrived a little before six things got really tight.

Mom assigned her to work on quiches and cookies. We all bumped elbows and sucked in our stomachs to scoot past one another in route to the fridge or for supplies in the pantry. I was used to this from the ship. We had a shorthand language we'd speak: "hot pan," "behind," "coming through." It's understood when working in a busy kitchen that you have to watch your back.

Thank goodness Linda had taken off early. I didn't know how we were going to make five people work in this space.

Andy ducked in a little after six. He removed his baseball cap and fired up the espresso machine. "Sorry I'm late, boss," he said, as I brought a tray of hot loaves of bread up to the front case. "I have a midterm later today and had to pull an all-nighter."

"It's fine." I placed the tray in the case, but left it cracked slightly open so the heat wouldn't steam up the glass. "But since you're here, I'll flip the sign to OPEN."

As I reached for the sign, the door jingled. Sterling was exactly on time for his front counter duties. I held the door open for him, and Thomas appeared behind Sterling with a box of sunflowers. "Special delivery."

"Wow, you're up and about early," I said, taking the box from him and resting it on the front counter.

"You know what they say—the early bird gets the—what is it? The muffin?"

"Something like that." I took two vases of sunflowers and set them on our bistro tables.

Thomas followed behind me, grabbing the vases with wilting flowers to return to his family's shop.

"Any news on Marco's murder?" I asked.

"Jules." Thomas raised his brow. "I thought we talked about this yesterday."

I walked to the front to get another handful of flowers. "We did, but I have some news," I said, making sure no one was listening.

"What kind of news?" Thomas looked skeptical.

"It's about Philip," I whispered.

Nina interrupted us. "Thomas, I thought that was you." She held a plate of chocolate cookies. "As promised, here is one of my most popular cookies at the Garden of Vegan."

Thomas smiled and plucked a cookie from the plate. He munched it in two bites and took another. "These are great," he said through a mouthful of chocolate.

Nina offered one to me. "Try one, Jules."

I took a bite of her vegan creation. The chocolate flavor came through nicely and the cookie had a chewy density to it. I'd almost swear she'd used butter. The nutty flavor I'd tasted in her futter yesterday didn't come through at all.

"You'd never know they don't have butter, would you?" Nina beamed at Thomas.

He polished off the cookie and took one more. "Nope. I don't think so, but you'd have to ask Jules. She has the palate, not me."

Nina waited for my response.

"They're really sophisticated." I broke a cookie in half. "Great texture."

Nina fluffed her curls. "And the futter?"

I hesitated. "I'm not picking up any hint of the coconut oil. I'm surprised actually."

Nina's hands trembled as she held the plate of cookies. Thomas helped her steady them. Was she worried that he wouldn't like them?

I took another bite of the cookie and concentrated on pulling out each ingredient. I had to give Nina credit, the decadent chocolate flavor must have overpowered the coconut. No wonder Thomas scarfed down two more cookies.

Having a discerning palate is a critical skill for a chef, but one of the things that irritates me about chefs is that as a general rule they tend to believe their palates are more sophisticated than the average person. There's truth to the fact that training strengthens the palate, but I've found most of our customers are quite savvy when it comes to what they like and don't like.

Nina scooted closer to Thomas. "I was wondering if you might be free to show me around town later."

Thomas started to reply. The bell on the door rang and a handful of locals walked in for their morning fix. I excused myself to go place the remaining sunflowers on the tables and make sure we had stocked pastry cases.

I couldn't help but watch as Thomas and Nina chatted

like old friends. *Jules, knock it off.* I flicked myself on the wrist and returned to the kitchen.

Mom and Stephanie were immersed in baking. I pulled coconut and lemon muffins from the oven. The smell reminded me of the tropical lotions that guests would lather on themselves on the cruise ship. I washed my hands (a constant task in our busy bakery) while I waited for them to cool.

Nina hurried back to remove her cake. "Thomas is going to walk me up to the theater. See you there in a while." She left with her workstation a mess. Apparently he's not busy solving a murder, I thought to myself.

"Mom, how are we going to make this work?" I asked, taking muffins out of the tins and arranging them on a tray.

She directed Stephanie to add more parmesan to the quiche. "I didn't want to say anything in front of Linda and Nina," Mom said, dusting her hands in flour before rolling out sweet bread dough. "Philip left a message on the answering machine. It was waiting for us when I got in. He's going to pay us extra to have Linda here too. Apparently the theater kitchens are closing with the show. Although he didn't exactly ask if it would work. It was more like an order."

"That's how he is. I can't decide if it's just because he's used to directing people around—literally—or if he's a self-obsessed jerk."

Mom sprinkled flour on the dough and her marble rolling pin. "What do you think? Can we make it work?"

"I think we're going to have to rotate shifts or something. Maybe have one of them here in the afternoon and the other in early evening?"

"That could work," Mom replied.

Stephanie tipped the bowl to show Mom her quiche mixture before she began pouring it into pie crusts. "I think it's weird to have all these people here. I had no idea that things were so chaotic behind the scenes when I watched the show."

"I agree," Mom said, nodding her approval for Stephanie's quiche.

"That makes three of us. Something's not right with the *Take the Cake* production." I stuck the last muffin on the tray and took the tin to the sink.

Stephanie's violet eyes perked up. "Elliot thinks so too. He told me last night that Philip's in some kind of trouble."

Mom and I glanced at each other in surprise. Stephanie's not exactly forthcoming with any details. Hearing her gossip caught me off guard.

"What kind of trouble?"

Stephanie shrugged. "I don't know. He didn't say."

Sterling came around the counter to get the muffins. "Am I interrupting something?"

"No, why?" Mom asked.

"'Cause everyone shut up when I came in."

Mom laughed. "What could we possibly be talking about that you couldn't hear?" She winked at him. "Unless we were discussing how all the girls in town seem to be especially hungry for pastry and coffee these days now that you and Andy are manning the front."

Sterling almost blushed. Only Mom with her playful banter and warm brown eyes could make the übercool Sterling momentarily lose his bad-boy persona. I hadn't had a chance to mention to her that things were weird between Stephanie and Sterling, so I hoped she didn't tease him about that.

I jumped in. "Sterling, what's your take on the show? We were just talking about how something feels off with it."

Sterling stared directly at me. Stephanie kept her gaze focused on a row of quiche. "I think it's whack."

"Whack? Is that a technical term?" Mom joked.

"I don't get why a show on a big network like the Pastry Channel wouldn't have their stuff more organized." He turned his gaze to Stephanie. She didn't look up, but I knew she had to feel the intensity of his stare. "And your boy Hollywood is sketchy."

Stephanie finally tore her gaze away from the uncooked quiche and shot him a glare. "He's not sketch."

Sterling flared his nose. "How would you know? 'Cause you hung with him for one night." He ran his finger along the tattoo on his forearm.

"Stay out of my personal business." She picked up the tray of quiche with such force that egg batter sloshed all over it. "Thanks. Now look what you made me do."

"I didn't make you do anything. You're making a fool of yourself with that cheesy Hollywood kid. I thought you weren't into that whole scene."

Mom looked at me and frowned. I mouthed, "Tell you later."

"I'm not into any scene, and not that I care, but Elliot's pretty chill, actually."

Sterling made a snorting sound under his breath.

"Hey, Sterling, would you mind taking those muffins up front? I see a couple theater people heading our way." I pointed across the street.

"Gladly." He hoisted the tray on the palm of his hand and shook his head as he returned to the front.

Stephanie pursed her lips and gave him a death stare. "I don't know what his deal is." She wiped her hands on her apron with force.

"Why don't you go wash up in the bathroom?" Mom suggested to Stephanie. "We can salvage the quiche, can't we, Jules?"

"Of course." I walked over to the tray of quiches. "Not a problem."

With Stephanie gone, I quickly filled Mom in on their love spat.

"I haven't met Elliot," Mom said. "What's he like?"

"He's pretty much exactly like Sterling's description. He looks like he's already had work done and he's only in his mid-twenties. He seems nice enough, but I'm with Sterling. There's something off-putting about him. He kind of went after Marco last night." I paused. He had. If Elliot was consumed with his *sexy* baking and Marco threatened the show, could that be a motive for murder?

"Plus, I wonder why he had such a sudden interest in Stephanie. That's always a red flag for me."

"I don't know, sometimes love at first sight can be magnetic." Mom coated her sweet bread with a jar of our apricot jam.

"Yeah, tell me about it." I knew from the second that I first saw Carlos that I was destined to be with him. I'd never had that feeling before. I'd heard people talk of falling in love at first sight and liked the romantic idea behind it. But until I met Carlos I'd never experienced a visceral draw to another person. It was as if there was a string of energy attaching us—pulling us toward one another. Look where that got me, though. I hoped Stephanie didn't jump in too fast with Elliot. I didn't want to see her make the same mistakes.

Chapter Sixteen

I popped the quiche into the oven and ripped a piece of paper out of the spiral notebook we keep by the whiteboard, to map out a schedule for Linda, Nina, and myself. If I allotted each of us a three- to four-hour window of time with a little overlap, I thought that should be enough to complete one dessert, and maintain sanity at Torte.

The bakeshop rose to life just like the bread baking in the oven as locals streamed in for a latte on their way to work or to talk shop over a chocolate croissant. I removed my cake from the refrigerator and finished it off with some shaved chocolate curls.

"Is that your cake?" Mom asked. "It's absolutely gorgeous. You're totally going to win. Don't you think so, Andy?"

Andy brought the sugar canister from the coffee bar to refill. "What's that, Mrs. C?"

"Juliet's cake. Isn't it beautiful?"

He scooped sugar in the raw into the canister. "Yeah, good job, boss. If you win does that mean we all get raises?"

"Only if I get one first." I laughed. "Are you guys set for the morning? I've got to head up to the Black Swan. I have no idea if the show is going to take an hour or all morning."

"We've got this." Andy looked at Mom. "Right, Mrs. C?"

Mom nodded emphatically and waved me toward the door. "Go. Go."

I placed my cake in a flat cardboard box and gave the kitchen one last inspection before heading out. Nina's organic vegan ingredients and supplies took up one corner of the island, and Linda's pastel cupcake liners and hot pink custom spatulas and cookware took up the opposite side. Their workstations couldn't be more different. Linda's supplies were neatly stacked in colorful Tupperware with laminated labels. Nina's idea of organization was more free-flowing, or in other words, it looked like she opened a tub and threw it all over the counter.

I'll tackle the mess later, I thought as I positioned the box between my arms and left Torte in Mom's very capable hands.

As I turned off Main Street, I heard the sound of men shouting. The voices were coming from the Merry Windsor. One of them sounded familiar, but I couldn't place it. The other was Elliot Cool, who came storming out of the Merry Windsor's back entrance and nearly knocked me off my feet.

"Sorry." He helped steady my cake box. "I didn't see you there."

"That's okay." I checked to make sure the cake hadn't touched the sides of the box. It hadn't. "No damage done," I said to Elliot, shifting the box in my arms.

"You on your way to the theater?" he asked, walking in step with me.

"Yep. You?"

"Looks that way." His chest muscles flared underneath his skintight T-shirt that read BAKING IS SEXY.

"Is everything okay?" I asked.

He glanced behind. "Yeah, why?"

"No reason. I thought I heard the sound of someone fighting back there."

"You did?" He looked behind us again. "I didn't hear anything."

That was impossible, but I played along. "Hmm. Must have been Richard Lord. He's always yelling at someone."

Elliot gave one final glance behind us. Was he checking to see if someone was coming after him? "So what's the deal with your pastry apprentice, Steph?"

"Steph?" I raised my eyebrow. Stephanie hates being called "Steph."

He nodded. "She's single, right?"

"I try to stay out of my employees' private lives."

"Come on. You must know if she's hanging with anyone. In a town this small." Elliot flashed me his most bedazzling smile. I'm sure that worked for his fans, but I was not buying his slick act, and I felt protective of Stephanie.

"My lips are sealed. You're right, in a town this small, whatever you dish out in terms of gossip finds its way back. I've learned it's best to stay out of that loop."

Elliot frowned. "Whatever."

I had the sense that Elliot's level of self-confidence led him to believe that most of the women he met were easily charmed.

He changed the subject. "So word on the street is that you're the one to beat."

"Really?"

"Duh. Yeah." He rolled his eyes. "Philip thinks the camera loves you. I hear he wants to make you a star." His tone shifted. He sounded bitter. "A word of advice: be careful what you wish for. This gig isn't all it's cracked up to be."

"Are all productions this chaotic?"

"No. I'd run away as fast as you can. That's what I'm thinking of doing."

This news surprised me, but I didn't have a chance to probe him further. We arrived at the Black Swan. Elliot held the door open for me and then headed to the stage, where he began practicing his opening statement.

"Jules. You're here, great." Philip motioned from the set.

My stomach felt jittery as I walked through the theater. At this time yesterday I'd discovered Marco's body right here. I knew that Thomas and the Professor must have completed their initial investigation since we were filming. That meant that any evidence of a crime here had been scrubbed clean, but still I couldn't shake my unease as I moved toward the set.

I took a deep breath. You can do this, Jules, I said as I stepped into the kitchen. The overhead lights glared on the shiny countertop where I set my cake.

"Now that is a work of art." Philip admired my cake.

Lance stood behind him. He smiled broadly as I stopped in mid-stride at the sight of him. "I told you she was good, Philip. Now if you could do something about this atrocious lighting. You're wasting that absolutely perfect complexion under these god-awful things."

Philip turned his attention to Lance. "How many times do I have to tell you that the stage and set are two totally unique beasts?"

"Set? Please." Lance rolled his eyes. "Juliet, did you know that my dear friend Philip had quite an impressive career on the stage before he decided to slum it in television."

"Slum it? Let's talk salaries, Lance. What do you say?"

Lance tightened his tie and gave Philip a dismissive wave.

"Exactly!" Philip smirked. "Jules, what do you say? You can stick here with Lance and live the small-town life, or come to Hollywood with me, where the real money is."

The banter between them seemed friendly enough, but I wasn't about to get in the middle of their argument.

"Keep me out of this."

"But do put her on television." Lance walked to me and tilted my head toward the lights. "I mean, can you believe this bone structure? It's to die for."

"Believe me, I have big plans for her," Philip said. "She's star material."

Elliot shot Philip a nasty look, and cleared his throat on the stage. "Uh, I'm trying to work here, guys. Can you keep it down?"

Philip pulled out his cell phone. "You're due for makeup anyway, Jules. We'll talk later. They're in the back."

"And you're sure it's okay to keep filming?" I asked.

"Fine. Fine. It's all been cleared. I came back up here and worked it all out with that detective late last night. What do you call him, the maestro?"

"Professor."

"Right. Right. The Professor gave me the green light. We're wasting green money every minute we're not shooting, so do me a favor and get back into the makeup chair so we can get this baby rolling."

Lance held out his arm. "Let me escort you to makeup, darling. Philip, fix those lights."

On our way backstage, Lance whispered, "What else have you learned? Any new delightful suspects in our little investigation?"

"Not really. I know for sure that Linda lied about being at the theater last night. She called *Othello charming*."

Lance threw his hand to his heart. "Say it isn't so. If I produced a charming *Othello* I should be banned from the company for life."

"I know. She's obviously lying."

"What else?"

"That's all I've got so far."

"Keep your ears open, darling. And remember, you promised to keep me in the loop." He blew me a kiss as he deposited me behind the stage where the hair and makeup team had set up a temporary workstation.

Nina sat in one of the chairs simultaneously having her curls teased and her lips glossed. One of the makeup artists called me over to her station and immediately set to work. She dusted my entire face with a translucent powder and enhanced my cheekbones with blush. "Let's dust gold on your lids," she said, holding a small tub of gold powder for me to see.

"You're the expert."

"It's going to look amazing."

I shrugged and let her finish. She offered me a handheld mirror. "What do you think?"

Maybe I should rethink my feelings on gold. My eyes looked like the top of Linda's sparkly cake. The gold shadow brought out the green and yellow flecks in my eyes, but wasn't so overdone that I didn't look like myself.

I handed the mirror back. "It's great. Thank you."

A wardrobe assistant helped us all tie our aprons at the same level so that the *Take the Cake* logo was displayed prominently on our chests.

Philip bellowed into a megaphone. It seemed unnecessary since there were only five of us, plus a handful of workers from the production crew. "Gather round, chefs."

Linda, Nina, Sebastian, and I all crowded into the kitchen, where Elliot stood talking into his mic and directing the lighting crew to reposition the overhead lights for the best angle.

"Elliot. Knock it off. That's my job. You look fine." Philip rolled his eyes and handed each of us a sheet of paper with our stage directions and a minute-by-minute schedule. "I want to get this as tight as we can. We'll start with a quick little backstory to get to know each of you. I'll be sending out a crew to film on location as well, so try to keep it short." He checked his phone. "We're just waiting for one more contestant."

Nina raised her hand. "What contestant?"

"I found someone to fill in for Marco. We need five chefs in order to make this thing work." There was something about Philip's intensity about the show, and total lack of acknowledgment that a man had just been killed, that made me feel like I was living in some sort of alternate reality.

Maybe he read my mind. He continued on. "We'll be doing a special segment before the first episode, paying our respects to Chef Marco. I have it all planned out. I'm sending a crew to New York to get some shots of Marco's restaurants. They'll interview some of his customers. I haven't had confirmation from our publicist yet, but it sounds like we might even get a couple celebrity interviews."

Okay, maybe the guy had a heart after all.

Philip continued. "It's going to be real a tearjerker. We're going to run a whole ad campaign leading up to the tribute episode telling people to grab tissues. I have a feeling that ratings are going to be through the roof for this one."

Or maybe not.

He pointed at Nina. "You go first. We'll start these interviews. Then I'll get a group shot of you all together for the intro." He tugged her toward an *X* on the floor. "Here's your mark. Stand here. Look at that camera and act natural."

The intense overhead lighting shone on Nina's face as she stood with her hands at her sides staring at the camera aimed at her face.

"What should I do with my hands?" she asked, holding them up like goalposts.

"Not that," Philip said.

Nina stuck one hand in the front pocket of her *Take the Cake* apron and rested the other on her hip.

"Or that," Philip said. "Just be natural."

I caught Nina's eye. She reminded me of a skittish mouse. Acting natural with a camera in your face and the knowledge that you're going to be on national TV was easy enough for Philip to demand, but I had a feeling I was going to look just like Nina when my turn arrived.

Philip tried to position Nina's hands for her. That made it worse. Finally he shooed her out without asking a single question. "Linda, come show everyone how it's done."

Linda practically danced over to her mark and started right in with her Southern drawl. She moved her hands and flirted with the camera. Nina stood watching with her arms crossed and a scowl on her face.

Sebastian didn't need any guidance from Philip either. He played the role of snooty French chef to perfection, looking at the camera with disdain and throwing out a number of culinary terms that the average viewer would never know.

My palms were sweaty when Philip called my name. I arched my shoulders and took a deep, centering breath, trying to stay ahead of my nerves.

"The camera loves you," he fawned as I introduced myself to our not-yet-existent viewers.

My speech may have been a little rushed, but my cheeks felt like they'd retained their normal amount of heat and hadn't flushed in front of the camera. The last thing I wanted to look like was an overripe tomato. I was glad to have the first little piece over. Philip assured us all that as we spent more time under the lights and in front of the camera we'd forget they were even there. I wasn't sure about that, but I was happy that I hadn't bombed like Nina.

Philip made her do her intro over. If possible, she appeared to be even stiffer the second time around. I felt sorry for her. If her workstation was any indication of her attitude, I thought she would have been the loosest of all of us. Maybe she'd do better once we were all interacting with each other. I thought it would be easier to talk with my fellow contestants versus just hearing my own voice.

Nina hunched her shoulders and came to stand next to me. "That was horrid."

"Don't sweat it," I whispered as Philip went over our marks, directing us to where he wanted us to stand next. "He says it's going to get easier."

Nina didn't look convinced.

I squeezed her arm. "Really, don't worry. It'll be fun."

At that moment a booming voice echoed in the theater. "Hello, anyone home?"

"Back here," Philip called. "Our final contestant has arrived."

Heavy footsteps sounded in the theater. I didn't need a visual of the new contestant. I'd know that voice anywhere. Richard Lord was joining the show.

Chapter Seventeen

"What's *he* doing here?" Nina muttered under her breath.

"One guess," I said, pointing to the cake Richard carried in. I'd bet good money he'd purchased it at the grocery store. How had Richard schemed his way onto the show? I had a feeling it probably had to do with money too.

"Richard." Philip greeted him with a slap on the back. "You are saving my hide, man. Thanks for being here."

"My pleasure." Richard stared in my direction and gave me an evil grin. "Anything I can do to give our little town some visibility."

Philip took Richard's cake and placed it next to the others. Then he sent Richard back for makeup and continued to direct us on our next tasks. "Elliot, you ready for this?" Philip asked.

Elliot did a couple jumping jacks and gave his entire body a shake. I'd seen actors at OSF go through similar preshow rituals to get their nerves settled. He took his mark in the center of the kitchen. The instant Philip gave him the sign that the cameras were rolling, Elliot snapped into his TV persona.

"Hey, hey, home bakers. Are you as excited as I am to

kick off another season of *Take the Cake*?" He whipped a spatula in the air like a weapon.

Elliot paused, watching Philip for the next hand sign. Philip shot his index finger in the air and Elliot continued on.

"Why are they pausing so much?" Nina whispered.

"I think they must add in applause or something."

"Like a laugh track."

I shrugged. "Not sure. It's just a guess. He stops at all the points when an audience would respond, though."

Nina leaned closer as Philip shot us a look. "It's kind of cool to watch it happen. I'd never guess things were so chopped up."

Elliot finished his exaggerated opening, explaining the rules of the competition to viewers, introducing each of us, and drooling over the cakes lining the counter. He'd obviously done this before. He acted completely at ease in front of the camera, and knew before Philip signaled when to pause and start again. I had to agree with Nina, watching a television show from the comfort of home was a completely different experience than watching it come together in front of me.

Richard returned from the makeup chair with a thick of layer of powder attempting to cover the ruddy color of his cheeks. "Juliet, don't look so surprised to see me. You're not the only chef in town."

"I never said I was." I tried to keep my tone even, but Richard had a way of getting under my skin.

"Too bad about that chef's death, but kind of a bonus for me."

"I'm not going to dignify that remark with a comment." I folded my arms across my chest. "What did you do, bribe your way in?"

Richard answered my question with a grin. He took

great pleasure in making me angry. If we were going to work on set together, I was going to have to find a way not to let him get me riled up. Being camera shy was suddenly the lowest problem on my list.

We spent the next two hours shooting and reshooting. Once Philip was confident he had the shots he needed, we moved on to the taste-testing portion of the show. Elliot and two professional judges would taste each entry, provide their personal critiques, and crown a winner for each round. The judges looked like they belonged in a courtroom with their starched black aprons and matching dark expressions.

"Okay, home bakers, things are about to get real." Elliot jumped to center stage, and cracked an amused smile. His gaze lingered on us for a moment before he whipped around and introduced the judges.

Elliot teased out each word, putting just the right emphasis on every syllable as he announced the first judge. "Home bakers, put your hands together for the one-and-only, world-class patisserie chef, joining us all the way from Paris, France . . . Maaa—dame Duuu—bois!" He sounded like the football announcer from Thomas's high school games.

A petite woman wearing thick black glasses about the size of her head gave a curt nod. Elliot leaped off the stage and walked over to Sebastian. "A French chef and a French judge, *oooh*, this could get interesting, you guys."

Madame Dubois adjusted her glasses and squinted at Sebastian.

"Any thoughts on how your fellow countryman is going to fare in this bake-off?" Elliot asked, casually resting his arm on Sebastian's shoulder.

Madame Dubois peered at Sebastian from behind her glasses. Her eyes disappeared in a thin slant as she appraised him. "Non, I do not know dis chef."

Elliot nudged Sebastian, who threw him off with such force I thought Elliot might wind up on the floor. Sebastian avoided Madame Dubois's gaze, while Elliot quickly recovered.

"Man, the tension in here is on fire. I love it!" He hopped back on stage and stood next to the other judge. "Home bakers, I'm superexcited to have you meet our other judge, coming to us from the C—I—A! That's right, the CIA."

Nina started. "CIA?" she mouthed.

Before I could answer, Elliot chuckled. "I see some of our competitors are looking a little green." He stared at Nina. "Running from the law, or something?"

Nina shook her head. She looked uncomfortable. I couldn't tell if it was from having Elliot's attention focused on her, or if she was skittish about something else.

Elliot grinned at the camera. "That's right, home bakers, joining us from the CIA, also known as the Culinary Institute of America." He winked at Nina. "Is master chef Harold Maaar—shall!"

Harold acknowledged each of us with a stern grimace. Elliot clapped. "Let's do this!" Perfectly plated slices of each of our cakes appeared before the judges. "Home bakers, hold on to your cookbooks. Watch your pastry knives. *Take the Cake* has officially begun!"

I held my breath as each judge took a bite of my cake. Philip had instructed the judges to stay neutral during taste-testing and reserve their comments until they'd tasted all the offerings. I tried to read their expressions, but everyone's face remained stoic.

Finally, after what felt like an eternity, Elliot jumped onto center stage again and announced that the judges were ready to weigh in. Linda faced the gauntlet of judges first. She received rave reviews for her design and use of embellishments. Her cake also received high marks for taste and texture, but both Elliot and Madame Dubois agreed with my assessment, that her frosting was too sweet. Nina's non-dairy cake was met with mixed reviews. They liked the overall flavor, but weren't thrilled with the texture. Richard's cake (shockingly) didn't make the cut. He was declared the clear loser for round one, and stalked away pretending to be angry. I knew he could care less. He was just happy to get his mug on TV.

It came down to Sebastian and me. Sebastian's intricate marzipan design wowed the judges. I could feel my stomach flop as I waited in front of the three of them to receive my feedback.

"Stunning cake, Jules," CIA president Harold Marshall said, sticking his fork back into the piece of cake in front of him. "I can't stop eating it. It has such a great balance of sweetness, with the bitter chocolate. Not too rich. Super-moist. Mouthwatering. This one's a winner in my book."

I smiled. One down. Two to go.

Madame Dubois had similar kind words for my creation. I'd never considered that I'd be so nervous hearing what they thought. I felt like I was back in culinary school.

Working on a large cruise ship rarely gave me an opportunity to talk directly with passengers about my pastries. On a rare occasion, I might get called to a table, and in those cases, passengers usually had great things to say about my creations. The same was true at Torte. Our customers tended to rave about our products. I couldn't remember a time in recent history when anyone had ever complained about taste.

Once this summer we had a tourist complain that her drink order was taking too long. Andy was the fastest barista in town, but when we get slammed during the busy season it can take a couple extra minutes. My motto is: great coffee is worth the wait. But my other motto is: the customer is always right, so we gave her a complimentary cookie and a gift card for a free coffee. She was back the next day with a group of her friends.

For this part of the competition, the judges were critiquing us on presentation, design, and taste, which included the overall flavor and texture of our cakes.

Elliot was the last judge to provide feedback on my cake. "Not bad." He held his plate for the camera to pan closer, then he stabbed his slice of cake with his fork. "See how the cake holds on to the fork? Great texture." He took a bite. "Nice flavor density. I like the balance of the chocolates. What kind of chocolate did you use?"

"A Bavarian milk chocolate and a dark chocolate ganache," I replied.

"What's the frosting?"

"A chocolate cream cheese."

"That's what I thought." Elliot nodded. He turned to Madame Dubois seated next to him. "It's missing something I can't put my finger on."

Madame Dubois caught my eye.

Elliot snapped his finger in the air. "Got it. Salt."

"Salt. Oui." Madame nodded in agreement.

"A finishing salt, just to enhance the forward finish of the ganache."

Philip called everyone to the front while the judges deliberated over a winner. Elliot might have a point about salt. Finishing salt is also known as sea salt, not table salt that comes from a shaker. We use finishing salts in a variety of pastries, breads, and savories at Torte. Our vendor harvests the salt off the Oregon coast. The delicate flakes enhance the flavor of everything from fresh-cut tomatoes to chocolate. One of the additional benefits of using a finishing salt is that you don't have to use very much. A little sprinkle goes a long way. I kicked myself for not thinking of it. I'd have to try adding salt when I made the cake for the bakeshop.

The judges huddled together, speaking in low tones, while Philip went over the next phase of the competition. "All right, everyone." Philip tapped on his clipboard. "Once the judges declare a winner for this first round, we'll go ahead and get that on film and then you're free to go for the afternoon. We'll resume the shoot first thing in the morning. As you'll see on the production schedules I passed around this morning, the second round is signature desserts. I'll be sending a camera crew out on location to get some footage of all of you at work in the kitchen. You'll each need to submit one dessert that defines you and your style. Ideally, I'd like it to be something that represents the region you're from. I know that might be kind of hard with Jules and Richard since you're both from around here, but just do whatever you think represents your pastry shop."

It was everything I could do to stop myself from blurting out a snide comment about Richard's signature dessert being stale, day-old, warehouse pastries.

He beat me to it. "Shouldn't be a problem. The Merry Windsor is known all around town for our world-class pastries." He gave me a smug look. "Right, Juliet?"

The judges announced that they'd come to a decision, saving me from entering into a battle with Richard Lord. It was futile anyway.

"I want you all lined up on your marks in the kitchen," Philip directed.

We complied, as the cameras focused on Elliot who gave a quick recap of each of us and our desserts.

He paused dramatically. "Before I announce our winner, I have to send someone to the kitchen for dish duty."

Dish duty? This was news to me. No one mentioned anything about dish duty.

"That's right, home bakers, whoever's cake gets cut is on dreaded dish duty," Elliot continued. "Someone is about to be in hot water."

This must be a ploy for the show. Philip didn't really expect the loser to go from kitchen to kitchen to do the dishes? Or did he? I hoped it was just an attempt to make the show more dramatic, because I certainly didn't have time to go do everyone else's dishes.

Elliot looked at each of us intently. Finally he landed on Richard Lord. I was pretty sure this is where they would add dramatic background music. I could almost hear the "Dun, dun, dun . . ." beat in my head. "Richard Lord, your cake was a recipe for disaster. It's dish duty for you." Elliot stabbed Richard's cake with a sharp knife and pointed him out of the kitchen.

Watching him stab the cake sent a shiver down my spine.

"Nina and Linda, you're both free to leave the kitchen. While both of your cakes were decent, they weren't great. Nina, your cake was just off. The flavor just wasn't there. We want to see stylized dessert—think seductive and spicy next time."

Elliot acted like he was enjoying this part of the show. I knew that he was supposed to make viewers at home feel the pressure and intensity of someone being named the clear winner of *Take the Cake,* but he was obviously playing up the drama. He continued, waving a spatula in Linda's face. "Linda, your cake was over-the-top sweet. Go easy on the sugar next time. Both of you hang your aprons on the hooks and get out of the kitchen."

They both exited the set. Elliot fixed his hair, and then nodded for Philip to keep filming.

"That leaves us with Jules and Sebastian. Step forward." Elliot motioned us closer to the stage with his spatula.

Sebastian and I moved closer to the judge's table.

"We had some debate on this, but after much deliberation, we've decided on a winner. Jules, your cake impressed us with its simple design and rich chocolate flavor, nicely balanced with the tangy cream cheese frosting. Sebastian, you knocked it out of the park with your marzipan work."

Sebastian wrapped his arms around his waist.

I just wanted Elliot to get it over with—tell us already. I wondered what I looked like on camera. Probably a nervous wreck.

Elliot held up a brown spatula with the *Take the Cake* logo. "Today's winner is . . ."

A cameraman zoomed his camera on both Sebastian and me.

"Sebastian!" Elliot cheered. "Come take the spatula."

Sebastian smirked and walked to the judge's table to take the spatula from Elliot.

"Well done," Elliot said as he leaned down and handed the spatula to Sebastian. "Congratulations."

Off to the side of the set, Nina and Linda clapped along with the crew. I quickly joined in the applause. I didn't want to look like a sore loser to my fellow contestants or when this aired on TV. Although I did have to admit that I felt a bit dejected that I hadn't won. I'm used to people raving about my pastries, especially since my only competition in town was Richard Lord. Let's face it, that's not really competition. I could feel my competitive spirit starting to rise. I wanted to wow the judges on my next entry.

Philip called it a wrap for the day and reminded everyone to be prepared to be on camera later in the day. Nina asked if she could take the first shift at Torte. Linda would take the afternoon shift and I'd stay late. That was fine by me. I needed time to decide on what my "signature dessert" was going to be. Plus, I was hoping I'd have a chance to find Thomas this afternoon and finish our conversation about Marco's murder.

Chapter Eighteen

By the time I made it back to Torte, the lunch rush was in full swing. I didn't have time to dwell on Marco's murder or think about what to make for tomorrow's competition. Nina worked on her dessert, a fruit and nut compote that she planned to serve with a nondairy ice cream, while Mom and I made sandwiches and packed boxes to go.

The tension between Stephanie and Sterling was palpable. Whenever he came into the kitchen for a tray of fresh scones or to drop dirty dishes in the sink, she pounded the bread dough so hard, I thought she might do permanent damage to her knuckles. Mom and I were going to have to do an intervention with the two of them if they couldn't figure things out—soon.

Nina finished her compote and set it aside to work on her ice cream. "How did you think that went?" she asked as I wrapped up the last boxed sandwich order.

"Good, I guess. It was a bit more intense than I expected it to be."

"Exactly. I can't believe they picked Richard to take Marco's place. He doesn't even bake, does he?"

"Nope. His idea of baking is prepackaged pastry that

comes in the freezer. Don't worry though, he's all bark. No bite."

Nina mixed together the ingredients for her ice cream. The camera crew arrived to film her at work. Mom and I gave them space in the kitchen, and used the opportunity to grab a bite to eat ourselves. Finding time to eat is always a challenge. It seems like the minute one of us sits down, the door will jingle and a new rush of customers will flood in.

Mom and I split a baguette with Havarti cheese and rosemary and sun-dried-tomato-encrusted ham.

"How did it go this morning?" Mom asked, pouring us each a glass of soda water. Carlos always called it "gas water." It used to make me laugh when he'd order "gas" when we went to a late-night dinner at port.

"Good. I didn't win."

Mom looked injured. "What? That's impossible. Let me go have a word with those judges. Obviously someone made a mistake." Her brown eyes sparkled as she teased. "Who won?"

"Sebastian. He's a French chef from Portland."

"That sounds about right." Mom tore a hunk of bread from the baguette. "Were you nervous?"

"A little." I nodded through clenched teeth.

"Do you remember how nervous you were when you did your first performance of *A Midsummer Night's Dream*? Your dad and I thought we were going to have to call the director and tell him that you couldn't do it. You were green for days before the show, and then when opening night came you walked out on stage like a pro. I think it was the anticipation. Once you actually did it you were fine."

"Some things never change." I took a sip of the fizzy water. The bubbles hit my nose. I coughed. "I thought about bailing this morning."

The door jingled. So much for the lunch break, I thought as I looked up from my drink.

Thomas and the Professor were heading our way. Mom sat a little taller and pinched her cheeks when she noticed the Professor had arrived.

"Stop. You look perfect." I batted her hand from her face. I wasn't lying. She did look perfect. Her bronze skin glowed against her sunflower-colored linen shirt. Her shoulder-length bob appeared unfazed by the heat and humidity of the kitchen.

The Professor strolled to our table. He had an easy yet commanding presence. It was clear he was comfortable in his own skin. Thomas turned and headed to the kitchen. I couldn't help but watch as he leaned on the counter, waiting for Nina to finish filming her segment for the show.

"Juliet, nice to see you." The Professor greeted me with a slight bow. He slid into the booth next to Mom and kissed her on the cheek. "Helen, you look like a vision as always." Both of them beamed at one another. I felt like I was intruding on something, and started to excuse myself.

The Professor held out his arm as I inched out of the booth. "Many apologies. I didn't mean to interrupt your lunch."

"No, no, it's fine. I should go check in with the team anyway. You two chat."

"Actually, I was hoping you might have a moment to spare." The Professor reached into the breast pocket of his tweed jacket and removed a Moleskin notebook and pencil. His auburn beard, streaked with gray, matched his jacket. I smiled as I read the inscription on the front of the notebook: "A Fool Thinks Himself to Be Wise, but a Wise Man Knows Himself to Be a Fool."

"Is that Shakespeare?" I asked, pointing to the quote.

"None other than the bard himself could have such wise words, don't you agree?"

The Professor moonlights as Ashland's resident Shakespearean scholar. It would be hard to debate whether or not

he was more well-versed in Shakespearean sonnets or police procedures. Thomas had confided that even with taking extensive notes on his iPad, he sometimes couldn't
follow the Professor's cerebral musings.

Mom, on the other hand, blushed like a schoolgirl whenever the Professor was around. I loved seeing her like this,
but it also made me hyperaware of how neglected my love
life was at the moment.

"What did you want to ask me?" I gathered my plate and
glass together.

"I was hoping you might be able to go over what you remember from the night before the murder and the morning that you discovered the deceased."

"Sure, but I already went over all this with Thomas."

The Professor flipped through his notebook. "Yes, I
know, but Thomas and I have a few more questions that
have arisen as we've explored some leads. Do you have a
free moment?"

Mom nudged him. "Scoot out. I'll let you two talk. I
need to go check on a batch of cookies anyway." She gave
me a quick smile. The Professor stood so she could exit the
booth. He kissed her hand and their eyes lingered on each
other for a moment before she hurried to the kitchen.

"Lovely woman, your mother, Juliet." The Professor's
eyes looked glassy as he watched her.

I turned and followed his gaze. "I know. She's the best."

"That's what she says about you." He stroked his beard.

"You wanted to ask me about Marco's murder?" I
nodded toward his notebook.

He chuckled. "Thanks for keeping me on task." He removed his tweed jacket and rested it on the back of the
booth.

"It's what I do."

Flipping through the notebook, he paused on a page and

studied it for a moment. His face was slightly weathered, but I could understand why Mom got giddy around him. He was distinguished and quite handsome for someone his age. "Could you humor me and walk me through what you remember from that night again?"

I told the Professor exactly what I'd said to Thomas. He stopped me when I got to the part about Marco and Philip's fight.

"What time was this?"

I shrugged. "I'm not exactly sure. Sometime after nine. We all left shortly after."

He raised an eyebrow. "Everyone left?"

"Uh. I think so."

"Can you remember? Was anyone still in the theater when you left?"

My mind churned over the images of that night. Nina and I left together. Where was Linda? Had she stayed behind? And Sebastian and Marco? I couldn't remember if either of them left before us or not. I'd been so distracted by Marco's drunken rage that I wasn't sure my observations were worth noting. I told the Professor as much.

He stroked his beard. "Hmm."

"Is it important?"

"Perhaps."

The Professor didn't offer any more. He scratched something in his notebook and continued with his line of questions. Once he was done, he folded the notebook and returned it to his breast pocket. "Thank you for your time, Juliet. You've been most helpful." He stood to leave.

I didn't feel helpful. I hadn't told him anything new. However, now my head was humming about the possibility that either Linda or Sebastian could have been at the Black Swan with Marco.

Thomas came to the front of the shop to check in with

the Professor. "Hey, Jules." He held a handful of vegan cookies that Nina had baked. "Want one?" He popped one in his mouth and offered one to the Professor.

The Professor declined. "Shall we continue on our quest?"

Thomas glanced to the kitchen where Nina was being interviewed by the television crew. "Sure. Catch ya later, Jules," he said, shoving another cookie in his mouth and following after the Professor.

He didn't even give me a chance to follow up on our discussion earlier this morning. Not to mention that he seemed more than a little distracted when Nina was around. I couldn't decide if her vegan sweets really were that tasty, or if Thomas was really sweet on her.

Linda Belle breezed in with a new outrageous outfit before I let myself stew on Thomas. She'd changed into a teal pantsuit since earlier in the morning. Her arms and neck were adorned in gold jewelry. I could never pull off such a gaudy look, but somehow it worked on her.

"Sugar, you are just who I was looking for."

"What can I do for you, Linda?" I asked, glancing at the clock. Linda wasn't due for her turn in the kitchen for another hour.

"I can't find my recipe for Southern banana cream pudding anywhere. I know that Chef Marco stole it. I've searched my hotel room. It's not there. I swear I had it in my special file that I keep on me. You can't trust anyone in a competition like this."

My eyes must have widened.

"Well, excepting *you*. Is it okay if I go check through my things here? I see Nina is filming. I'll stay out of her way."

"It's fine by me."

She fanned her hand in front of her face. "I don't know what I'll do if I can't find it. It was my great-great-grandma's recipe. Been in the family for years now. I bet you that nasty Marco stole it."

"Can't you re-create it?" I asked. Most chefs tend to use recipes like a rough outline. I'll use a recipe as my base and tweak it to fit my mood, or whatever ingredients I have on hand. Recipes we bake daily, I know by heart. It surprised me that Linda would need a recipe to bake a dessert that had been in her family for years.

"I don't know if I can." She fanned her face again. Her cheeks were splotched with color. "I don't know what I'm going to do if I can't find that recipe."

"Let me help you look," I said, waving her toward the kitchen. "I'm sure it'll turn up."

The camera crew was finishing with Nina when Linda and I entered the kitchen. "You ready to roll?" one of the camera guys asked Linda.

She looked flustered. "No, not yet. I still need to do all my prep work." Her smile was broad, but her voice sounded tight.

The camera crew agreed to come back in an hour. Nina hurried out after them, leaving the kitchen island cluttered with dirty mixing bowls, dishes, and all her vegan supplies. "Richard's on dish duty, right? I'm leaving all this for him to clean up. That's a little something I call karma. Police headquarters are just a couple doors down, right?"

I pointed her in the direction of the police station, and turned my attention to helping Linda find her missing recipe.

She tossed shakers of sprinkles on the island, and unpacked all her baking tools. "It's not here. Are you sure you didn't move it?"

"Look at this place." I motioned to the messy island and countertop. "Where would I put it?"

Linda threw her head in hands. "What am I going to do?"

I walked around the island and put my hand on her shoulder. "Don't panic. I'm sure you can re-create it. Do you want some help?"

She composed herself, smoothing her hair and shifting the bracelets on her wrist. "You don't need to do that. Although it is mighty sweet of you to offer, but I'm sure you have your own dessert to worry about."

In fact, I did. I still hadn't decided what to make for tomorrow's show. Torte doesn't really have a signature dessert, we do a little of everything. That's my style—dabbling, playing around with a recipe or new ingredient. I wasn't worried about it. I'd figure it out.

"I've got plenty of time," I said to Linda. "How about this? I'll make you a deal. If we work on it together and it turns out well, we'll feature it here at Torte tomorrow. It can be our show special. Give people in town a chance to taste something Southern."

Linda smiled. "Are you sure you're not from the South? That's the kind of hospitality I know and love. Thank you. I think I'm rattled from Marco. He's always trying to steal my family recipes."

"Always? I thought you just met him."

She didn't make eye contact and quickly began grabbing her sprinkles and rearranging them. "Right. I did. I meant he was sneaking around, trying to watch me in the kitchen. I know he was after my recipe." She excused herself to refresh her face before getting started on the pudding.

I thought about the first day Marco had been here at Torte. He was sloshed, that was for sure. Going after Linda's recipe sounded like a stretch, especially since he could barely stand upright. I had to drag him up the hill to the Black Swan. Come to think of it, when would he have snuck out to go in search of Linda's recipe? He'd been at Torte, and she was at the Merry Windsor. I had the sense that Linda was lying, but I couldn't figure out why.

Chapter Nineteen

I spent the next hour helping Linda re-create her banana cream pudding recipe. It was fairly simple and standard, but I didn't tell her that. She planned to make a basic vanilla cream pudding base. I suggested we try adding bananas into the actual pudding.

She worked on a cookie crust while I stirred heavy cream, butter, eggs, and vanilla on the stove. Making homemade pudding is really simple and well worth the effort. Mainly it requires a lot of stirring, which in my opinion is fine given the flavor difference between a handmade pudding and store-bought mix.

I added a dash of salt and a half teaspoon of Mexican vanilla to give it a hint of coconut. The smell reminded me of my childhood. My dad would often whip up a pudding for an after-school snack. By the time I came home from school, he'd have puddings chilled in parfait cups in the fridge and send me to the back to grab one.

"Juliet, what should we top our pudding with this afternoon?" he would ask while setting chocolate sauce, fresh berries, and whipping cream on the counter.

He'd always act impressed with whatever choice I made. "Excellent. Excellent decision. That flavor combination should pair nicely." We'd eat our puddings on bar stools at the island while he asked me about my day.

I smiled at the memory. He'd been gone for so long, I had a tendency to forget how magical the time we had together had been.

The camera crew returned to shoot footage of Linda at work. She pounded shortbread cookies into a fine powder for the crust, and put on a supersweet smile for the camera. I tried to stay out of the way while they interviewed her about her signature dessert. She acted like a pro, not giving off even a tiny hint that things hadn't gone as she planned.

Linda finished her cookie crust after the crew told her they had everything they needed and would be back to shoot me in an hour. She sliced bananas lengthwise.

"Why do you slice them like that?" I asked, removing the pudding from the stove.

"That's the way my mama always did it."

"Can you mash a few for me and I'll blend them into the pudding?"

She reached for a potato masher. "That I can do."

I added the fresh bananas into the cooling mixture, then I whipped it in the mixer and handed it to Linda.

"It looks absolutely divine, doesn't it?" She swiped a taste.

The pudding had a creamy, pale yellow color. The vanilla smell hit my nose as I took a bite on a spoon. "Really good," I agreed. "I like the banana finish. It's subtle. That should work nicely with the fresh banana slices you've got in there."

Linda spread the warm pudding over the crust. "Delish. I'm going to let this set overnight. I'd like to wait until morning for the whipping cream. Thanks again for your help, sugar. I need to scoot out of here and go have a little chat with Philip. Richard's on cleanup duty, so I'll just leave this mess for him too."

I knew that there was no way Richard was actually going to come do any of our dishes. Plus, the camera crew was due to return in less than an hour to film me. I wanted Torte to shine on TV.

Mom and the rest of the team offered to stay late and help me, but I like working by myself, especially in the evening. It was such a rarity to have any alone time when I was working on the ship. Being home I've created a ritual of sorts I like to follow in the evening—I uncork a bottle of wine, pour myself a glass, and blast some tunes. It's cheaper than therapy and gives me a break from my own head.

I sent them on their way, promising that I'd try to sleep in in the morning. I locked the front door after them, and cranked on some Carlos Santana. On top of my signature dessert, I wanted to test out a few ideas for Lance's end-of-the-season party, but before I could do anything else I needed to organize the kitchen.

Linda's and Nina's things were easy to tell apart. I started with Nina's supplies, stacking everything into her plastic tubs and placing them on the front counter. I threw all her dishes in the sink and left them to soak. Linda's sprinkles and jewel embellishments were all over the island and the floor. I swept the floor and brushed everything else into the garbage. Then I piled her supplies together on the edge of the island. I wanted to use the entire space while I was cooking, so I decided to move her things into the office for the evening.

When I opened the office door, I forgot that Thomas had stored all of Marco's things inside. Why hadn't the Professor taken them this afternoon? As soon as I was done with my segment for the show, I'd have to call him and make sure they were still coming back for Marco's things.

I pushed the cart with Marco's supplies closer to the filing cabinet on the far wall. It bumped into the cabinet and everything spilled onto the floor. Great. Just what I needed. I bent down to pick up Marco's things. As I grabbed a stainless steel pastry cutter, I paused with it in midair. Was I tampering with evidence? Should I put on a pair of gloves?

Thomas and the Professor couldn't be too worried about fingerprints if they'd left Marco's things, right?

Too late now, Jules, I told myself as I scooped his other supplies from the floor and placed them back on the cart. His index card holder with recipes had tipped over and scattered handwritten notes all over the floor. I gathered those together too. Blame it on the chef in me or my inquisitive mind, but I couldn't help thumbing through Chef Marco's recipes. Not that I'd ever consider stealing them, but I always find it interesting to look at recipes. I must have dozens of cookbooks at home. Some people spend their spare time reading romance novels, I spend mine flipping through pages of perfectly styled food. Carlos used to tease me about this habit, calling it my food porn.

Marco's recipes included everything from a beef Wellington puffed pastry to a chocolate soufflé. Looking at his handwritten notes about omitting or adding a particular spice, or cutting down the sugar content, made me feel sad for the deceased chef.

I returned the recipes to the holder. My eye focused on the recipe at the front of the box. It was for Southern banana cream pudding. Linda must have been right. Chef Marco had stolen her recipe.

A knock on the front door sounded before I could take a closer look. I wondered if what we'd come up with today was better than her original. I left the recipes and Marco's things and headed to the front of the bakeshop.

It wasn't the camera crew. It was Nina.

She waved from the other side of the door. "I forgot something. Is it okay if I come in?"

I unlocked the door and let her in.

"I'm glad you're still here. I was sure everyone had gone home. The front of the shop looked dark."

"Nope. I'm still here. Going to be for a while."

Nina looked like she was dressed for a show. She wore a simple black halter dress with a hemp-colored shawl over her shoulders and strappy black sandals. Her curls spiraled around her face.

"Are you going to closing night?" I asked, flipping on the front light.

"No, why?"

"You're all dressed up."

"Oh, that." She blushed. "I guess I kind of have a date. Well, I'm not sure if it's a date, but I'm going to dinner with that nice cop, Thomas."

Cop? Maybe I was being snooty but I thought of Thomas as a detective in training, not a cop.

"That's great," I lied. Why did my stomach start to turn? *Knock it off, Jules.* I smiled at Nina. "Did you need something?"

She fluffed her curls and giggled. "Oh, yeah, I did. I made a special batch of vegan brownies earlier and I want to grab them for Thomas. I'll just scoot past you and get them."

"Of course." I stepped to the side and pointed to the front counter. "I moved all your stuff up here so I could have the workspace in the back. I don't remember seeing any brownies though."

Nina glanced at her neatly stacked supplies. "Wow. Did Richard come clean?"

"Nope. That would be yours truly."

"Oh, sorry. It looks really good. My brownies are in the fridge. I'll just run grab them and get out of your hair."

Her curls bounced as she trotted to the fridge. Was she really Thomas's type? Why did it matter? I had to get myself out of this weird Thomas loop—quick.

She returned with a glass pan of brownies. "Got 'em. See you bright and early."

I felt my jaw clench as she skipped outside. There's a chance I might have been exaggerating about the "skipping." Across the dimly lit plaza I could see the *Take the Cake* crew assembling. I hurried to finish cleaning the kitchen before they came to film me. As I finished wiping it down with a basic mixture of warm water and vinegar, the door jingled again.

"You ready?" the main cameraman asked. His lip curled a bit as he scanned me from head to toe.

I hadn't even thought about looking good on camera. I'd been too distracted trying to think of something to make. "Can you give me a couple minutes?"

The cameraman agreed, muttering something about the lighting.

I raced into the bathroom to assess myself in the mirror. I was as bad as the kitchen had looked a few minutes ago. My Torte apron was splattered with flour, pudding, and water. Stray hairs escaped from my ponytail and my face looked worn out. Fortunately Mom keeps a nice little stash of bathroom accoutrements for us and our guests in a set of wicker drawers next to the sink. Things like hand lotion, wet wipes, and individually wrapped toothpicks and mints.

I splashed water on my face and dug through the bottom drawer for a brush. We keep a stash of personal supplies on hand in case we need to freshen up after a busy morning baking. Yanking my hair free from the ponytail, I gave it a comb-through and tied it back up. I pinched my cheeks to give them a little color and ran a peony-colored shimmer gloss on my lips.

My apron would have to go. I threw it in the wicker basket and grabbed my *Take the Cake* apron. After I tied it on, I gave myself a final check. Much better.

"Ready to roll," I announced as I stepped into the kitchen.

The cameraman had placed lights and screens on the windowsill and the far wall near the sink. My eyes squinted, trying to adjust to the bright lights. I'm not vain, but I did feel disappointed that the makeup team weren't on site. When I asked, the cameraman laughed.

"Philip wants these shots to be real world," he scoffed. "Like any baker would be working this late."

I didn't bother to tell him that I often stayed at the shop late. In fairness, I was unique. Most bakers aren't like me. I thrive on little to no sleep. I just wished I had spent more of my waking hours preparing a dessert, instead of helping everyone else.

We started the segment with a brief Q/A about Torte. I forgot the camera was rolling once I started talking about the bakeshop.

Then he asked me to start working on my dessert. I gulped. *What are you going to make, Jules? Think!* My eyes landed on a bottle of strawberry dessert wine that Mom had brought from her wine tour for me to sample. I'm not overly fond of sweet wines, but this one had been made with ripe-from-the-vine Oregon strawberries and tasted like I'd cracked open a jar of strawberry jam.

I'd make a panna cotta and serve it with the sweet wine. Panna cotta is like pudding for adults. It's an Italian dessert that translates to "cooked cream." I'm a fan of the simple, versatile dessert. It works for elegant parties and casual family gatherings. It's easy to dress up with fresh raspberries or, in my vision for my signature dessert, an exotic sweet wine.

The cameraman gave me a minute to assemble gelatin, cream, milk, and sugar. He cued me that he was ready, and

I somehow shifted into on-air mode. The panna cotta, like Linda's pudding, didn't require any special culinary technique, but I talked through the process and explained how to properly incorporate gelatin into the mixture. There's nothing worse than getting a lump of flavorless gelatin when you bite into a panna cotta or custard.

After a few minutes of zooming in and out on my hand whisking cream and sugar on the stove, the cameraman announced he had what he needed and that he was hitting the pub. "By the way, I'm supposed to tell you that your call time got pushed back to nine tomorrow morning. Guess you can sleep in."

"A baker never sleeps in," I said with a laugh as I walked him to the door. After he left, I poured myself a glass of wine and completed assembling the panna cotta. It would set overnight and I could finish it off with the sweet wine and garnish it with a flourish of fresh herbs in the morning. I considered trying out a few ideas I had for Lance's party, but I was beat. I did a quick wipe down of the island and wondered what I should do about Marco's things.

Thomas and Nina were at dinner. I didn't want to disturb his date, but this was related to a murder case. I figured he'd be angrier if I didn't call him, so I punched his name on my phone.

He answered on the second ring. I could hear the sound of music and chatter in the background. "Jules?"

"Sorry to bother you, but I was cleaning up tonight and all of Marco's things are still here."

"Crud. I totally forgot about that." His voice sounded muffled like he had his hand over the receiver while he was talking to someone else. "Hang on one sec, Jules."

I waited while he finished talking to whoever was on the other end of the line.

"Jules?"

"I'm here."

"I was thinking maybe I could head over tonight, but it's getting kind of late. Can I meet you at the shop first thing tomorrow?"

"Sure. See you then." I hung up before he could respond. What was wrong with me? I hadn't been jealous like this since the seventh grade. Was I even jealous, or was it more that I was lonely and missing Carlos? That made Thomas an easy scapegoat.

Before locking up, I reminded myself that this was my time. I was here in Ashland for me. I didn't need the distraction or self-sabotage of worrying about what Thomas was doing. The late evening air was cold and a slight breeze rustled leaves from their branches as I stepped outside. I wondered if it might rain.

Nothing compares to a walk in the rain. There's something about a rainy walk that revives the soul. I scanned the dark sky. The moon was shrouded by clouds. Yep. Rain was coming.

Across the street a group had gathered in front of the Merry Windsor. Lance was speaking expressively with his hands. What was he doing downtown? It was closing night of the show. Shouldn't he be on stage?

I checked my watch. It was nearly ten-thirty. I had no idea it was so late.

Lance spotted me and called me over. "Juliet, come have a drink! It's a wrap."

I crossed the plaza. Lance and his crew of actors and stagehands looked like they'd already engaged in a round of merriment. I couldn't blame them; after running the production night after night for months, they deserved a celebratory cocktail or two. What surprised me was that they'd picked the Merry Windsor of all places. Richard and Lance aren't exactly friends.

"That's it for the season?" I asked as Lance greeted me with a kiss on each cheek. He smelled like gin.

"And what a season it's been." Lance bowed to the other members of the company. "My heartfelt thanks to all of you. Who wants another round?"

A shout of cheers erupted.

"You're drinking at the Windsor?" I asked.

Lance took a step backward and threw his hand to his forehead. "Darling, how could you say something so dastardly? We partook of a postshow martini backstage and now we're en route to Puck's Pub. You just happened to catch us waiting for a couple of the barmaids at the Windsor who are joining us."

"Got it."

A waitress exited through the carved wooden front doors of the Merry Windsor. She immediately tugged off her apron and threw her arms around one of the actors who scooped her up and swirled her in the air.

Lance leaned closer to me. "Did you learn anything new about our little case today?"

"How many martinis did you have?"

"One, darling. Maybe two." He intentionally slurred his words and swayed from side to side.

"Right."

Lance's friends pulled him in the direction of Puck's Pub. He called over his shoulder to me, "Join us?"

I laughed and shook my head.

"Ta-ta, darling. We'll talk tomorrow."

He was enveloped in the middle of his company. They crossed the plaza with linked arms, singing aloud. The sound of their cheery celebration echoed on the otherwise quiet streets.

I started toward my apartment. *Maybe I should join them for a drink?* One thing I'd been trying to work on was putting myself out there more. Working on a cruise ship for all those years led to a sort of unintentional isolation. It's strange because I was always surrounded by people, but not close to them, except for Carlos. It's the nature of the job. Workers tend to rotate between ships and go wherever the seas take them, so to speak. Being home for the past few months made it painfully clear that I needed to expand my social network.

However, my feet were sore from a twelve-hour day, and I knew I needed to be back at Torte bright and early to meet Thomas and to get my panna cotta ready for the show. Next time, Jules, I promised myself.

I shivered as a gust of wind sent a pile of leaves swirling on the sidewalk. Winter was just around the corner. I hoped I could handle it. I'd spent most of my recent winters on tropical seas. Adjusting to the cooler weather was going to take some getting used to.

Rubbing my hands together, I picked up my pace a little. As I crossed the plaza, I had the sense that someone was behind me. I stopped and turned around. Nothing.

I continued on, but couldn't shake the feeling that I wasn't alone. The sound of footsteps made me stop again. I glanced behind me. Nothing.

Knock it off, Jules. You're just imagining things. It's probably the wind. I tried to soothe the on-edge feeling in my stomach as I hurried toward my apartment.

I passed Puck's Pub where I could see Lance and his crew raising giant pint glasses in a toast. I considered ducking in, but felt silly thinking I was being watched.

I checked behind me one more time before speed-walking to the front entrance of Elevation, below my apartment, which was plunged in darkness. Everyone had gone home hours ago. I stuffed my hand into my pocket to feel for my keys. I wanted to have them out and ready.

Every hair on the back of my neck rose when the sound of footsteps and heavy breathing came near. I don't usually spook that easily, but I could feel my heart rate spike.

Should I run back to Puck's or up the stairs to my apartment?

Before I could choose, a figure in black came directly at me from up ahead and knocked me off my feet.

Chapter Twenty

I landed on my butt on the sidewalk, my hands bracing my fall.

"Hey, who's there?" a man's voice said. It sounded vaguely familiar, but I couldn't place it.

"Who are you?" I responded from the ground.

My eyes tried to focus as the figure bent closer. He was dressed completely in black from head to toe. No wonder he blended in with the night sky.

"Sebastian?" I asked. "Is that you?"

He extended his hand and helped me to my feet. The scent of cigarette smoke made me gag.

"What are you doing here?" I asked, brushing dirt from my hands and coughing. Had he been following me? I didn't think so. The sound of footsteps had been behind me. It was difficult to make out his features in the dark, but I'd swear he looked as surprised to see me as I was him.

"I was coming from ze Merry Windsor," he responded. "Until you ran into me." His accent was thick, much thicker than when he first bumped into me.

"Um, I was the one just on the ground. I think it's the other way around. You ran into me."

He crossed his arms. "Non. You should not be sneaking around in ze dark."

"I wasn't sneaking around. I was going home. You're one to talk." I pointed to his black outfit.

"I do not have time for dis." He brushed past me and turned across the plaza to the Merry Windsor.

He had claimed that's where he was coming from when he bumped into me, but that couldn't be true. He'd been coming from the opposite direction—Lithia Park and the steps up to OSF. Why would he lie? *Had* he been following me?

I watched as he disappeared into the darkness, and raced up the steps to my apartment. Once inside, with the lights on and door securely latched, I let out a sigh of relief. I had no idea why Sebastian had just lied, but I knew for sure that he had.

My apartment was starting to feel like home. When I first returned to Ashland, Mom had arranged with the owners of Elevation for me to stay in the furnished space for a couple weeks. Once I decided to make my stay more permanent, I worked out a temporary lease and unpacked my suitcase. What a concept.

I'd been trying to make the space homier once the tourist rush slowed down. I found a great wooden print that read EAT MORE CAKE that I hung over the sofa. I unwrapped some of the treasures I'd accumulated at different ports of call—like my collection of postcards. These I displayed on a cork board near the kitchen.

The kitchen was small but efficient, and I'd stocked it with baking supplies and some of my can't-live-without equipment, like my coffee grinder and vintage pie tins that I'd inherited from my grandmother.

My run-in with Sebastian left me feeling rattled. Maybe a late-night espresso would help take the edge off. Some people feel the effect of caffeine. Not me. I can drink coffee around the clock, and it doesn't seem to impact my ability to sleep, or give me the shakes. Carlos used to say that I was immune to the stimulant.

I unwrapped a bag of beans and sprinkled them into the grinder. Within minutes the entire kitchen smelled of coffee. I let the scent engulf me. *Ah, heaven.*

With a hot espresso in my hands, I returned to the living room, kicked off my shoes and flopped onto the couch. Most people would probably be watching late-night talk shows at this hour. I've never really been drawn to television. In fact, I hadn't even invested in a TV for the apartment yet. I guess if I was going to be on TV, maybe I should at least own one before *Take the Cake* aired. I had time. It wasn't slotted to run until February.

Most people probably wouldn't be knocking back an espresso at close to midnight either, I thought as I flipped through the latest issue of *Cooking Light*. That's okay, I was content to polish off my coffee and browse the glossy pages of the magazine.

I must have fallen asleep because I woke a few hours later with the magazine on my chest and my empty coffee cup on the floor.

The clock ticking on the wall read 4:15. I didn't want to do the math in terms of how many hours of sleep (or not) I'd had. I used to think it was a phase—part of the adventure of working on a cruise ship where people were literally awake around the clock. I thought once I returned to land I'd outgrow it, but apparently I hadn't. At least not yet.

Falling back to sleep was out of the question, so I took a minute to center myself and stretch before returning the magazine to the stack on my coffee table and retrieving my coffee cup from the floor.

I'd left the beans open on the counter last night, fully

intending to return once I'd finished my espresso. It felt like déjà vu as I retraced my steps to brew another cup of coffee. Hadn't I just done this a few hours ago?

This morning I opted for French press. While I waited for the water to boil, I hopped in the shower. The warm water rejuvenated my skin. I let it cascade down my back. One of the things I missed the most about not being at sea was the sound of the water. I didn't expect to miss it, but I did. I missed the sound of waves lapping against the bow and crashing on the horizon. There's something so peaceful and soothing about the sound of water. Maybe that's part of the reason I was drawn to Lithia Park, with its fountains and meandering river.

I downed my coffee and laced up my tennis shoes. The caffeine felt like it took immediate effect. I grabbed a jacket and zipped it up before stepping out into the crisp air.

It had rained overnight. The sidewalk was damp and wet piles of leaves gathered on the storm drain. The air smelled fresh, as if the rain had wiped everything clean. After last night's run-in with Sebastian, I practically sprinted to the shop. By the time I made it to Torte, my heart was pumping, my cheeks had heat, and my nose dripped. I felt great.

That quickly changed as I pushed opened the front door. Mom stood near the pastry case with a broom in her hand. Glass had shattered all over the floor.

"Mom. What happened?" I stepped around the glass and shut the door behind me.

"I don't know. Someone broke in last night. Look." She motioned to the tables in the front and then to the kitchen. "Vandals. It's a mess."

Chapter Twenty-one

It looked like something had exploded inside. All of the flower vases on the tables had been shattered. Glass, water, and flowers littered the floor. Coffee beans had been spilled near the espresso bar and napkins and salt and pepper shakers intentionally knocked from the counter onto the floor.

"Oh my God, what happened?" I maneuvered through the carnage on the floor to the kitchen.

If possible, the kitchen looked worse. Flour, sugar, recipes, and Linda's and Nina's supplies had been strewn all over the island and on the floor.

"Who would do this?" I asked Mom.

She continued sweeping glass into a pile near the pastry case. "I have no idea."

"Vandals? Kids?"

"But who, and why?"

"Yeah, good point. I don't know. It looks like someone wanted to make it look like we'd been vandalized. Is anything missing?"

Mom shook her head. "Not that I can see. I checked the cash register. Everything's intact. It looks worse than it really is. Mainly someone shattered our vases and threw some flour around."

"That doesn't make any sense. Who breaks in and doesn't steal anything?"

"I was wondering the same thing."

"Did you call the Professor?"

Mom swept glass into a dust pan and then dumped it in the garbage. "Not yet. It's so early."

It was almost five A.M.

"Thomas is meeting me here early. Do you think we should wait until he gets here to clean up? There could be evidence, fingerprints or something."

Mom paused with the broom in her hand. "I didn't even think about that. I was focused on trying to get it picked up before customers start arriving. Maybe you should call him."

I agreed. Thomas sounded like he was still asleep when he answered. Once I explained that Torte had been vandalized, he perked up and promised to be over in a few minutes.

The way the flowers and our baking supplies had been tossed around didn't make any sense to me. Someone must have been intentionally trying to make it look like kids. Could they have been after something else? But then why wouldn't they have stolen cash out of the register, or any of our expensive bakery equipment?

"Is the door broken too?" I asked, craning my neck toward the front.

"No. It was unlocked when I got here," Mom replied. "Did you give anyone a key?"

"No. I didn't give anyone a key. The only people with keys are you and me. Well, and Andy, Stephanie, and Sterling."

Mom frowned. She rested the broom on the pastry case. "You don't think one of the kids could have been involved in this?"

"No way."

She looked relieved. "Me neither."

I walked to the counter, careful not to slip on the flour coating the floor. "Do you think this could have something to do with Marco's murder?"

"We agreed that we're going to leave that to the Professor and Thomas." Mom gave me a stern look.

"I know, but it's just really strange. What if someone broke in looking for something? I realized last night all of Marco's things are still here. Maybe there was a clue in his supplies. Maybe someone broke in to steal that and tried to make it look like a break-in."

Mom swatted me on the back with the broom. "Listen, young lady, I know that Doug doesn't want either of us mixed up in this investigation."

I pretended to be injured from the broom. "Child abuse."

She laughed. Then her face turned serious. "Juliet, think about what happened this summer." She pointed to my shoulder.

Without thinking I covered my scar with my hand. "I know. You're right. It's just once I get on a loop like this I can't stop myself. I wish I hadn't been the one to discover Marco's body. Maybe then I could separate myself from it a little more."

Mom reached out and squeezed my wrist. Her hands were warm and soft on my skin. She held my gaze. "Have you considered the idea that one of the reasons you've immersed yourself in this case is because of Carlos?" She ran her hands over my fingers. "I noticed you haven't been wearing your wedding ring."

I looked at my bare hand. It felt weird not to wear my ring. Sometimes I caught myself trying to twist it and would be taken aback when I only felt my own skin. I wasn't even quite sure why I'd taken it off. I guess when Carlos and I agreed to take a break until next year, I figured my ring would be a constant reminder. Having it resting safely in the nightstand next to my bed felt symbolic of our relationship. He was often in the back of my mind, but not actually present.

She released my hand and stared at me. Her wise brown eyes seemed to know exactly what I was thinking. Thankfully she didn't say more, she just gave me a nod and propped the broom near the window. If I was honest with myself, I did wonder if there was something more than symbolic behind my bare finger.

It had been surprisingly easy to push my longing and nagging worry about what was next for Carlos and me from my head. If I didn't think about him, was I even missing him? Or had I manufactured a way to protect my heart? The truth was that I was no closer to figuring it out.

Thomas appeared outside the window—a welcome reprieve from having to dive any deeper into my thoughts, at least for the moment.

Mom opened the door for him and greeted him with a welcoming hug. She's not someone who holds back when it comes to expressing her feelings. Whether someone has known her for five minutes or five decades, she makes everyone she meets feel welcome and at ease.

"Morning, Mrs. Capshaw." Thomas towered over Mom. I inherited my height from my dad's side of the family. Thomas whistled as he looked around the bakeshop. "You weren't kidding, someone really messed this place up."

"I started to sweep the floor." Mom motioned to the broom. "But I haven't touched anything else yet."

"Good thinking." Thomas pulled out his iPad. "When did you arrive this morning?"

"A little after four-thirty."

"No sign of forced entry?" Thomas surveyed the door and front windows.

"It was unlocked when I arrived," Mom replied.

Thomas typed something onto his iPad. "Anything missing?"

"Nothing." Mom shook her head.

"Really?" Thomas looked up from his notes. "Did you check the register?"

"Yep."

"What about the office? Do you keep any cash in there?"

"No. I checked everywhere. There's nothing missing. It's just one big mess. Like someone was mad."

Thomas scowled. "I don't like the sound of that."

"Exactly!" I jumped in. "This has to be related to Marco's murder. Who would do something like this to Torte?"

"Uh-oh." Thomas gave Mom a knowing look. "Here we go again."

"You tell her, Thomas." Mom waved her finger at me. "I don't want her involved in this at all. We both know what a close call she had."

"I've already told her that." Thomas addressed Mom like I wasn't even in the room.

"Knock it off, you guys. I'm right here, and for the record I'm not inserting myself into the investigation, I'm simply sharing my thoughts as a witness to this vandalism."

"Right." Thomas scowled and looked at Mom. "She's not going to stay out of this, is she?"

Mom sighed. "Doesn't look like it."

Thomas placed his iPad on the counter. He reached behind him and held a pair of handcuffs up. "I thought so. I came prepared." He turned to Mom. "Where should we keep her?"

"That front booth might be nice." Mom grinned. "She'll have a good view from there."

Thomas stepped toward me, dangling the cuffs. "Let's go, Jules. Get moving."

"You are not cuffing me." I took a step back.

He was quicker than me. Within a flash he grabbed my hands and slapped a cuff on my wrist. He smelled like he just stepped out of the shower, like Ivory soap. I could feel heat radiating from his trim body, and feel the warmth of his breath on my cheek.

My heart skipped a beat.

He looked down at me and gave me a sly grin. His eyes lingered on mine for a moment. They reminded me of the sea in Capri. His breath sounded shallow. He caressed my free hand. I could feel the heat of his touch like a pulsing beat up my entire arm. He must have felt it too.

The moment vanished. He dropped my hand and grabbed the cuffs. "Let's go, trouble. You're coming with me." Thomas started to drag me toward the front of the bake-shop.

"All right. You've made your point." I threw my free hand in the air as a sign of surrender. "I promise. I'll stay out of the case. Just let me go. We have so much cleaning to do and customers are going to be here soon."

Thomas scrunched his face and looked at Mom. "What do you think, Mrs. Capshaw? Should we trust her?"

"Well, she did promise." Mom caught my eye and winked.

Thomas unlocked the cuff, but before he loosened it, he gave me one final warning. "You heard your mother, you promised. It's just baking for you, no more murder. Got it?"

"You two are ridiculous." I shook my hand free.

Thomas scanned the dining room. "Let me do a walk-through. I need to call the Professor. I'm pretty sure he's going to want to dust for prints."

Mom rubbed her temples. "Does this mean we can't bake?"

"I'm afraid not. I'll try to be as quick as I can, but you're probably going to need to tell customers that it's going to be a little wait for their morning fix."

Mom sighed and looked at me. "What about the guest chefs? When are they coming in this morning?"

"Not this early," I said. "We're not filming until later this morning. I don't think either of them has anything major to do. Linda is going to whip some cream, and I think Nina's basically finished with her dessert."

Thomas walked through the front of the shop and the kitchen in a grid, stopping every once in a while to examine a spot on the floor or to inspect something on the counter. When he finished his initial survey he returned to Mom and me. "I'm calling the Professor. I don't like the looks of this."

"Why?" Mom bit her fingernails.

"Hold on a sec." Thomas stepped outside and made a call. I assumed he must be calling the Professor. When he returned his face was solemn. "What about the office? Did you check in there?"

"No." Mom swallowed. "What are you worried about?"

Thomas went straight to the office. Mom and I followed him, giving each other quizzical looks. What was he so fired up about?

The office was untouched, except for one major thing. All of Marco's supplies, recipes—everything was missing.

Chapter Twenty-two

Thomas shook his head. "I should have taken all this to the police station." He blew out a long gasp of air. "I take it someone unlocked this door."

"It was locked." I looked at Mom. She agreed.

Thomas scowled.

"So the Professor thinks this *is* related to Marco's murder?" I asked.

"Looks that way. I should have come by last night."

Mom patted his shoulder. "It's not your fault. Doug will understand."

"Thanks, Mrs. Capshaw." Thomas gave her a glum smile. "I knew better, but I thought it could wait."

"Thomas, Mom's right. Don't sweat it. I should have called you earlier. I've just been so busy with the competition. Here's the thing though, Linda Belle said that Marco stole her recipe for banana pudding. I found it in with his recipes last night. Do you think Linda could have done this? Maybe she came back looking for her recipe?"

"Why would she damage the rest of the bakeshop?" Mom asked.

"Good point." Thomas let out another long breath. "No, I should have come by last night. This is my fault."

Mom snapped into counseling mode. "Thomas, whoever did this is to blame, not you. Now what do we need to do to help you and get this place cleaned up?" Her voice was calm and commanding.

Thomas responded by shaking his head and squaring his shoulders. "Let me run over to headquarters and grab some supplies. The Professor's on his way."

"Is there anything we can do in the meantime?" Mom asked.

"No, thank you. I'll be right back." He hurried away.

Mom shook her head. "He's always been too hard on himself."

"What do you mean?"

"Don't you remember back when you two were in high school? If the football team suffered a loss he took it on his shoulders. When your dad died, he took such responsibility with you, like it was his duty to help heal you."

"He did?" I remember Thomas always being around to drive me to the bakeshop or OSF for rehearsal after school and how he used to plan thoughtful dates—hikes on Mount Ashland, rafting on the Rogue River, and late-night picnics in Lithia Park. I didn't remember him seeming consumed with my dad's death. More with me. He was just always there, like another member of our family.

Mom raised an eyebrow. "Don't you remember how you complained about how he didn't give you any space?"

"Yeah, but how was that about Dad?"

"It was." Mom fiddled with a button on her linen shirt. "He was trying to watch out for you."

The Professor rapped on the door. Mom fluffed her bob and scooted to the front to let him in.

I thought about what she said. Had Thomas really been

trying to help me get over losing my dad? I never considered that. We were so young, and by the time we graduated all I wanted was to get out of town. I wanted freedom. I got it too. Maybe more than I intended.

That was food for thought. Had I been drawn to Carlos because he was the opposite of Thomas? Why couldn't self-reflection be easy? It all felt like too much work right now.

The Professor stepped cautiously over the broken glass as Mom led him to the office.

"Juliet, good morning. Or is it even morning? Not in my book."

I grinned. "What are you talking about? Mom and I have been up for hours."

"What can I say, beauty does dawn with the rising light."

"Shakespeare again?" I asked.

"No, that's me." The Professor bowed.

Mom fanned herself. "So romantic, isn't he?" She pretended to faint.

The Professor scooped her in his arms. "My lady. Doth jest."

Thomas sprinted in, out of breath. He held a box of supplies in his arms. "I'm really sorry about this, Professor. I know I should have followed protocol. This one is all on me."

The Professor released Mom. He took the box from Thomas. "Not to worry. Let's proceed with the investigation, shall we?"

Mom and I tried to stay out of their way as they dusted the countertops, filing cabinet, and doorknobs for fingerprints. The Professor knelt by the broken vases in the front. He removed his moleskin notebook from his jacket and jotted something down.

"What are you looking for?" Mom asked.

"Shoe prints." The Professor pointed to a set of prints leading to the front door. "I think we can safely assume that our perpetrator wasn't book smart. He broke vases filled with water and then stepped through it to make his get-away."

I came closer to see what they were looking at. Sure enough, there were shoe prints from the farthest table underneath the chalkboard all the way to the front door.

"Why do you say he?" I asked. "You think it was a man?"

"A man, or a woman wearing men's shoes." The Professor shone a pocket flashlight on the prints. "Those are big feet. From the looks of it, I'd say size eleven or twelve in men's shoes."

So much for Linda as a suspect.

The Professor called Thomas over to take photos of the prints and the damage. Thomas snapped shots of the large prints on the floor. There was only one person who I thought the prints could belong to, and he'd been sneaking around town dressed in black last night—Sebastian. The only question I had was why? What could he have been looking for in Marco's things? Maybe a clue that would have led Thomas and the Professor to him as the murderer?

A chill ran up my spine. I could have been alone with a murderer last night.

Chapter Twenty-three

"Jules, are you okay? You look a little pale." Thomas looped the camera around his neck.

"Huh?"

"Is everything okay?"

"Yeah. Fine. I was just wondering when we can start to clean up this mess. Customers are going to start lining up outside soon." I glanced behind me at the window. It was true. The sun had begun to rise, warming the dew on the pavement and illuminating the glistening leaves.

Thomas asked the Professor, "Are we done here?"

The Professor stood and tapped his fingers on his beard. "I do believe we have everything we need."

"Who do you think did this?" I couldn't help asking. Mom shot me a warning look.

"As the bard says, 'suspicion always haunts the guilty mind.' I believe we'll know the identity of our suspect soon." He tucked his notebook back into his breast pocket and gave it a little pat.

Thomas caught my eye. He gave me a look that said, don't ask. Translating the Professor's words can be a challenge. It makes me wonder if he knows more than he lets on, or if he has a unique approach to solving crime.

He kissed Mom's hand, then turned and bowed to me. "Sadly, my fair ladies, I believe you are familiar with cleaning up our dust."

Last summer Torte was the site of a murder. Mom and I had had to have the space professionally cleaned before reopening to our customers. This time all it needed was a good dusting and mopping. We were up to the task.

The Professor asked Thomas to accompany him to headquarters where they'd go over the evidence they'd collected. Mom and I stretched rubber gloves over our arms and started scrubbing. She tackled the floors. I took on the countertops. By the time Andy and Stephanie arrived for their shifts, the shop sparkled. We were ready for customers. The only problem was that we didn't have anything baked to sell them.

We pride ourselves on baking all of our cakes, pastries, and breads fresh daily. Missing out on our prep time was going to set us back for the entire day.

Mom instructed Andy to fire up the espresso machine and get drinks cranking as fast as he could. At least customers could get their caffeine hit while waiting for breakfast. Stephanie started in on breakfast bars. Basically a glorified cookie bar that we chock full of oats, cranberries, and walnuts to make it healthier. The bars were quick. We could slice them in large portions and serve them warm.

I assembled fruit parfaits with fresh berries and yogurt. Then I whipped eggs, milk, fresh herbs, and cheese together. I'd scramble the eggs and serve them in warm tortillas with sausage or veggies. Mom began mixing bread dough like a possessed woman. Years of running a bakeshop meant that she didn't even have to look at what her hands were doing or consult a recipe. By the time my parfaits were lined up in the pastry case and my eggs warming on the stove, she'd mixed three different batches.

Our morning offerings were going to be modified for the

next couple hours, but as I looked at the assortment of dishes we'd pulled together in less than thirty minutes, I was pretty proud of our little team. Customers would still have breakfast options, and we wouldn't lose out on a morning's worth of sales.

Sterling slipped in right as Andy flipped the sign on the front door to open. I noticed he and Stephanie refused to greet one another.

We all worked at lightning speed for the first hour, trying to catch up. I didn't have a chance to run interference between the two of them or think any further on Marco's murder. Customers loved the parfaits and egg wraps. Maybe we'd have to add them to the menu. Mom, Stephanie, and I whizzed around each other, kneading bread dough, stirring sauces on the stove, and pushing tins of muffins and cakes into the oven.

By a little after seven, we'd baked enough to fill half of the pastry case. Nina and Linda arrived together. Thank goodness neither of them had tried to get an early start on their signature desserts this morning. That would have been a disaster.

"You're all buzzing like bees around honey this morning," Linda said as she removed a peach-colored tailored raincoat and hung it on a hook.

Nina's hair was tied in one large braid down her back. Her open-toe sandals peeked out from beneath her flowing peasant skirt. "I have to say it's been kind of a nice break not to have to rise before dawn. I could get used to sleeping in like this."

Most people probably wouldn't consider seven sleeping in, but in a baker's world sleeping in until any time after four in the morning is pure luxury.

The kitchen quickly became cramped. My panna cotta was resting in the fridge and Torte was under control, so I decided to pop over to the Merry Windsor before I had to be on set. I wanted to have a chat with Sebastian about what he was really doing lurking around in the dark last night.

I wanted to tell Linda about finding her recipe in Marco's things, but Thomas had been so uptight about me being involved in the investigation, I thought I'd better let it be.

I ducked out of the kitchen and checked in with Andy before leaving.

"How's it going?" I brushed away coffee grounds that spilled as he tamped a shot.

"Not bad, boss. Customers are sucking down the special." Andy foamed milk and had to raise his voice over the sound of the steam. "We might need more pumpkin."

"Really?"

"Yep. They're flying out the door."

"I have to step out for a moment anyway. I'll swing by the store and grab some more on my way back."

"Cool." Andy cut the steam and poured hot milk in a circular motion into the white paper cup in front of him. He finished off the latte by hand, designing an outline of a pumpkin in the foam.

"Gorgeous." I nodded my approval and hurried out of the bakeshop before anyone stopped me to help with another project.

The temperature had risen by a few degrees since the early morning. I crossed the plaza toward the Merry Windsor. A group of middle-school students gathered in front of the tourist information booth. They scrolled on their phones and snapped selfies while killing time before school.

I had to admit Ashland without the throng of summer tourists was nice. Crossing this way in peak season would have required weaving in between out-of-town visitors sporting fanny packs and cameras around their necks and trying to dodge the big tour buses that shuttle visitors in.

The Merry Windsor may have looked the part of traditional Elizabethan Tudor with its exposed beams and whitewashed walls, but it was anything but merry. Richard Lord sucked any hint of merriment from the dated space with his entitled attitude.

His employees were surly and slow. Anyone showing up to work at Torte with an attitude like most of Richard's staff would not be invited back to work the next day.

I took a deep breath in as I pushed open the heavy doors and tried to avoid a stain on the forest-green carpet. The carpet had been well worn from years of tourists weaving a path in it. I couldn't tell if the stain was new or decades old; the floor was pocked with stain marks and smelled of baking soda trying to mask something—probably mold.

There was no sign of Richard as I strolled past the kid manning the front desk. I've found that if you act like you're supposed to be somewhere, most people don't ask many (if any) questions. It didn't matter anyway. The kid didn't look up from his cell phone as I passed by.

The long, dark hallway leading to the kitchen and dining room was adorned with a variety of Shakespearean items—a bust, paintings of Stratford-upon-Avon, and butcher paper with sticky notes where guests rated OSF plays. It smelled of mildew and chlorine from the pool. Richard had dumped a bunch of money into upgrading his new espresso bar, but the rest of the hotel was in desperate need of a face-lift.

In the dining room, a couple was helping themselves to the breakfast buffet. By the looks of things there wasn't going to be much competition for the heaping piles of scrambled eggs and bacon in front of them.

My stomach rumbled. I guess I'd forgotten to eat breakfast in the flurry of police activity at Torte. I'd have to grab something before we started filming *Take the Cake*. I didn't want a growling stomach on national TV.

The Merry Windsor's kitchen was at least twice the size of Torte's. In the busy season they served three meals a day to a packed hotel of guests. We weren't equipped to turn out that amount of food at Torte. I glanced with just the slightest hint of envy at the brand-new industrial ovens and indoor grill that Richard had had installed.

A chef and sous-chef were going over the lunch menu when I walked in. They stopped their conversation. "Can I help you?" The chef looked up.

"I'm looking for Sebastian. The French chef. Is he around?"

The chef nudged his sous-chef and rolled his eyes. "Sebastian's out back taking a phone call, but I'd use the term 'French' loosely."

I must have looked puzzled.

The sous-chef cracked up and began speaking in a mock French accent. "Dis is not how you prepare cakes, non?"

It must have been an inside joke because they both broke into fits of laughter and ignored me. I decided to take a walk to the back alley and find Sebastian myself.

I exited through the far end of the hotel. The Merry Windsor's alley has shops on both sides. I stepped outside and heard the sound of a man arguing. I could see Sebastian, still clad in all black, two shops down near a Dumpster. I couldn't see who he was arguing with.

I tried to creep closer, keeping my shoulders in contact with the Merry Windsor's wall.

Sebastian had his back to me. Where was the person he was arguing with?

I inched closer. There was no sign of anyone else in the alley.

Were my eyes playing tricks on me, or was Sebastian holding a phone up to his ear?

He was. But that couldn't be right. He was speaking without the slightest hint of a French accent.

Chapter Twenty-four

I bumped into a recycling bin. A loud thud sounded in the alley. Sebastian snapped his head around and narrowed his eyes on me. He sprinted off the other way before I could say anything.

He wasn't French! Why would he lie about being French?

A delivery truck rumbled up behind me and tapped his horn. I jumped out of the way and tried to enter the Merry Windsor from the back door. It was locked. For a brief moment I considered taking off after Sebastian, but after Thomas's warning and attempt at cuffing me to a booth this morning, I decided I should probably stay out of it.

Instead I'd go get more pumpkin for Andy and report to the Black Swan for hair and makeup. It was a good thing that someone was going to make my face look presentable this morning. I had a feeling that after my late night, my face could use a touch-up.

After picking up pumpkin at the market, I paused to chat with two fellow shop owners on my way to Torte. "Heard you're going to be a regular old-fashioned TV star," the owner of the Fountain Pen said as she positioned wrapping paper and embossed envelopes in her window display.

"Looks that way." I gave her my best movie star pose.

"You know from here on out I won't be able to associate with the common townspeople."

We laughed. She stepped off the curb to get a better vantage point. "What do you think?"

"It's great. I love all the color. And the wrapping paper. It's so rich. Fall just might be my favorite season. I'd forgotten how much I missed our changing seasons."

"We're one of the lucky places that actually has four seasons. I tell that to all the tourists. Winter, spring, summer, and fall—there's always something new to experience around here. I've lived here for fifty years and it never ceases to amaze me how beautiful our little town is during each season."

She stepped back onto the curb and gave her window display a nod of approval. "It does look nice, doesn't it?"

I agreed and started to continue on.

She stopped me. "Juliet, you tease, but thank you for being on the show. It's a great thing for Ashland. You're helping all of us out. It's all the downtown association is talking about."

Maybe I needed to stop being so flippant about *Take the Cake,* I thought as I crossed the plaza. Of course, given how things had been going so far, I wasn't sure how Ashland or any of us were going to end up being portrayed on the show.

Torte wasn't too busy, a handful of customers were waiting in line for espresso drinks and pastries, but otherwise only a few tables were taken.

I rested the pumpkin on the espresso bar. "Just grabbing my dessert," I called, as I slipped past the line. "You guys are good?"

Sterling ran his hand over the top of the pastry case. "It's under control."

I grinned and hurried to the back. Linda and Nina must have already left for the Black Swan. Mom and Stephanie each held dishrags. A bucket of water with vinegar sat in the middle of the island. I could smell the natural cleaning solution.

"Another mess?" I scrunched my brow.

Mom wrung her dishrag in the water.

Stephanie scowled. "Why are we cleaning up after those two? It doesn't seem fair."

Mom held the dripping rag above the bucket. "At the moment, I'd have to agree with you, Stephanie. I didn't count on the fact that our guests wouldn't be cleaning up after themselves."

"Me either. I'll talk to Philip about it this morning. Yesterday the 'loser' was supposed to come clean up after the other contestants. Richard lost. I knew there was no way he'd do dish duty. Plus, I got the sense it was a gimmick for the show." I watched as Stephanie scrubbed the wooden counter. Her fingernails were painted black. They matched her antiestablishment persona, but as I'd come to know she had a much lighter interior. Once you got past the tattoos, purple hair, and her tendency to act aloof, a sweet girl was inside.

I could relate. I'd learned to protect myself by putting up a cool exterior. I'm not entirely sure why, but I think it was the combination of losing my dad at a young age and to my early time in the theater. It's worked for me so far. It keeps people who don't know me at a safe distance, and those I trust and love close. Like Mom, I'm pretty good at reading people. I usually know within minutes of meeting someone if I like them or not.

Those who really know me also know that I'm fiercely protective of my friends and family. Stephanie was family now. Our entire little team was.

I promised I'd talk to Philip about the cleanup situation and retrieved my dessert from the fridge. Please let this go better than yesterday, I thought, walking to the Black Swan. It couldn't be worse, could it?

Don't even go there, Jules.

The small theater was a flurry of activity when I arrived. Philip barked out orders to his crew.

"You're late!" He tapped his cell phone and gave me an exasperated look. "This is always how it goes with talent. You're costing me money for every second we're not shooting."

"Me?"

"Yes. You!" He waved off a lighting technician who was holding a broken light.

Before I could respond he pushed me to the back of the theater. "Make it quick. We gotta get rolling."

I wasn't late. We were supposed to arrive by nine, and I knew it was definitely earlier than that.

Makeup brushes, compacts, and palettes of eye shadow covered a folding table. The makeup artist stared at my dessert.

"What's that doing back here? Philip needs those on set."

"I know. He told me to come straight here."

"We can't have dessert around my makeup." She caressed the tip of a tiny eyebrow brush.

"I'll go put it on set and be right back."

"You should get a move on. You're late, and Philip is not happy when people are late."

"I'm not late." I started to protest, but she waved her eyebrow brush at me. "But I was told to be here at nine."

"Who told you that?" She dusted the brush with brown powder.

"The camera crew last night."

She shrugged. "I don't know how they got that information. We've all been on set and waiting for you."

Great, I look like a flake, I thought. Why would the camera crew have told me to arrive late?

Sebastian and Philip stood nose to nose in the kitchen as I hurried in with my panna cotta. Philip didn't notice me.

His attention was singularly focused on Sebastian, and he didn't look happy.

Spit sprayed as Philip spoke. "I'm not doing this again. We're shooting this morning. End of story. You and your little problem can wait. I'm giving you the opportunity of a lifetime. A lifetime. Do you understand? You walk and you're done. You'll never work with the Pastry Channel again."

Sebastian threw his hands in the air. "I cannot work like dis." His French accent had returned.

Philip caught my eye. "Jules, what are you doing? I thought you were in makeup?"

I pointed to my panna cotta. "I just needed to set this down." I bit my bottom lip and tried to squeeze around Sebastian to place my dessert next to the others.

Sebastian narrowed his dark eyes at me. "She is spying."

"I'm not spying. What are you talking about?"

"I saw you sneaking around." His accent was thick.

Philip clapped his hands together. "Enough. Both of you. Jules get to makeup. Sebastian, we're done."

Sebastian said something I couldn't decipher. I slid my panna cotta on the counter and hurried back to the makeup chair.

The makeup artist quickly coated my face in foundation and patted on a layer of fine powder. She dusted my cheeks and filled in my eyebrows.

"You remind me of someone," she said as she unscrewed a tube of bronze lip gloss.

"Who?"

"Someone famous. I can't place the name. She played a detective on a TV show. Vera or something like that."

"Veronica Mars?"

"Yes. That's it." She told me to stay still as she ran the gloss over my lips.

"I used to be so addicted to the show. It was really popular on the ship. I've never heard anyone compare me to her."

"You kind of look like her. Taller of course, but I think it's more in the way you talk or something." She studied my face. "I think you're good. Take a look." She handed me a mirror.

The makeup smoothed my skin and hid any shadows under my eyes. I looked refreshed, bright, and like I belonged on a Las Vegas stage. "It's a lot." I frowned.

"You'll look great under the lights. Speaking of which, you better get out there. Philip is in a mood today and you're late."

"I'm not late. Like I said, they told me to arrive at nine. I'm on time."

She tapped her wrist.

I shrugged and grabbed the *Take the Cake* apron she held out for me. Everyone was positioned under the lights. Nina whispered as I took my place next to her, "Where have you been?"

Philip shot us a look and pressed his finger in front of his lips. Elliot stepped onto the judge's stage and began his opening monologue. "Hey, hey, home bakers, welcome back to the second round of competition. Today our pastry chefs are going to dazzle us with their signature desserts." He snapped his fingers and gave the camera a cheesy wink. From my vantage point he looked like he had as much—or more—makeup on than me. I couldn't imagine Stephanie's attraction to him. I get the whole thing about being dazzled by meeting a real-life celebrity, but Elliot's manicured and coiffed personal style couldn't be more different than Stephanie's grunge.

Elliot introduced the judges again. Then the camera panned on each of us holding our signature dessert. We had exactly thirty seconds to explain our concept.

"I opted for a panna cotta with a strawberry wine sauce

and fresh mint," I said as the camera zoomed in on my hands.

"What makes this a signature dish?" Elliot asked, thrusting a handheld mike in my face.

"The simplicity. It's foolproof, and a really elegant and indulgent dessert that people can create at home. At Torte all of our pastries and baked goods are stripped down. We want the flavor to shine."

Richard Lord, who stood two people down, made a snide comment under his breath. When Elliot made it to Richard, he made a big production about the Merry Windsor's focus on serving Renaissance food. He offered a gingerbread cake as his signature dessert. I'd wager a guess that he couldn't list a single ingredient in gingerbread. "Unlike my fellow Ashland contestant, my signature dessert reflects our Shakespearean town and roots. Guests at the Merry Windsor keep coming back just for our sweets."

When the camera panned away from him, he craned his head forward and shot me a smug smile. I wasn't going to let Richard get under my skin. Taste mattered, and I was confident that my fresh panna cotta would outperform Richard's gingerbread.

Like yesterday, each judge was served a taste of our desserts on small plates. They jotted down notes and carefully assessed flavors. Sebastian was positioned at the opposite end of the set. I noticed that he glared at Madame Dubois as she sampled his dessert. What was his deal? Wouldn't he want to try and butter her up? Or maybe he was worried that she knew he wasn't really French. I wanted to try to get him alone and see if he'd fess up to faking his French accent.

The judges finished their deliberation. Elliot sprang in front of the camera and congratulated Nina on winning the round. I couldn't believe her nondairy ice cream and fruit and nut compote had won. She squeezed my hand and practically skipped to the stage. Her eyes were wide with delight as the judges showered her with praise.

After Nina left the stage and joined us again, Elliot increased the tension and heightened the competition by announcing to the imaginary viewers at home that Richard Lord was on the brink of being voted out permanently. Two last-place votes in a row sent the contestant packing.

Philip directed the camera crew to switch from Richard's face to his gingerbread and back again. "Cut. Cut." He halted filming and addressed us. "Look, you guys, this is television. We're filming a show here. I can't have you all looking like you don't care. I want to see some emotion in this next shot. Your faces should reflect the drama. Richard could be out, one of you could be next. Let me see that."

Linda Belle batted her fake lashes at him. "You got it, sugar. We'll play it up for you, right, ladies?" She nudged Nina and stared at me.

Maybe I was becoming jaded with age, but the idea of faking emotional distress over a baking show seemed over the top. Plus, if Richard got booted today, I'd be thrilled.

You signed up for this, Jules, I thought as I tried to tap into my internal bank of turmoil for Philip's shot.

He seemed satisfied that we'd all put on our best vexed faces. "That's it. Let's roll, boys." Filming continued, and Elliot ratcheted up the tension with long, dramatic pauses before announcing the results.

It didn't come as a surprise when Elliot sighed and said, "Richard, bad news, my friend. Bad news." He put his hand to his cheek and shook his head. Today he wore another skintight T-shirt that read I BAKE HOT. He jumped off the stage and sauntered over to Richard. As he rested his arm around Richard's shoulder, his voice turned conciliatory. "Richard, you will not *take the cake*. I'm afraid it's the chopping block for you, my friend."

Richard got into character. He threw Elliot's hand from his shoulder. "It's a setup, I tell you. This competition is rigged." He yanked off his apron, revealing a pastel golf shirt stretched over his bulging belly. "I'll be back. You just wait. Next time I'm winning this." He tossed his apron at Elliot and stalked off the set.

Elliot gazed into the camera. His bright blue eyes almost looked glossy. He wasn't going to cry, was he?

Nina leaned over and whispered, "Oh, he's good. He's really good."

Turning his head in the direction that Richard left, Elliot sighed and held his hands in a namaste pose. "That exit just goes to show how intense this competition is. Things are heating up. It's going to get smokin' hot in this kitchen over the next few weeks. Be sure to tune in next time when the contestants will be judged on pies." He whipped a spatula from his apron pocket like a gunslinger. "This is your *Take the Cake* host, Elliot Cool, signing off and reminding you all that baking is a piece of cake. Stay sexy!"

Chapter Twenty-five

The camera light shone on all of us as Philip counted down with his fingers. "That's a wrap," he announced, and the camera went dark.

Off to the side Richard Lord broke into a throaty laugh. Philip raced over and clapped him on the back. "You were perfect. That was genius."

Richard puffed his cheeks. "I think the acting bug has rubbed off on me."

Philip turned to us. "That's what I want to see, people. That's television. Drama. Let's have a round of applause for Richard." He clapped his hands. The cast and crew followed suit.

Richard ate up the attention. He bowed. "It's back to the busy world of business for me. Good luck to the rest of you." He paused and stared at me. "I'll be rooting for my girl Juliet. We have keep it here in the family in Ashland, so to speak."

I felt like my jaw must have dropped to my chest. Richard stepped closer and lowered his voice. "You don't have to look so shocked, Juliet." He sounded sincere, and almost remorseful. Before I could sputter out a response, he left. Could Richard Lord actually be softening a little, or did he have some ulterior motive? I didn't have time to figure it out at the moment, but watching him walk off the set made me feel a tad guilty. I hadn't exactly made an effort to be kind to him. That's something you're going to have to work on, Jules, I thought to myself.

Philip passed around info sheets with the rules for our pies. From the crust to the filling everything was to be made by hand. That wasn't a problem for me, but Linda looked distressed as she read through the list. I figured she had a vision of a pie adorned with candied pearls.

I stuffed the list into the back pocket of my jeans and removed my apron. It was almost lunchtime. I couldn't believe the shoot had taken so long. It felt like we'd only been at the theater for an hour or so. Sebastian snuck past me and out the front door before I could grab him.

Nina looked like she was waiting around to speak with Philip, so I headed outside. Maybe I could catch up with Sebastian. I was dying to know why he was faking a French accent. I had a feeling it had to do with Marco's murder, but I couldn't figure out why.

I scanned the bricks across Pioneer Street and looked down the hill. Sebastian was nowhere in sight. He must have run off. Oh, well. I should probably just tell all of this to Thomas anyway, I thought.

The noon sun warmed the sidewalk and danced on the trees. Everything smelled fresh and clean. I inhaled, thankful to be outside.

"Jules!" someone called from behind me.

I stopped and turned around to see Nina running down the hill.

"Thank goodness I caught you." She slowed her pace.

"What's up?"

"I was hoping I could talk to you about Thomas."

"Thomas?" I felt my body tense.

She wiped brown eyeliner from under her eyes. "This

stuff is so gross." She took two fingers and smudged it. "I need to take a shower."

The makeup felt thick on my face. I imagined it seeping into my pores as we spoke. "I agree," I said, patting my unfamiliar face. "You wanted to talk to me about Thomas?"

"You guys are old friends, right?"

"Yep."

"He seems really nice." She twisted her peasant skirt.

"He is really nice." I could feel my body loosen. It was true. Thomas was probably one of the nicest guys I'd ever met. Maybe that's why it didn't work out with us.

A light mist drizzled from the sky. She blushed through the layer of foundation on her face. "I was sort of wondering if you knew if he's seeing anyone."

"I don't." I shook my head. When I returned home this summer Thomas told me he was dating someone, but I'd never heard any more about the woman and I'd never seen him around town with anyone. "I mean, I don't think he is, but honestly, I don't know."

Nina looked disappointed. "Okay, don't worry about it. It's kind of embarrassing to ask you anyway. I just can't get a read on him. We went to dinner last night and it was really fun. He was so sweet, but I couldn't figure out if he thought it was a date or if he was just being nice."

"Thomas is nice to everyone."

"That's what I thought." She sighed.

"I didn't mean it like that. I meant he is *nice*. You should ask him."

"No. No way. I'm not that forward. I am going to work on making him some vegan treats that he can't refuse."

She thanked me and said she'd forgotten something at the theater. I continued on to Torte, trying not to let Nina's interest in Thomas make me feel weird. She had every right to pursue him. My claim on him had long expired.

Torte smelled like chilies and onions when I stepped

inside. Most of the tables were taken by locals lunching together. The Professor was on his way out with a box of pastries tucked under his arm.

"You're becoming a regular fixture around here," I teased him.

His eyes twinkled. "You know what they say about officers of the law and doughnuts."

"Somehow, I don't think you're the type." I laughed and held the door open for him.

"Ah, but you never know, dear Juliet, do you? As the bard said, 'Don't share your top secret with anyone.' " He looked me straight in the eye, nodded, and departed.

I wondered what he meant by that.

"How was the show, boss?" Andy asked, as he poured whole coffee beans from a ten-pound bag into the grinder.

"Not bad. Richard Lord got booted off, so that was a bonus."

Sterling's intense eyes studied my face. "That's, uh, some serious makeup."

I laughed and posed for them. "What? Don't you think I should come to the shop every day looking like this?"

"No!" they both shouted in unison.

"Ouch. That hurts. That really hurts, you two."

Sterling glanced behind him to where Stephanie was working in the kitchen. "Don't end up letting those Hollywood types rub off on you, like someone else we know."

"Like that would ever happen." I reached out and squeezed Sterling's hand. "These Hollywood types are heading home soon. Don't worry about it."

Sterling shrugged and shuffled back to the pastry case as a new customer entered.

Andy folded the bag of remaining beans and clamped it shut with a large clip. "You want a coffee, boss? I can fire something up for you."

"That would be great."

"What do you want?"

"Surprise me." I left Andy and went straight to the sink to wash my hands. "What smells so good in here?" I asked Mom and Stephanie, drying my hands with a paper towel.

"Chili. It's your dad's recipe," Mom said. She lifted the lid off a cast-iron pot on the stove.

The smell of tomatoes, onions, and chilies infused the kitchen. I walked closer and leaned over for a better whiff. "That smells so good. I think I could eat the entire pot." My stomach gurgled on cue. "I forgot to eat breakfast and then the morning got away from me with the show and everything."

Mom reached for a bowl and ladled the hearty chili. "I've got an assortment of toppings on the counter." She nodded to a tray with ramekins of sour cream, shredded Colby jack cheese, diced green onions, crushed tortilla chips, salsas, and black olives. "Help yourself. It felt like a chili kind of day with the rain this morning, and the changing leaves. When I think fall, I think chili."

"Me too, Mrs. C." Andy delivered my coffee. "Because fall is football season and nothing goes better together than football and chili."

Mom gave him a half hug. "And you are our own football star, who needs some of this sustenance."

Andy grinned. "Dude, I won't ever turn down your chili, Mrs. C."

Mom ladled another bowl for Andy while I brought the tray of toppings to the island. Andy added extra salsa and chips to his. I went for a dab of sour cream, a sprinkle of cheese, and olives and green onions. It would be interesting to study how our food choices pair with our personalities. I already knew Andy liked heat. This summer he created an espresso drink with dark chocolate and chili powder. It sold so well that it became a permanent fixture on our drink menu.

"How about you, Stephanie?" Mom asked. "Are you ready for a lunch break?"

Stephanie declined. "I'm fine. I'm having lunch with a friend after my shift."

"Friend?" Sterling whipped his head around from the front counter. That's the drawback of working in a small space. It's hard to have a private conversation. "Or Mr. Hollywood?"

Stephanie glared at him, and concentrated on brushing olive oil on sliced baguettes in front of her.

I dug into my chili without letting it cool. It burned the tip of my tongue, but I was so famished I didn't even mind. It had been years since I tasted my dad's chili recipe. Everyone does chili a bit differently. My dad's recipe revolves around using fresh tomatoes. We score them, steam them, and then sauté them with celery, onion, and tons of garlic. This veggie base makes the chili taste like it has been picked ripe from the garden.

With my mouth tingling, I scooped another taste. Mom used a combination of ground beef and stew meat and three kinds of beans. The spicy finish exploded with flavor.

Andy devoured his bowl of chili and went in for seconds. "This is like, seriously, the best chili I've ever had, Mrs. C."

"I'm glad you like it, Andy. It's been quite a while since I made a batch for the shop."

"You should make more. Customers are into it." Andy wiped his bowl clean with a hunk of bread.

My mouth burned from the heat of the chili. I wiped my chin with a napkin. "Andy's right, Mom. I've been wondering about selling soups to go in the fall and winter. We could package them in family-sized containers so that customers could grab a loaf of bread, some soup, and be all set for dinner."

Mom ladled more steaming chili into Andy's bowl. He

wisely blew on his spoon to let it cool. She held the ladle above the pot and turned to me. "Do you want more?"

I declined.

She rested the ladle on the counter and placed a heavy cast-iron lid on the pot. "I like that idea. I would want that for myself, especially on a busy night when I don't feel like cooking. A homemade batch of soup and bread to go. See, Andy, that's why I pay her the big bucks."

"Ha!" I tried to launch my napkin at her, but it floated onto the floor.

A customer came into the shop. Andy left his cooling chili to go craft one of his semifamous espresso drinks.

"Should we try the soup-to-go idea, Mom?" I asked, rinsing my bowl in the sink. "I think it could bring in a little extra cash. If you're game I'll look into ordering some containers. Maybe we can test it for the next couple weeks and see how we do?"

Mom brushed her hands on her apron. "Of course. I think it's a great idea." She walked to the sink and gave me a playful hip bump. "Get out of here, would you?"

I flicked her with water. "What's that supposed to mean?"

Her face turned serious. "I'm worried about you. You look tired, and I have the sense that even though you're putting on a good front, this murder has you rattled."

I didn't meet her eyes as I reached for a clean dish towel to dry my hands.

"It's understandable. I'm sure it's bringing back all kinds of feelings about what happened this summer. That's normal," she continued.

"I'm okay, Mom." I looped the towel on a hook next to the sink.

"I know you're okay, but I want you to go get some rest. Take a little time for yourself." She pointed to the front of the shop. One table was occupied and two customers stood at the front counter trying to decide what afternoon sweet to partake in. "It's slow. You're working too hard. Go home. Take a nap. We've got it covered here."

"Yeah, but Linda and Nina are going to be here to work on their pies."

"Do I bite?" Mom winked.

"No, but."

"Stop with the 'buts.' Go home. Get some rest. We've 'got this' as the kids like to say."

I had to admit that I was dragging a little. The last couple days were catching up with me. A nap sounded divine. If I could sleep, and that was a big *if*, then I could come back to the shop in the evening when it would be quiet to work on my pie.

Mom swatted me on the derriere. "Stop worrying about the kitchen. We're fine. Go take care of yourself."

I covered my rear with my hands and ducked away from her. "Okay. I'm going. Call me if it picks up, though."

"Sure," she lied.

I gave the shop one final glance before scooting out the door. A nap. Maybe that would help erase some of the craziness from the last two days.

Chapter Twenty-six

I don't even remember walking home or falling asleep. The next thing I knew I woke up on my couch to a numb right arm. Somehow I'd twisted myself onto one side, cutting off the circulation.

What time was it? Had I slept all afternoon?

I checked the clock. It was just after four. Not bad, Jules, I thought as I shook my arm to get blood flowing again. Mom was right. I must have needed sleep.

Was she also right about reliving last summer's memories? And was she talking about the murder, or was she also hinting about Carlos? I'd never really thought about it, but I guess I did associate him with returning home and my first murder investigation.

I wondered what he was doing right now. I knew he was back on the ship, but short of that I hadn't let myself think about him. Wondering where he might be—on a smooth stretch of sea, swaying his sultry hips to the sound of Latin rhythms in the ship's kitchen—made my throat tighten.

Carlos took leave for a week after I left and returned home to Barcelona to see his son—the son he somehow managed to never tell me about. The lump in my throat grew as I allowed the painful memories to resurface.

Maybe trying to shove thoughts of Carlos to the back of my mind hadn't been the best idea after all. I could picture his olive skin, slightly tanned like a perfect piece of toast. I could hear his thick accent and the way he'd roll his *r* when he called me "*mi querida*."

My hand absently went to the back of my neck. I could almost feel his breath, his tender kiss on pale skin. Being around Carlos made me feel warmer, sexier, stronger.

Our friends on the ship used to call us beautiful opposites. Carlos, with his Latin charm and dangerously attractive dark eyes, and the fair Juliet, with ash-blond hair and skin that glows pinkish with the slightest touch of the sun. I knew we made a striking couple. I guess I just never saw myself striking out in love.

Mom had encouraged me to let things sit for a while. She reminded me that I didn't have to figure out what was next for Carlos and me right away, but pretending he didn't exist wasn't working for me either.

I hugged my knees to my chest as I pictured him in his kitchen whites, chopping onions and infusing his food with his playful and sensual spirit. A tear rolled down my cheek. I let it fall. It felt welcome. I needed to cry.

One tear turned into a steady flow of salty liquid streaming from my eyes. I read somewhere once that tears shed for different reasons have different chemistries. That the tears that form when dicing an onion or laughing hysterically contain different compounds than those spilled from grief. My tears felt like my body was tapping into the ocean. It was fitting to associate their salty grittiness to my time on the sea.

My breath slowed, and I inhaled through my nose. I guess I needed that. I knew my emotional purge was triggered by my memory of Carlos, but I'm sure the events of the past few days had something to do with it too.

I cleansed my face with a washcloth and grabbed a

sweatshirt from my dresser. The evening would most likely be cool, and I wasn't sure how long I'd be at Torte working on my pie. Hopefully Linda and Nina had finished their pies by now, and hopefully they hadn't left a giant mess for me.

Drat. That reminded me. I'd forgotten to ask Philip about contestants cleaning up after themselves. Before I headed to the bakeshop, I made sure to leave the light on in the front room and lock the door. My run-in with Sebastian last night had me a tiny bit rattled, and I didn't want to take any chances.

On my way to Torte I stopped in for a quick chat with Mark, the owner of Elevation. He was a serious rock climber in his mid to late forties.

"Jules, how's everything upstairs?" He was stacking boxes of hiking boots at the front of the outdoor store when I stuck my head in.

"It's great. I'm starting to make it feel a little like home. I actually hung a picture on the wall."

"Whoa, you're really living on the edge, aren't you?" He laughed.

"That's how I roll." I tried to wink. I don't know why it never works for me. My face just ends up looking like I'm contorting it in some weird way.

Mark put down the boxes and strolled to the front of the store. His brow furrowed, revealing the beginning of age lines in the center of his forehead. "I'm glad you stopped by actually. There was a guy in here this afternoon asking about you. He wanted to know where you lived. Said he heard you lived by the store. I don't know. It was weird. I didn't tell him."

"Who was it? Do you know?"

"Didn't recognize him. He's not from town, but he had a French accent."

I gasped. "Sebastian."

"You know him?"

"He's a contestant on the Pastry Channel show."

"Okay, well, don't worry about it then. I'm probably being an overprotective landlord."

"No, thank you. He gives me the creeps too. I'm really glad you didn't tell him I live upstairs."

"I'd never tell anyone that. I guess everyone in town already knows, but you know what I mean. Not a stranger. Are you cool? Do you need me to watch out for anything?"

"Thanks, I'm good, but if he comes around again will you let me know? I'll tell Thomas too."

"Good idea, and yeah, I've got your back, Jules. We all do."

That's what I love about being home again. I smiled. "I better get to the bakeshop. I've got a pie to make tonight."

"Feel free to swing by if you need a taste-tester. I'm always happy to help." He picked up a pair of hiking boots on the front window display and tied the laces. "Catch you later, Jules. Be careful out there."

I didn't like that Sebastian was asking around about me. He already knew where I lived. I didn't want to say that to Mark, but he'd seen me go upstairs last night. What possible reason could he have for asking where I live?

Locals took advantage of the break in the weather, sitting at outdoor bistro tables being warmed by portable gas heaters. Fall is such a lovely time to dine al fresco. Most restaurants have invested in heaters or fire pits to allow customers to enjoy the fresh air and changing foliage for as long as possible. Soon winter would arrive with snow and more rain showers. I greeted familiar faces as I made my way along Main Street.

The door at A Rose by Any Other Name, Thomas's family's flower shop, stood propped open. I breathed in the scent of roses and fresh cut lavender.

"Hey, who's sniffing around out there?" Thomas yelled from behind the counter.

"I'm so glad you're here," I said, stepping into the shop.

A cement-block counter stretched the length of the small shop. Thomas and his parents use it as a workspace to assemble bouquets. This evening it was piled with sprigs of lavender, evergreen boughs, and pale purple roses. Buckets with bunches of flowers waiting to be sold were arranged around the room, and in the far corner of the space was a glass case displaying preassembled bouquets in vases and tied with raffia and brown paper.

I've always loved the quaint, country vibe in the shop. It almost feels like stepping into a farm flower stand.

Thomas set a pair of heavy-duty shears on the counter. "I'm here for all your floral needs. This sounds like an emergency. Probably calls for orchids. My mom says when in doubt, go with the orchid."

I picked up a sprig of lavender and ran it between my fingers. The friction intensified its scent. "Sadly, no, I'm not here for flowers."

Thomas scrunched his face. "Let me guess. I'm not going to like the reason you are here, right?"

I smelled the lavender. I should make lavender shortbread cookies, I thought. I could dust them with sea salt, a nice balance with the herb and a hint of sugar.

"Jules?" Thomas interrupted my thought just as a recipe was solidifying in my head.

"Yeah." I sniffed the lavender again.

"Why are you here?"

"Right." I put the lavender back in the pile. "Sebastian."

"What about him?"

"I think he's the killer."

"Juliet Montague Capshaw. You just broke our deal!"

"No one calls me that, *Tommy*." I pretended to snarl at

him. Even Mom didn't call me by my full name anymore. I'd thankfully shaken off my Shakespearean title years ago.

"You got me." Thomas grinned. "So do tell. How has that lovely brain of yours deduced that Sebastian is our killer?"

I folded my arms across my chest. "Now you're just making fun of me."

"Me? Never." Thomas gave me a dopey look. "Do I ever make fun?"

I tightened my arms around my chest.

Thomas brushed pollen from his hands and came around the counter. "Okay, okay. You're not going to drop it, are you?"

I shook my head.

"Tell me what you know, then." He grabbed his iPad.

"Sebastian followed me last night."

Thomas started to click something on the iPad, stopped and looked up. "He followed you?"

"Yeah." I nodded and let my arms fall loose. "He was dressed completely in black and sneaking around the plaza. He ran into me in front of my apartment."

His voice lost any trace of playfulness. "This is serious, Jules."

I explained my theory about Sebastian breaking in at Torte, how I overheard him in the alleyway speaking perfect English, and about him asking the owner of Elevation where I lived.

Thomas's phone rang. It was the theme song from *Skyfall*. Thomas is a huge spy movie fan. When we were dating in high school we used to argue about our polar-opposite tastes in movies. I preferred romantic, and sometimes weepy romantic flicks. He opted for as much action as possible. Although he usually let me win. When we'd walk to the little video store on the plaza (that's now long gone) we'd browse each section. He'd usually come up to me with puppy-dog eyes and a stack of guy flicks. We always left with a romantic comedy (my choice) and a box of Junior Mints (his).

I figured he could have the Junior Mints if he was willing to sit through two hours of a sappy movie with me.

He nodded into the phone and tapped his iPad. Holding the phone to his ear with one hand, he navigated the iPad with the other. "Got it," he said. "I'm right across the street. I'll head over now."

"Who was that?" I asked when he ended the call.

"The Professor." He frowned. "It sounds like you might be onto something here. Apparently the fingerprints we pulled from Torte this morning came back with a match."

"Sebastian?"

"Yep. Only according to his police record, the French chef is actually from Ohio. He has quite the record. An assault charge from ten years ago. Guess who filed the charges?"

"Who?"

"Chef Marco."

Chapter Twenty-seven

"I knew it!" I punched Thomas in the arm.

He rubbed his shoulder. "Easy, there. We have this thing in law enforcement and the justice system called 'innocent until proven guilty.'"

"You have to admit, that's some pretty compelling evidence."

"Nope. Not evidence in Marco's murder." Thomas clicked the iPad off. "Evidence that he was at Torte, but those prints could be from anytime. We need more proof. Or better yet, a confession. All we have now is some circumstantial evidence. I'm heading over to the Merry Windsor to question him right now."

"You're not going to arrest him?"

"On what charge?"

"What do you mean? You can't just let a killer have free rein around town."

"Slow down, slow down." Thomas held his arm out in an attempt to stop me. "We have procedures we have to follow, Jules. I'm not about to let a potential murder suspect out of my sight, but I don't have anything to hold him on at the moment. Prints at the scene don't prove that he vandalized Torte. We found multiple prints. You run a successful business. Half of the town's prints are in there."

"But in the office?"

Thomas hesitated. "Listen, I'm following the Professor's orders. I need to go interrogate the suspect." He squeezed his iPad under his arm and stepped toward the door.

"So you did find his prints in the office?" I followed him.

"Jules, this is a murder investigation. I can't discuss specific details of the case. I could get myself in big trouble." He held the door open for me.

Thomas may not have been able to share details, but I knew that he'd found Sebastian's prints in the office. It was what he wasn't saying that was a dead giveaway. Bad pun, Jules, I thought as I tagged after Thomas.

He stopped in mid-stride. "What do you think you're doing?"

"Coming with you."

"No way."

I batted my lashes at him. "Please."

"Knock it off, Jules, you are so not the girly type."

"I had to give it a shot." I tried to wink and continued walking across the plaza. "Come on. I'm not going to interfere with your investigation, it just so happens that I have some important business with Richard Lord."

Thomas threw his head back and laughed. "Yeah, right." His shoulders slacked a little. "Fine, but I don't want you saying a word. Not a single word, understood?"

"Of course." I crossed my heart. "You'll never know I'm there."

Thomas sighed. "How do I get myself into these situations with you, Juliet Capshaw?"

I figured it was better if I kept quiet now and followed him past the bubbling fountains and across the street to the Merry Windsor in silence.

The same apathetic kid sat behind the reception desk. Thomas flashed his badge and said he needed to speak with Sebastian. The kid pointed toward the kitchen without looking up. "He's one of those chefs, right? Kitchen's that way."

Thomas gave me a warning look as I tiptoed behind him.

"I'm so quiet," I whispered.

He pursed his lips and smiled. "Jules, I'm serious. Not a word."

I gave him a salute as he flashed his badge again. The dining room was practically deserted. Not a good sign for Richard. Sure, it was the off-season, but clearly Richard wasn't pulling locals in the way we were at Torte. Could his bravado be an act? Maybe things weren't as merry at the Merry Windsor as Richard would like to have us all believe.

Thomas peered into the kitchen. He flashed his badge again. "I'm looking for Sebastian."

The cook pointed to the back door. "He's having a smoke."

I followed Thomas, retracing my steps from earlier in the morning, to the back alley.

Sebastian had his back propped against the building and a long, thin cigarette hanging from his mouth. He didn't react when Thomas held up his badge prominently. "Sebastian, I need a word," Thomas said.

Sebastian took a long drag from the cigarette. He held the smoke in his lungs before exhaling. "Yes."

"I have a few questions for you." Thomas secured his badge on his chest and opened the cover to his iPad. "We can either talk here, or I can walk you over to the station."

"Here is fine, yes." Sebastian maintained the French act, while puffing on the cigarette.

Thomas launched into a round of questions. At first Sebastian acted completely unimpressed by Thomas's questions. He smoked his cigarette, snuffed it on the ground with his shoe, and lit another one while Thomas asked him where he'd been last night.

"In ze kitchen."

Thomas continued to push, asking for specific timelines and who might be able to confirm Sebastian's whereabouts.

Sebastian answered all of Thomas's questions with the French accent, smoking like a grease fire the entire time. I coughed and waved smoke away twice when Sebastian blew it in my direction, but otherwise I followed Thomas's order and blended into the wall.

It was all I could do to keep from jumping in. I could feel my muscles tense as Thomas continued his slow and steady style of questioning. This wasn't working. Sebastian didn't even look nervous.

Thomas swiped something on his iPad and held it out for Sebastian to see. "Do you know what this is?"

Sebastian choked on his own smoke.

Thomas slid his finger over the document. "This is on your public record. It looks like you failed to mention that you and Chef Marco were previously acquainted during our initial investigation."

Sebastian dropped the cigarette and mashed it into the ground.

"Not only were you and the late chef acquainted, but it seems you were involved in an altercation which led to your subsequent arrest. Is this sounding familiar?"

Sebastian tried to remove another cigarette from the pack but his hand shook. He gave up and tucked the pack into his pocket.

Thomas was on a roll. "The way I see it, you lied to us about knowing the chef. You lied to us about your record, and you lied to us about killing him."

"Non, no." Sebastian's accent faded.

"It gets worse for you, I'm afraid." Thomas clicked onto

a new document on the iPad. "We found your prints at Torte, which was vandalized last night. Murder, vandalism, prior assault conviction. It's not looking good for you, Sebastian."

I'd never seen Thomas interrogate a suspect before, and I had to give him credit. Somehow he managed to strike a balance between being a tough detective and actually sounding like he was sincere.

It may have been the sincerity that finally made Sebastian crack. He covered his face with his hands. His arms trembled. I almost felt sorry for him.

"You don't understand." Sebastian's voice held no trace of an accent. "It's not what you think."

Thomas tapped the iPad. "This has nothing to do with what I think and everything to do with the facts right here in front of me."

Sebastian removed his hands from in front of his face. "I know, but can I explain?"

"Get started." Thomas caught my eye. "I'm waiting. First, I'd like to know what happened to your accent."

Sebastian looked at me. "Is she with the police or something? I thought she was a bakeshop owner."

I started to answer, but Thomas cut me off. "She's here because it's her shop that was vandalized. She's probably going to press charges. That is, if I don't book you for murder first."

Sebastian swallowed. "I didn't murder Marco. I swear. I didn't."

Thomas waited.

"Okay, I confess. I'm not French. In fact, I've never even been to France."

"Go on."

"I've always wanted to be a pastry chef. I'm originally from Ohio, and no one in my family cared about pastry the way I did. I can remember being a kid and practicing my sugar art on our dining room table. My dad used to get so mad at me for staining the table with food coloring."

I could relate. Not necessarily to staining the table, but to having an interest in the culinary arts from a young age.

Sebastian continued. "After I graduated, I took off for New York."

Maybe we had more in common than I thought.

"I didn't have a plan. I didn't have a job, any money, but I knew I had to be in New York. That's where all the top pastry chefs were. I figured I'd get my start in New York and then I would have a résumé that would take me to France. That's always been my dream. I've studied French on my own, read every book by some of the most famous French chefs that I can get my hands on, and I spend all my spare time watching videos of French chefs."

Thomas waited with iPad ready to type. Apparently none of this was worthy of including in notes yet.

Sebastian reached for his pack of cigarettes, patted it but didn't pull it out. "Things didn't exactly go as I planned. New York is a hard city. Really hard when you're an eighteen-year-old kid."

I knew a little something about that too. Although unlike Sebastian I was fortunate enough to attend one of the top culinary schools during my stint in the city.

"I couldn't get anyone to give me a shot. I tried every single high-end restaurant and dive bar in town. No one would hire me. I worked odd jobs for a while and lived in this nasty studio apartment with two other guys. It was terrible. I almost moved home to Ohio."

Thomas gave me a look I couldn't quite decipher.

"Right when I was about to call it quits, I got a break. One of my buddies was working as a dishwasher at a swanky pastry shop in midtown. The restaurant kept losing wait staff and the kitchen help due to a horrid head pastry chef. He'd just fired the latest busboy. I didn't care. It was my shot. I showed up for my first shift the next day, like a kid at Christmas. I was riding high with my first real job. I knew that if I busted my ass bussing tables and washing dishes I could work my way up and get some real training as a prep cook."

Sebastian pulled the pack of cigarettes from his pocket. "Hang on a sec. I need a smoke," he said as he lit a cigarette. "Turns out my buddy was right, the head chef was a nightmare to work for. He belittled the staff, and was always drunk in the kitchen. He'd break things, ruin a dessert and then blame everyone else. We all tried to avoid him. The sous-chefs did all the work anyway, and they were pretty decent to me. I worked there for three years and yet the head chef never even knew my name."

He inhaled another hit of nicotine. "I finally got another break when one of the prep cooks left in the middle of a shift. The sous-chef knew I was eager and had me fill in. I took abuse from the head chef. I can still remember his slurred voice in my ear and the smell of alcohol on his breath."

"Marco?" I asked. I couldn't help myself.

Thomas raised his eyebrow.

Sebastian nodded. "Yep, the world-famous Marco. The only reason he was famous was because he had a staff that did everything for him. The man didn't lift a finger. I'm not even sure he knew how to bake. He spent all his time with a bottle under his arm, making life miserable for the rest of us."

I kept quiet after Thomas's warning, but Sebastian's confession was making him sound guiltier to me.

"But I didn't care, because I knew I was training at the best pastry shop in town. Having that on my résumé was going to open doors. The sous-chef really took me under his wing." He waved smoke from his face. "One night I was working late and had a pan of custard cooling. Marco stumbled in drunk and spilled the custard all over the floor. He slipped on it, and then claimed that I'd pushed him. Fired me on the spot. Not another word, then called the cops. Said I had assaulted him. Threw the custard at him. I didn't."

Thomas stopped him. "I'm not entirely sure that this story is helping your case. Do you want to speed it up a bit?"

Sebastian smashed his cigarette. The ground near his feet was littered with cigarette butts. "I'm getting to that. Marco firing me ended up being the best thing that ever happened to me. That night I hit the bar. I used to pretend that I had a French accent to impress women, and there was a woman at the bar who was starting a new bistro. What started as my attempt to try and hit on her with a fake French accent ended up landing me a job as her head pastry chef. She thought I was really French, and I told her I'd worked for Marco for years. That was enough. I've been a French pastry chef ever since."

"I'm still not sure how this clears you as a suspect," Thomas said.

"Don't you see, I owe my career to Marco? If he hadn't fired me that night, I'd probably still be working for Marco and be bitter, but in a weird twist of fate he helped me get my first break. I worked as the head chef of Le Dish for five years. Last year my grandmother died and left me her diner in Portland. No one knows me in the city. I've played the part of a French chef for so long, I guess I didn't even think about just being me when I moved."

"This doesn't explain your prints at Torte." Thomas pointed to the iPad.

"Yeah, about that." Sebastian looked at me. "Sorry. I'll pay for everything."

"So you did break in?" My voice sounded shrill.

Sebastian hung his head a little. "I did."

Chapter Twenty-eight

"If you didn't kill Marco then why break into Torte?"

Thomas shot me another warning look. "Yes, you're going to need to explain yourself."

"It was for a recipe."

"A recipe?" Thomas and I spoke at the same time.

"Back when I worked at Marco's, the sous-chef and I came up with a masterful fruit torte. It took us weeks to perfect and then the recipe disappeared. I tried to re-create it at Le Dish, but never quite got it right. I'm sure Marco stole it years ago. I'm just not sure why. He never put it on the menu or anything. When I saw that old black binder he was carrying around, I wanted to see if my recipe was still there."

"So you broke into Torte?" Thomas looked doubtful. "Why wouldn't you have asked to see his recipe book, and why break all the vases?"

"I figured if I asked to take a look at the recipe book then this entire story would come out and it wouldn't look good for me. Chef Marco didn't recognize me, so no one would ever associate the two of us together." He patted his cigarette pack again. The guy had a serious addiction. He must have smoked five cigarettes in the ten or fifteen minutes we'd been talking. "Sorry about the vases. Like I said, I'll pay you for any damage. I'm pretty good with a lock, but after I broke in I realized that if I went through Marco's things, someone would think it had to do with his murder. I broke the vases to make it look like someone had vandalized the shop."

Thomas typed something on the iPad. "I'm not sure what to think about this. I'm going to need to talk to the Professor. In the meantime, Jules, do you want to press charges?"

Sebastian wouldn't meet my eye. "I am really sorry. That's why I broke the vases. I figured they'd be the easiest to clean up and replace. I didn't touch anything else in the shop, I swear."

I wasn't sure I believed him. The man had to be a good actor if he'd spent the last decade pretending to be French, but I also wasn't sure I wanted to go through the process of filing a complaint against him. "No," I said after a moment of deliberation. "But you are going to need to buy us new vases. I want them at the bakeshop before we open to customers tomorrow morning."

Sebastian let out a breath. "Thanks, I appreciate it. I'll get you new vases. No problem."

"Not so fast there." Thomas held up his index finger. "Jules may be letting you off easy, but I'm not done with you yet. You are not to leave town until the Professor or I say you're free to go. Understood?"

"Where am I going to go?"

"Regardless. I don't want you to put a foot outside of Ashland."

"I won't." Sebastian pointed to the back door of the Merry Windsor. "Can I get back to work?"

Thomas nodded. "And I need you to bring anything of Marco's to the station immediately."

"Okay." Sebastian flipped the pack of cigarettes. He gave

me a nervous look. "You're not going to say anything about the French thing, are you?"

"No." I wanted to ask him a thousand more questions, but I knew Thomas wouldn't approve.

Sebastian slipped back inside. Thomas extended his arm. "How about if I walk you to Torte?"

I accepted his hand. His touch sent a tingling sensation up my entire arm. Maybe a decade had passed, but the chemistry between us still felt palpable and familiar. And yet entirely different than my chemistry with Carlos.

Carlos and I ran hot. From the first time we met on the ship, the heat between us was impossible to deny.

I dropped Thomas's hand. His posture stiffened as we walked down the alley.

"Do you believe him?" I asked.

Thomas didn't answer right away. I wondered if I'd offended him by pulling away. Had he felt the connection between us too?

The only thing I could compare the two men to was pastry. Thomas was like a soft oatmeal cookie, served warm from the oven with a chewy center. Carlos was like cherries jubilee, flaming hot on the outside. Once the flame burned out, though, what was left?

Thomas was speaking. I was only half listening. "Sorry, what did you say?" I asked.

"You always were a dreamer, Jules." His voice sounded husky.

He must have been reminiscing too. He held my gaze for a moment, his blue eyes searching for a memory, or maybe a sign that I still felt something.

I broke the tension with a flippant response. "Not sure any of that dreaming has paid off. Look at me now, I'm right back where I started—literally." I pointed to the wooden sign that hung above Torte.

"Maybe you should think about it more like you're right

back where you belong." Thomas leaned close to me. I could smell a hint of lingering pollen mixed with aftershave. Like his touch, the smell was familiar. Although fortunately he didn't smell like he bathed in aftershave the way he used to in high school.

I wondered for a moment if he was going to kiss me. My back rested on the window, he leaned forward and propped one arm on the window too. Our noses were an inch apart. I could feel my breath quicken. Did I want this?

At that moment someone rapped on the window from inside. Both of us jumped. Thomas backed away. I turned to see Nina waving from inside.

Thomas cleared his throat. "You better get in there. Looks like you might be needed."

"I think you're the one she's looking for." Nina was still waving with one hand and holding a plate of treats with the other.

"Come in!" she called.

Thomas muttered something under his breath I couldn't make out. Nina danced toward the door and flung it open.

"I was just hoping that I would see you," she said to Thomas, ignoring me. "I made you another vegan delight." She pushed the plate in front him. "Cookies. Wait until you taste these. You'll never go back to butter."

She bounced back and forth on her open-toed sandals while waiting for Thomas's reaction as he took a bite. "So what do you think?"

Thomas chewed the cookie. "It's good," he said with his mouth full.

"Good. Come on." Nina batted her hand. "They're better than good. Here, try another one." She shoved the plate at Thomas.

I wanted to ask him more about Sebastian, but I could tell Nina had no intention of sharing him, so I left them and the vegan cookies in favor of an empty kitchen.

Nina's workstation was a disaster. I pushed her stuff to one corner of the island, washed my hands, and tugged on a clean apron. Pies were one of my specialties. They're such a simple yet elegant dessert option.

The wine Mom brought from her trip sat within arm's reach. I grabbed the bottle and poured myself a glass. The question was, what kind of pie? I had a feeling that Linda's pie entry would be something cream based, Nina's was most likely to be an apple or some kind of fruit. I'd put money on Sebastian bringing in a rustic tart, to keep up with his fake French act.

What could I make that would set my pie apart from the rest of the competition? I took a sip of wine and flipped through our recipe book. The farther I went in the competition, the more I wanted to win.

Nina scurried into the kitchen with a half-empty plate of cookies. "I'll get all this tomorrow." She set the plate on the island and noted her mess. "Thomas and I are going to go grab a drink. Don't work too late." She winked.

I swirled the wine in my glass and watched them stroll across the plaza. The smooth wine slid down my throat and warmed my stomach. In the excitement of tagging along with Thomas to interview Sebastian I hadn't eaten anything—again. This seemed to be a pattern. One I needed to fix. Mom had been on me since I'd come home about being too thin. I eat. That isn't the problem. It's just that sometimes I forget that I need to eat more than one meal a day, or more than cookies.

Andy and Sterling had cleared and cleaned the pastry cases. We donate day-old bread and pastries to the shelter in town, so there was nothing left for me. Maybe I'd get lucky and score a sandwich in the fridge. Sometimes we wrap them overnight so they don't go bad before we deliver them to the shelter.

I walked into the fridge. It was jam-packed with extra

supplies for Nina and Linda. I found eggs, pineapple, a box of organic apples and pears from an orchard nearby, and an assortment of meats and cheeses for tomorrow's sandwiches. But alas no leftovers. I grabbed some farmer's cheese, a couple eggs, mushrooms and onions. I could make myself a quick egg-scramble.

As I started to close the door to the fridge, I noticed Nina's pie on the second shelf. I could tell it was hers because, like her workstation, a two-foot section of the shelf was littered with her baking supplies. She must have seen Thomas and me outside and dropped whatever she was working on.

I would have just left everything as it was, except that my eye caught a glint of a silver wrapper in Nina's mixing bowl. I picked up the bowl. Sure enough, it contained not one, but four silver wrappers. Silver *butter* wrappers.

The vegan chef was baking with butter.

Chapter Twenty-nine

"That cheater!" I said out loud to no one. Nina was baking with butter. Butter! She'd been giving me nothing but grief for the last few days, making me feel like I was serving my customers poison, lecturing me on the fair and equal treatment of animals, only to be secretly using butter herself.

This was rich. I couldn't wait to tell Thomas.

I hurried out of the fridge and rested my ingredients on the counter. What was the deal with these contestants? Was everyone putting on an act? Sebastian pretending to be French, Linda and Philip having an affair, and now Nina using butter in her clean-living "vegan" pastries.

Cracking two eggs into a mixing bowl, I thought back to Nina's other *Take the Cake* entries. Had she used butter in all of them? I whisked in a splash of cream, and lit one of the gas burners on the stove. The flame burned low, as I drizzled olive oil in a skillet and set it on the flame. While I gave that a minute to heat up, I added a pinch of salt and pepper to the eggs.

Next I rinsed and chopped the mushrooms and onions and added them to the skillet. The skillet responded with a delightful popping sound. I sautéed them on medium heat until the onions went from being opaque to slightly golden and the mushrooms caramelized in their juices. I whisked in the eggs and scrambled it all together.

I plated the scramble and topped it off with a sprinkling of cheese. I poured myself another splash of wine and pulled out a bar stool. Not bad for a five-minute dinner.

The mushrooms were the perfect texture, slightly chewy with a big finish of flavor. I tucked into my meal, sipping my wine and considering the craziness surrounding all the contestants on *Take the Cake*.

I wondered what they were saying about me. At least I wasn't pretending to be something I'm not.

My small plate hit the spot. I polished off the eggs and finished my glass of wine. Time to get baking, Jules.

If Nina was cheating by using butter, then I didn't care about making a fruit-filled pie as well. Her excuse of having to compete against non-vegan ingredients didn't hold up now that I knew she'd been using butter the entire time.

What did Nina gain by lying about being a vegan chef? Maybe the opportunity to be on the show. Philip had said from the start that he wanted interesting contestants. What if Chef Marco had found out that Nina was using butter, and threatened to tell Philip she wasn't really a vegan?

Would that really be motive for murder? It sounded weak to me, but then again I'm not exactly the murdering kind, so how would I know?

I cubed butter for my pie crust. It's much easier to incorporate flour into small cubes of butter when making a crust. The key to making a light and flaky crust is in using a full-fat butter. Some professional bakers use lard in their crusts to ensure an indulgent finished product. Personally, I prefer the taste of butter, but I do have a secret ingredient I always use in my pie crusts—vodka.

I learned the trick from the head pastry chef in culinary school. He taught us to swap vodka in most basic crust recipes for the water. The alcohol doesn't allow gluten to form in the baking process and results in a tender, flaky crust. It works like a charm every time.

While I added flour and vodka to the butter, I couldn't stop shaking my head. Nina of all people sneaking the luscious yellow milk-fat product into her sweets. Man, and the way she'd buttered Thomas up (I couldn't resist) with her vegan treats, and lecturing Mom and me for using the foul stuff.

She and I were going to have a chat first thing in the morning. I could hardly wait.

I sprinkled the island with flour and began rolling out the crust. The doorbell jingled. Stephanie and Elliot came in. They both looked surprised to see me.

"What are you doing here?" Stephanie held her arm up to stop Elliot from entering any farther. "I thought everyone went home."

"Nope." I raised my hands, which were white with flour. "I'm working my magic. What are you two up to?"

Stephanie started to reply. "Elliot wanted to—"

Elliot swooped in front of her and cut her off. "I was hoping to sneak a little time in the kitchen. I'm having withdrawals being away from the kitchen for so long. I asked Steph if she wanted to learn some tips from a professional. She's really eager to learn. I like her attitude. I may have to poach her from you, and bring her back to New York to train with me."

Stephanie gave him an odd look.

Elliot moved toward the counter and rested his hands on his elbows for a better look at what I was doing. There was something about him that I didn't trust. Maybe it was the way he consumed the entire counter space like he owned the place.

"Vodka?" He pointed at the bottle. "You don't strike me as a drinker."

"It's for my pie."

"Vodka pie. Vodka pie. Yes! You could be onto something. I can see it now—a cocktail-themed pie display. Supersexy. I might have to steal this idea, don't you think, Steph?"

Stephanie hovered behind him. Her cheeks were bright with heat. They clashed with her purple hair.

"It's not for the pie. It's for the crust," I said, as I pressed the crust into a pie tin.

Elliot straightened up and clapped his hands together. "Even better. Booze-infused crust and filling. You are a genius. No wonder Philip thinks you're going to take home the cake this season."

"He does?"

Elliot ignored me and turned to Stephanie. "Forget baking. Let's go get a drink at the pub. I'll sketch this out. Cocktail pies. I can serve them in mini tart forms, so people can have them like a shooter. I love it. This is going to go big. Real big. I think we're sitting on the hottest new trend in food in years. I should call my agent. He can trademark this."

Stephanie looked uncomfortable. "Well, it was kind of Jules's idea."

She got more than a few bonus points in my book for sticking up for me in front of her crush.

Elliot paused and flipped his head in my direction. "You want in on this?"

"I'm good. It's all yours. Knock yourself out." I took the pie crust and slid it into the oven.

Stephanie looked unsure. "It is a good idea . . ." She trailed off. Elliot was already halfway out the door.

"I promise. It's fine. Really. We're not going to serve alcohol-themed pie shots here."

"But a trademark. If he gets that we couldn't make them."

"He's not going to get a trademark on pies. I'm sure someone has already done it. Go. It's fine." I nodded.

She twirled a strand of her eggplant-colored hair and stood in the doorway.

I twisted the handle on the sink and waited for the water to warm. "Stephanie, is everything okay?"

She didn't meet my eyes. "Yeah."

"Are you sure?" She still wasn't moving.

"Huh?" She looked up.

"You're okay?"

"Yeah. Sorry. I better jet." She raced after Elliot before I could probe more. I wondered if she was torn between Elliot and Sterling. I could certainly relate to that feeling. Maybe she wanted input on the two very different guys, but wasn't sure how to broach the subject with me. I'd have to try to find some time to pull her aside tomorrow. Although I wasn't sure what help I'd be. It was hardly like I had my own love life figured out.

The smell of the buttery pie crust baking in the oven reminded me I still needed to work on the caramel apple filling. I finished washing my hands and removed a bag of organic apples from the fridge.

Peeling apples is like meditation for me. Time drifted away as I swayed to the sounds of Latin salsa. It was a habit I was finding hard to break. When Carlos was at the helm of the ship's kitchen, he always blared Latin rhythms. He said it made his cooking and the staff loose. I think it did. I'd been conscious of trying to listen to my own music while finding my own rhythm back at home, but when it came to baking I found myself clicking play on the old standby without even thinking.

I stopped in mid-peel, walked over to the CD player, and clicked off the Latin music. I searched through a stack of CDs, and found one of Mom's Beatles collections. That should do the trick, I thought as I returned to the apples. "Yellow Submarine" is about as far from Latin salsa as I could get.

Peels piled up in the bowl. I cored the naked apples and sliced them thin. When working with fruits that brown easily, I always keep a fresh lemon within reach. After slicing each apple I squeezed lemon juice over the slices to keep them from browning, and the acidity of the lemon juice would give the filling just a little bite.

The timer on the oven rang for my crust. I pulled it out to cool on the counter before filling it. Lightly baking the crust before filling helps to make sure it doesn't end up with a soggy center.

I stirred the apples with cinnamon, brown sugar, and a pinch of salt. I cut open a vanilla pod and scrapped the seeds into the mixture. Then I added an egg and flour and spread the mixture evenly into the crust. Usually with an apple pie I place a crust on the top as well. Mom likes to do lattice crusts, while I like a more rustic look—a simple sheeted crust brushed with an egg wash and dusted with sugar and nutmeg.

Since this was a baking competition I decided to forgo a double crust and do a caramel and whipped cream topping. However, I'd have to prepare both in the morning. I'd serve the caramel warm over the pie and top it with a touch of fresh vanilla whipped cream.

While my pie baked, I washed the dishes and wiped down the countertops. Both Nina and Sebastian had lied—majorly. If they could lie about being vegan and French, what else could they lie about? The question I kept coming back to was, why?

Would Nina have killed to keep her non-vegan practices a secret? Could Sebastian be making up the story about Marco? It sounded true, based on my short-lived experience with the world-famous chef, but Sebastian could be lying to save his own skin. If I was being honest with myself, I was no closer to figuring out who killed Marco, and no closer to deciding what I was going to do with my personal life.

If this was my attempt to distract myself from Carlos and my failing marriage, it wasn't working. Maybe I needed a new distraction.

My pie finished baking. I took a whiff of the sweet, fall flavor as I removed it from the oven. The apples simmered in the cinnamon and had baked to a toasted golden color on the top. It looked and smelled divine. I could probably serve it plain, but a subtle caramel sauce and dollop of cream to cut the sweetness just might make me the winner tomorrow.

I locked Torte for the night and headed straight for my apartment. I wasn't taking any chances that Sebastian might be lurking in the shadows.

The cool night breeze matched my pace, as I kept my head straight forward and my senses on high alert. There was no chance I was going to take a late-night stroll through Lithia Park or stop at the pub for a pint. I was on a mission to get home and get this day behind me.

I made it to my apartment without incident, except for the sweat beading on my forehead and the thumping in my chest. Taking the stairs three at a time, I was to the top in a flash, gasping for air. I fumbled for the key, unlocked the door, stepped inside and quickly locked it again.

Whew.

My head fell against the back of the door. I let out a long breath of air.

Breathe, Jules.

I stood up, and started to laugh at myself. Really, what did I think was going to happen on the short walk home? Some crazed killer was going to jump out from behind one of Ashland's charming little shops and take me out?

My heart rate slowed as I set my keys and phone on the bookshelf and kicked off my shoes.

That's when I looked at my feet.

An envelope with "Jules" scrawled in red pen had been shoved underneath my front door.

My stomach tightened as I bent over to pick it up. Something about the sloppy handwriting put me on edge.

I ripped open the envelope, and pulled out an index card. Written in the same red pen were these words: "One clue. Two clue. Three clues. You're through."

Chapter Thirty

I dropped the envelope and note on the floor and put my hand to my chest. My heart was racing again. What did that even mean? Was someone trying to be funny? Or was that a threat?

Maybe I shouldn't have touched the envelope. Would the Professor or Thomas want it for prints?

My hand shook slightly as I picked it back up and rested it on the bookshelf near the front door. Was it too late to call? Could it wait until morning? No, Jules, the voice in my head yelled. Call Thomas.

I tried to hold the phone steady as I punched in Thomas's number. He didn't answer. I left him a scattered message, and told him not to come over. We could meet at Torte in the morning.

I left the note and collapsed on my bed. I was probably making too much of nothing. Maybe Lance was trying to play a silly joke on me for not including him in the investigation. Yeah, that was probably it.

I doubted my attempt at calming myself, but thinking that the note came from Lance helped me sleep. When I woke in the morning, I had myself pretty convinced that I was imagining the entire thing. Until I padded my way on the cold hardwood floors to the kitchen to make my morning java and saw the note.

"Forget it, Jules," I said aloud as I dumped beans into the grinder. "There's nothing you can do until you get to the shop."

I went through the motions of my morning routine with an unsettled feeling nagging at me. Was I missing some critical clue? Did the note hold more meaning than I was giving it?

The smell of coffee brewing permeated the entire room. That should help raise your spirits and your energy, Jules, I told myself as I warmed a mug with hot water in the microwave.

With a hot mug of coffee in my hands, I moved onto the couch, where I sat to slowly savor my morning drink and try to center myself before going to Torte. My list of things to do was miles long—finish my pie, order and start to prep all the food for Lance's end-of-the-season party, see if I could help mend things between Stephanie and Sterling, and get Torte ready for the day. The problem was I kept coming back to Marco's murder. Clearing my mind wasn't working. I couldn't stop worrying about the note under my door and puzzling over Sebastian's and Nina's lies.

It was no use looping every detail through my head as I sat here on the couch. My coffee turned lukewarm in the bottom of my mug. I set it in the sink and grabbed a sweatshirt from my closet. Without looking I'd grabbed one of Carlos's. I didn't have to see it to know it was his. It smelled like him. I buried my head in it, took a whiff and placed it back on a hook. I didn't need the distraction of thinking about Carlos today.

Outside, the breeze danced through treetops, making the leaves flit through the air as if they were greeting me for the morning. I kept my pace quick and my eyes on alert en route to Torte. While I was probably overreacting, the note had me spooked. Working on the ship for so many years provided me with an easy sense of my personal safety. It might have been an illusion, but I never even considered that harm could come to me on the ship.

When I'd walk the upper deck in the predawn the only thing I had to worry about was not waking one of the guests who'd indulged in too much merriment the night before and was sleeping it off on a lounge chair. Growing up in Ashland had been the same way. I'd hike through the upper trails of Lithia Park alone. My only concern was making sure I didn't bump into a mama cougar trying to protect her cubs.

Since I'd returned home, my sense of personal safety had taken a beating. Maybe this was a part of the natural evolution of aging into my thirties. That idea that I was losing a slice of the easy sense of freedom that I'd enjoyed in my youth. Mom says that as we get older we develop a better understanding of everything we have to lose. That felt particularly true as I turned the key in the lock at Torte and shut and locked the door behind me.

I wasn't taking any chances this morning.

The bakeshop was completely dark. I flipped on the lights, not realizing that I was holding my breath. After Sebastian trashed the place yesterday, I guess I was half expecting to find Torte in disarray. Fortunately as the lights hummed on and illuminated the cheery dining room, everything looked exactly as it should—the floors gleamed as the light reflected on them, each table sat cleaned and ready for customers, the pastry case and espresso machine looked as if they had been polished.

I let out a sigh. It's a new day, Jules.

I got straight to work on the morning prep, warming the oven and pulling out batches of cookie dough and brownie batter that had been prepared yesterday. These would go in the oven as soon as it was at temperature. I washed my hands and removed sourdough starter from the fridge.

We've used the same sourdough starter for as long as I can remember. It's one of the many reasons that customers keep coming back to Torte for bread. My dad used to tinker with the starter like a chemist. He taught me how to maintain the fermented yeast that we keep in a glass container in the refrigerator.

I sifted dry ingredients for the bread dough and mixed them together with starter, milk, and butter. Then I went to work kneading the dough. There's nothing more therapeutic than kneading, in my humble opinion. I worked the sticky dough, letting the tension in my arms and spine soften with each pass.

Mom arrived as I was forming the dough into individual loaves and covering them with towels to rise.

"You're here early, honey. Were you able to rest yesterday?" She unbuttoned her pale green raincoat and hung it on the hooks near the office.

"Sort of. Is it raining?" I pointed to the coat, trying to keep my tone light. I couldn't tell her about the note.

"Not yet, but they say it's rolling in later this morning. Maybe thunderstorms. We definitely need to make sure we have a soup on the menu today." She wrapped a Torte apron around her slender waist. I hoped that I would inherit her genes when it came to aging. She looked like she could pass as my older sister. In part because her style was timeless. She wore a simple ivory shirt, with jeans and clogs. Her modern bob and subtle makeup contributed to her youthful appearance; the only giveaway that she was entering the second half of her life were the lines on her face and the wrinkles on her delicate hands.

I'm so lucky, I thought.

"What are you smiling about?" Mom asked.

"You."

"Me?"

"I was just thinking how glad I am to be here with you."

Mom came closer and squeezed me around the waist. She smelled like lavender soap. Wherever I traveled in the world, if I found fresh lavender I would always stop and pick a sprig. I remember Carlos teasing me about it, but when I told him it was how I got in touch with feeling like I was home, he just kissed my forehead and picked me a giant bundle.

"I think the same thing about you," Mom said, releasing me. "I love having you home." She stepped back and stared at me. "Is everything okay, though?"

"What? I can't give you a compliment?"

"I love your compliments, but I get the sense something else is going on." She reached on her tiptoes to the shelf behind us and pulled down a mixing bowl.

"How do you always know?" I threw my head back. "I can't hide anything from you."

"You'll understand when you have a daughter someday."

"Someday . . . I don't know, Mom. I'm getting up there. Kids might not be in my future."

Mom threatened me with the stainless steel dough hook in her hands. "Don't you dare go there, young lady."

I grinned. "I knew that would get ya."

She twisted the hook into the mixer and secured the bowl on the base. "Are you going to fess up on what's really bothering you? I have a guess. You haven't given up on Marco's murder, have you?"

I looked at my feet. "Not exactly."

Mom sighed. "I told Doug the chance of you staying out of this investigation was about as likely as him suddenly becoming golfing buddies with Richard Lord."

"Ha! I'd love to see that. I can totally picture the Professor in his tweed jacket golfing alongside Richard in one of his ridiculous golfing outfits. Maybe we should see if we can make that happen."

"Jules, I know what you're doing." Mom's tone turned into her serious "mother" voice. "You can't breeze out of this discussion. It's serious business. Murder. I'm worried about you. Doug is too."

Now I really couldn't tell her about the note. She'd probably call Thomas and have him lock me up in the one small holding cell downtown.

She measured sugar and butter and creamed them together on low. "Have you considered our conversation the other day?"

"You mean about Carlos?"

Her voice softened. "Honey, it's not a bad thing. I get it. I really do. You've spent so much time contemplating your life over the last few months. That's exhausting. I understand why the distraction of this murder is a good thing for you in some ways, I just wish you could find a different distraction."

I checked my loaves of bread. They were rising nicely. "I have thought about it, Mom. Maybe too much. I guess I just didn't think that I'd still be this confused. I really thought I could take a couple months and things would just sort themselves out. That I'd have a clear sense of whether I wanted to give it another go with Carlos, or whether I was done for good."

Mom added buttermilk and eggs to the mixer and waited for me to continue.

"You know the whole idea of not communicating with him until next year sounded like a good thing, but I'm not sure it is. I think I'm making it worse. I'm making myself crazy because anytime I start to think about him I shove it inside and tell myself to stop. That can't be healthy, can it?"

Mom pursed her lips. "I don't know, honey. Does it feel healthy?"

I shook my head. "Nothing feels healthy. I mean I love being home. I really love it. More than I ever thought I would. I hadn't realized how much I missed Ashland. I love working with you, the staff, thinking about expanding, but then always in the back of my head there's Carlos."

Mom nodded.

"I don't know if I miss him, or just the *idea* of him. Does that even make sense?"

"It does. It really does."

I removed the first batch of cookies from the oven and slid them onto cooling racks on the counter. The bakeshop quickly filled with the scent of chocolate, almond, and vanilla. I had to resist breaking one in half and chomping it. They needed to cool.

"Is there anything I can help you with?" Mom asked, sprinkling a handful of cranberries into her batter. "I wish I could fix this for you."

I gave her a half smile. "I know. You can't. This one's on me."

"Do you think maybe it's time for you to go see Carlos? Face-to-face."

I thought about that for a minute before responding. "I don't know. That's a good question. Let me think about it. I've told myself I wasn't going to do anything about it until next year, so I guess I've had that date firm in my head."

"You might consider being a bit gentler with yourself, Juliet."

The timer rang for the brownies. I pulled them from the oven and set them next to the cooling cookies. "What? I'm not gentle?"

"Not with yourself, no." Mom removed the bowl from the mixer and began scooping the batter into muffin tins. "You're so much like your father. Stubborn, but only when it comes to *you*. Here's a thought, what would you say to me or a friend in your situation?"

"What do you mean?"

"I mean what advice would you give me if I were you?"

"Mom, that's silly. You'd never be in this position."

"Uh—uh—uh. Hold it right there." Mom pointed her index finger at me. "That's exactly what I'm talking about. Stop being so hard on yourself. You'd never be like that with anyone else."

"Okay. I'll try." I scooped cookie dough in perfect balls onto the sheets.

Mom sprinkled the top of her muffins with an oatmeal and nut crumble. "I'm going to hold you to it."

I smiled. The cookies on the counter had cooled enough to taste. I broke one in half and offered part to Mom. "Breakfast?"

She took the cookie and bit in. "Oh, this is good, really good."

I tasted my half. The cookie was crispy on the outside with a chewy center. The combination of dark chocolate and almond was a rich treat for my palate. I polished off my half and had to resist grabbing another. I probably needed something a bit more substantial to make it through another morning of filming.

Mom started a new batch of muffins while I finished baking the cookies. I had something else I wanted to ask her, but couldn't quite find the courage to start the conversation.

Nina and Linda arrived with Andy and Stephanie, saving me from trying to figure out how to broach what I wanted to ask Mom. I had to find a way to talk to Nina alone. Now wasn't the time. The bustling kitchen became more like a boxing ring as we all ducked and darted around each other trying to put the finishing touches on our pies.

The bell on the door jingled before Andy had even warmed up the espresso machine. "Good morning, darlings!" Lance greeted everyone with his usual theatrical flourish.

Andy explained it would be a few minutes before he could make an espresso.

"Not a problem. I'm here to check up on a little *note* I sent over." Lance shot a dazzling grin my way.

Chapter Thirty-one

The marble rolling pin that I was using to roll out my crust slipped from my hand and landed on the island with a thud. Linda let out a little scream and Nina started.

"Juliet, are you okay?" Mom asked. "You look as white as that flour."

Lance peered over the counter. "Your mother is right. You look like you've seen a ghost, darling."

I shot him a look to keep quiet and brushed flour from my hands. "I'm fine," I said to Mom.

Mom wrinkled her brow as she looked at me. "What's this about a note, Lance?" she asked, leaving her muffin trays on the island and walking toward the front counter.

I followed after her, praying internally that Lance would keep his mouth shut. He must have sent the note, and was trying to call me out in front of Mom. What did "one clue, two clues, three clues" even mean? I couldn't ask him now, but I did feel relieved to know that Lance had been playing a silly prank versus the alternative—the note being left by a killer.

Lance leaned over the counter and kissed Mom on both cheeks. "Helen, I swear you get lovelier and lovelier every day."

Mom blushed slightly at his compliment and kissed him back. "Lance, you're too much, but please keep it coming."

The espresso machine hummed to life. Andy stepped to the side to make room for me at the counter. I drank in the smell of the beans he was grinding.

"Morning, Lance," I said, giving him a pleading look.

"Juliet, a vision as lovely as your namesake. Although I must agree with your mother's assessment. Your skin is looking a bit sallow this morning. Something's not bothering you, is it, darling?"

"I'm fine. Just a bit tired," I said, feeling my jaw clench.

"Lance, what note did you send?" Mom asked as she flipped through a stack of order sheets behind the counter.

"Oh, yes, the note! Didn't you get it, Juliet?"

"Me? No. I don't think so."

Mom rested the stack of order forms on the counter. "I don't see anything with your name on it. I'm so sorry."

"Don't give it a thought." Lance flicked his wrist. "That's what I get for sending a stagehand on an errand." His eyes pierced mine as he continued. "The *note* had all the final details for my soiree. I have complete trust in your culinary talent, but this party must be nothing short of flawless. You know us theater types."

"Let me grab something to write with," Mom said, turning to leave.

Lance stopped her. "No, no, Helen. I see that you're bursting with activity this morning. I wouldn't dream of interrupting. I'll track down the stagehand and send him back down."

"If you're sure?" Mom looked at me. I shrugged.

"Absolutely." Lance accepted a latte in a to-go cup from Andy and strolled to the front door. "Ta-ta."

After he was out of earshot, Mom turned to me. "That was odd. Am I missing something?"

"You know Lance—he *is* odd."

Mom agreed, and a customer walked in, saving me from having to elaborate. While Mom chatted with the customer, I snuck back to the kitchen.

I melted butter and brown sugar on the stove for my caramel sauce. It transformed into a rich, golden color as I whisked in a splash of vanilla and a pinch of salt. The sauce thickened on the heat. Mom returned to her muffins.

Linda examined the muffin batter. "That looks bowl-lickin' good."

Mom held out the mixing bowl. "Have a taste."

"Divine. I need the recipe." She licked the tip of her finger and scanned the kitchen. "Y'all want to hear a little gossip? Rumor has it that Sebastian is the number one suspect in Marco's murder," Linda said, sprinkling the top of her cream pie with brightly colored sprinkles. It reminded me of a kid's ice-cream sundae. "I'm not surprised. You know, the French are so nasty."

Mom handed Stephanie a list of items to start on for the morning rush. She smiled at Linda, but kept her tone even. "I'm not sure. I haven't heard anything."

Linda brushed sprinkles from her bejeweled hands. "Sugar, that's not what I hear. I hear you're cozy with that dashing detective that y'all call 'the Professor.'"

"You mean Doug?" Mom grabbed a pencil from a teal canister near the island and sketched something on Stephanie's to-bake list.

"That's the one." Linda picked up her pie and examined it from every angle. "He's so handsome and distinguished."

Mom pinched my waist as she scooted past me toward the fridge. "He and I are old friends," she said to Linda, not biting on Linda's blatant attempt to fish for information.

I grimaced as Mom continued on to the fridge. Was I as bad as Linda? Oh, man, I hoped not. No wonder Thomas was irritated with me.

My caramel sauce had thickened. I poured it into a glass

jar and secured the lid. Nina meanwhile had been working with her head down in the corner of the kitchen. I could tell she was listening to the conversation, but making a point to stay in the background.

I walked over to her. "Are you heading up the hill soon?"

She concentrated on zesting an orange. "What's that?"

"I was hoping we could walk to the Black Swan together. I want to talk to you about something."

Nina's hand slipped on the grater. She sliced the tip of her finger. A bright red spot of blood appeared.

"Let me grab you a towel," I said.

"It's fine," Nina said, sucking the blood from her finger. "I'm not usually that sloppy. I don't know what's wrong with me. I must need more coffee." She set the grater on the island and went to rinse her hand in the sink.

I suspected why she was jumpy, and I bet it had to do with butter. I kept quiet on that, and waited for her to return. "Are you ready to go?" I asked again.

Nina dusted the top of her pie with the grated orange rind. "Sure. What did you want to talk about it?"

I lowered my voice a bit. "Let's talk outside."

Her face turned as white as flour. "Okay." She sounded unsure.

"Let me get my pie out the fridge. I'll be right back."

Nina agreed and began boxing up her pie.

On my way to the fridge I caught Mom by the arm and whispered, "I'm heading to the Black Swan a little early. I need to talk to Nina for a second."

Mom frowned. "I thought we just went over this."

"It's not about Marco's murder—well, at least I don't think it is—it's about *butter*."

"Butter?" Mom looked confused.

"Shhh. I'll tell you later." I left Mom staring after me.

The icy air inside the fridge made me shiver. I retrieved my pie from the shelf and placed it in one of our Torte boxes. Then I headed to the front of the shop with a canvas grocery bag containing my caramel sauce and whipping cream. I'd assemble the pie on set.

Nina was nowhere in sight.

"Hey, have you seen Nina?" I asked Andy.

He sipped a cup of French press. "Yeah, she just left."

"Left Torte?"

"Yeah. She went that way." He pointed across the street. "She looked like she was in a hurry."

"Seriously?" I didn't wait for him to answer and hurried after Nina. She was obviously avoiding me. Why?

The moon sank behind me as the sun pushed its way through gathering clouds. Mom was smart to bring a raincoat. I probably should have done the same.

Crossing the plaza, I searched the empty side streets for any sign of Nina. She must have sprinted out of Torte. Where could she have gone? Not far.

A figure appeared in front of the Merry Windsor. I couldn't make out who it was in the dusky morning light. "Nina, is that you?" I called.

She didn't answer.

I tightened my grasp on my bag and headed in that direction.

Sebastian stood near the front entrance. He sneered at me. "Just who I was looking for."

Instinctively I clutched my pie and looped my hand through the bag. If he attacked, I could thump him with the bag. "Why were you looking for me?"

He reached behind him.

Did he have a weapon? I let out a little yelp. "Stop right there."

"What's your problem?" He held a box of delicate glass vases in front of him. "Kind of jumpy, aren't you? I was going to drop these by, but since you're here . . ."

"Oh, thanks." I felt like an idiot. "I can't take them right now, though. I'm headed to the Black Swan. You haven't seen Nina, by any chance?"

He looked at the vases. "What do you want me to do with these?"

"Can you walk them over to the shop?"

"I guess." He sounded put out.

"Listen, you're the one who broke them." Irritation crept into my voice.

"Sorry. I'll take them. About Nina. I saw her running up the hill a minute ago."

Running up the hill. Why was she running from me? I left Sebastian and the vases and followed Nina up Pioneer Street. I caught the eye of a couple of shop owners as I sprinted up the sidewalk. By the time I made it to the Black Swan, I was huffing and my forehead was damp with sweat. Running uphill isn't exactly my speed.

"Hello?" I called, pushing open the front doors. "Nina—are you here?" The lights were on, but there was no sign of motion inside the theater.

I was surprised the crew hadn't arrived, but then again I wasn't sure how long it took them to prepare.

"Nina?" I called again, stepping farther inside. "It's Jules."

The sound of a muffled cry came from the kitchen. I froze.

"Nina? Is that you?"

Another soft cry sounded.

I probably should have considered my choices, but instinct kicked in. I walked to the kitchen, leaving my pie and bag on the counter. Sure enough, Nina was crouched there on the floor, hugging her knees and sobbing.

Chapter Thirty-two

"Nina, what's wrong?" I dropped onto the floor next to her and put my hand on her shoulder.

She said something I couldn't understand through her sobs.

"Take a breath," I said, waiting for her to regain her composure.

Her body convulsed as she tried to suck air into her lungs. "I knew this would happen," she said between sobs.

I stood and grabbed a napkin from the counter. Sitting down next to her again, I offered it to her. "You knew what would happen?"

She dabbed her eyes with the napkin. "I'd do something stupid."

"What do you mean?"

"You know! I know you know. You're a great chef. Of course you know." She buried her face in the napkin.

I waited for a minute. The napkin stayed in front her face. Finally, I broke the silence. "You mean about the butter?"

She sobbed again. "Yes."

I couldn't help it. I'm not exactly sure what came over

me, but I broke into the giggles. Once I started laughing I couldn't stop.

Nina peeled the napkin from in front of her face. She looked up at me with bloodshot eyes. "It's not funny. I'm an idiot. I don't know how I thought I was going to pull this off on a nationally televised cooking show."

"We are talking about butter though, right?" My fit of giggles continued. "Sorry, I'm not laughing at you, but the whole thing is a bit over the top. You're crying about *butter*. I wish that's all I had to cry about."

She ran the napkin under her nose and stared at me for a second. Then she broke into laughter too. We sat on the floor laughing until neither of us could catch our breath. I knew this was a needed relief for both of us.

Nina released her knees and drew out a long breath. "I guess it is a little ridiculous."

"A little?" I raised my brow.

"Well, maybe a lot." She folded the napkin on her lap.

"Do you want to talk about it?"

"I do—obviously I've been a bit wound up."

"Me too." I pushed to standing and offered her my hand. "Why don't we go sit over there?" I pointed to the bar stools lining the counter.

She let me help her up. I moved the stools, wishing I had something else to offer her. At Torte, Mom always serves up a slice of warm pie and a cup of coffee when people come in for her wise counsel.

The only thing in the fake kitchen was my apple pie. I couldn't cut into it before the competition. I'd just have to wing it by asking lots of questions. I was good at that. I'd learned over the years that asking questions deflects attention away from myself.

Nina sniffed a bit. "You've been so nice to me. I feel terrible for lying to you."

I wanted to console her by telling her that she wasn't the

only one who'd been lying, but I'd made a promise to Sebastian. "It's okay. I'm not angry."

She gave me a small smile and launched into an explanation. "My shop wasn't vegan until a few years ago. I'd been known for my cupcakes. People came from all around for my cupcakes. I was doing a good business. In fact, I'd been thinking of expanding. Doing a second shop on the other side of town. Rent isn't cheap in L.A., so I spent some time researching the market. Thank goodness I did, because it was about that time that the vegan craze really took off."

That made sense. Trends on the West Coast tend to hit in southern California first and then slowly work their way north. We're usually a few years behind in Ashland.

Nina bit her nonexistent fingernails. "My cupcakes took a major hit. All of a sudden everyone was terrified of butter. Saying you used butter was like saying you were injecting your products with MSG."

I chuckled.

"No, I'm serious. I thought I was going to lose the shop. Baking has been my life. I couldn't let that happen, so I decided to give the whole vegan movement a shot. You know how people are in L.A. They're desperately seeking beauty and youth and will do almost *anything* for the promise of wrinkle-free skin. So, I poured myself into researching new recipes. I ate at every vegan restaurant in town to compare what the competition was doing. It turned out that I was pretty good with creating vegan treats. Business has been slowly picking back up since I made the switch."

"I don't understand. Why sneak butter into your products then?"

Nina shook her head. "I don't. I mean not in my products at the shop. Never. I wouldn't do that to my customers."

"But I found butter in your bowl at Torte last night. Isn't that what you were just so upset about?"

"Yeah." Nina's shoulders slumped. "I got intimidated by all of you. Everyone is so skilled. I mean even Linda. Her stuff is gaudy, but the taste and design are there. The only way I got invited to compete was because one of my good friends works for the network. She convinced Philip that I was the best vegan chef in all of L.A. I'm not. Not yet anyway. I still have so much to learn, but I really wanted—no, I really need—the prize money, so I figured it was worth a shot. I would play up the whole vegan-chef angle for the show and hopefully walk away with enough money to keep my doors open for another year."

"I know something about that," I said.

Nina's eyes widened. "You do? But Torte is thriving, and you're the best baker here."

"Thanks." I smiled. "I appreciate it, but Mom and I are barely squeaking by. Running a bakeshop, well, any business, in a tourist town is a struggle. We really need to update our equipment. We've been scrimping and saving every penny. That's the only reason I agreed to do the show."

"I never would have guessed that." Nina looked me over. "You're so put together and in control."

"Ha!" I chuckled. "I promise I'm not."

Nina bit her nails again. "Anyway, like I said I got intimidated and worried that I wouldn't have a chance competing against chefs like you and Marco with my new vegan recipes. I know I shouldn't have cheated, but I thought using butter would give me an edge, and no one would be the wiser. It's not like the judges are vegan." She looked me in the eye. "I promise I would never serve someone something with butter if they were."

"It's cool. I'm not judging you."

She sighed. "I'm judging myself. It was stupid. I guess I just thought no one was getting hurt, and if I won all my recipes really would be vegan."

"But they wouldn't be if they contained butter."

"No, I mean, yes, the judges would be tasting products with butter, but none of my actual recipes call for butter. The recipes I serve at the Garden of Vegan are all free of animal byproducts." She shook her head. "This is why I never should have even considered using butter. Now I've messed everything up."

"What are you going to do?"

She rubbed her temples. "I don't know. We only have one more day left. I hate to ask this, but if I run back to Torte and make a new pie this morning, would you be willing to keep my secret?"

I was becoming the town secret-keeper. Is this how Mom felt all the time?

"Nina, I won't say anything." I reached out and squeezed her hand. "But you have to promise you won't use any more butter. It's not fair to the competition, to viewers, but more than anything, to yourself. Look how upset this has made you."

"Thank you." She squeezed my hand back. "No wonder Thomas talks so much about you. You really are wonderful, Jules." She glanced at her bare wrist. "Do you know what time it is? I should probably fly if I'm going to have time to make something that's actually vegan before we start filming."

I don't wear a watch, or any jewelry for that matter, when I'm baking. It gets in the way, especially when I'm up to my elbows mixing dough. I stood and dug through the canvas bag I'd left on the counter. I pulled out my phone. "It's almost seven," I said, sticking the phone in my back pocket.

Nina jumped off her stool. "I gotta run. Thank you again."

She hurried toward the front door. I wondered if I'd do the same thing in her position. I understood the desperate desire to want to save a business, or a relationship, but would I lie to make it happen? I didn't think so.

The door closed behind her, and I was alone in the empty theater. If Nina could lie about being vegan was there a chance she could have lied about killing Marco? She seemed sincere, but if he'd discovered that she'd been secretly using butter, could she have snapped?

I didn't want to think so, but I couldn't rule it out either. I also couldn't stop thinking about Nina's parting words. What had she meant about Thomas always talking about me?

Chapter Thirty-three

I decided I might as well wait for the crew to arrive. At least no one would accuse me of being late for makeup today. I took the opportunity to assemble my pie. I got out a container of whipped cream, a spatula, and the caramel sauce.

The caramel sauce would be served warm. I spread the whipped cream in soft peaks over the apple pie. It reminded me of the top of Mount Ashland in the middle of winter. It had been a long time since I'd seen snow. I couldn't wait to break out my skis and hit the slopes.

Unlike Linda, I prefer my presentation to be simple. After I covered the pie with the whipped cream I wiped the spatula clean with a towel and returned everything to my bag. When it came time to serve the pie, I would drizzle each slice with the thick caramel sauce.

I kept looping the conversation I had with Nina through my brain. There was something important she'd said. What was it? I tasted the caramel sauce with my pinkie. It was beautifully balanced—sweet and salty.

That was it! *Beautiful*. Why hadn't I realized it before?

Nina's desperation to make her vegan bakery a success in health-conscious Hollywood reminded me of someone else who was obsessed with looking good and staying in the spotlight—Elliot.

Suddenly every interaction I'd had with Elliot flashed in my mind. Elliot had been fuming the night Marco was killed. Fuming enough to murder Marco? Maybe.

Elliot hadn't been pleased when Philip showed interest in me. Actually, he had warned me to stay away from television. Could that be why he'd been hanging around the shop and Stephanie? Had he been trying to spy on me? Maybe he'd wanted access to Marco's things.

It all made sense. Could Elliot be the killer?

I grabbed my phone and called Thomas. He didn't answer.

"Thomas, I'm at the Black Swan. I think I know who killed Marco—Elliot. Call me back."

At that moment the door swung open.

It caught me off guard. I jumped slightly and knocked over the jar of caramel sauce. Fortunately it didn't break.

"Hello. Is someone here?" I called.

The door banged shut. I thought I heard the sound of someone locking it. I stepped around the counter to see who was there.

Elliot Cool had his eyes locked on me. "Good morning," he sang in a mocking tone.

One look at his wild eyes confirmed that I was right. Elliot Cool had killed Marco. Why hadn't I figured it out sooner?

"Oh, hey, Elliot. You're here early," I said as he came closer, keeping my voice even and taking a step back.

"Looks that way, doesn't it." He snarled.

"Sounds like you could use a cup of what I call the nectar of the gods." I tried to laugh.

"You mean coffee? I don't need coffee. I need a word with you." He invaded my personal space. I could feel negative energy pouring out of him.

I inched back.

"That's right, keep backing up." He tapped my collarbone with his index finger. "Back it up. Back it up."

I took another step back. I had to get out of here.

"You've been putting on a nice little performance all week. Show's over, sweetheart."

"Performance?"

"Please. Like I don't know an actor when I see one." He ran his fingers through his normally styled hair. It looked disheveled. He snapped his fingers together. "You're trying to take my job, just like Marco. You saw what happened to Marco. You're next."

"Take your job? I don't want your job." I could feel my heart rate climbing.

"Right. I heard the whole thing. I was listening when Philip was giving you the full-court press to take the job." Elliot searched the countertop.

What was he looking for? A knife?

I held my hands up in surrender. "Let's cool down for a minute here, Elliot. I'm not hosting any show. You heard wrong. I told Philip no."

Elliot spread his legs in a wide stance, trying to block my exit. He tugged on one of the drawers. It appeared that the drawers, like everything else on the set, were just for show.

"Freakin' set," Elliot said under his breath.

"Why did you kill Marco?" I asked, trying to distract him.

"He deserved to die." Elliot's eyes shot to the judge's stage. "He was trying to boot me from the show. Fattie. Not sexy. Like he'd ever be able to replace me."

If that was the case, I wondered why Elliot had killed him. Elliot answered my question for me before I could decide whether asking would antagonize him more.

"Marco came to me last summer and wanted to partner

together. I think he was getting nervous that my pastry party shops were a hit. I didn't care, but he wanted to give me a big chunk of cash to partner and expand into other markets. That was fine by me. Then he shows up here and suddenly says the whole thing was his idea. I overheard him pitching it to Philip. Philip ate it up—loved the idea. Said Marco could host a whole series about rolling out the pastry parties across the country. When I confronted him about it, he was so trashed he didn't even know what I was talking about."

Elliot's eyes glazed over as he spoke. I could tell he wasn't even registering the fact that he was speaking to me. He was in some sort of trancelike state.

That's good, Jules, let him talk, I thought. Hopefully Thomas would check his phone.

"I'm the youngest chef in the history of the Pastry Channel to have a chain of restaurants, my own show, and a hosting gig. I wasn't about to let that old drunk fatso come in and steal everything I've worked hard for from me."

"What was Marco going to steal?" I should have kept my mouth shut. What was I thinking?

Elliot's face twitched. His eyes refocused on me. "Don't you listen? I already told you. He and Philip had devised a plan to take me out. Philip was going to let him take over as host of *Take the Cake* and give him his own miniseries. My miniseries! To the drunk idiot. I don't know what Philip was thinking. I overheard the whole conversation that night. I was backstage."

I had a feeling I knew why—blackmail. Philip had already confessed to me that Marco had found out about his affair with Linda. In order to keep him silent, Philip agreed to Marco's demands. Who knew if he was just trying to pacify the chef or whether he would have actually followed through on his promise? I had a feeling that Philip hoped that Marco wouldn't remember their conversation the next morning. Only, he never had a chance to find out. Elliot killed him first.

And if you don't get out of here, he's going to kill you too, Jules.

"I also heard all of Philip's little chats with you. He may think you're a beauty, but you don't have the killer instinct it takes to make it in Hollywood. But no, no, Philip had found his muse. He didn't even care when you showed up late. Do you know how much crap he's given me about wasting money and time?"

"No." I shook my head. That's why I was late yesterday. Elliot must have told the camera crew to have me arrive at nine. He wanted me to be late. He wanted me to look like a flake.

Elliot's hand fumbled on the countertop and landed on a marble rolling pin. "Right. Too bad it has to go down this way. You do have a gorgeous face, but not as gorgeous as mine." He flashed me his camera-ready grin.

I shuddered in response. He lunged for the rolling pin. This was my chance. I ducked under him and made a break for it.

Run, Jules!

Chapter Thirty-four

I sprinted out of the kitchen.

Elliot was right behind me. I didn't dare look back.

My foot slipped. I flailed my arms to try and regain my balance. It didn't work. I landed on the floor—hard.

Pain seared up my right arm. I thought I might vomit.

This isn't good, Jules. I crawled toward the exit.

Elliot jumped in front of me. He wound up the rolling pin. There was no escape. I thought about Mom, Thomas, Carlos, Torte, my years at sea. Time slowed in rhythm with Elliot's arm motion.

I watched him raise the pin, and start to lower it toward my head. This must have been how Marco felt in his final moments.

The doors rattled. Maybe Elliot hadn't locked them after all.

"Freeze!" the Professor commanded.

Elliot dropped the rolling pin. It landed on the floor near my feet, making a loud thud that reverberated on the floor. He ran back to the kitchen and leaped onto the stage as the sound of voices and heavy footsteps echoed.

The Professor and Thomas both ran to me. I signaled that I was okay and pointed them in Elliot's direction.

I didn't move from the floor, but listened intently to the sound of their feet hitting the stage, shouts for Elliot to stop and surrender, and ultimately what sounded like Thomas tackling him somewhere backstage.

They returned a few minutes later with Elliot in handcuffs. His face was covered in sweat and blotched with color. He certainly didn't look the part of a polished TV star at the moment. The Professor led him outside, while Thomas came to help me.

He fell to his knees. "Juliet, are you okay?" His voice caught as he said my name.

"I think my arm is broken."

Thomas gently covered my injured arm. His hand was warm to the touch. "It's already swelling, and that's one nasty bruise. Can you squeeze my hand?"

I tried to squeeze his hand. My fingers refused. A new wave of pain shot up my arm.

"Okay, stop. Stop." Thomas kept his hand over mine. "It's definitely broken. I'll call an ambulance."

"No. I don't need an ambulance."

Thomas reached out and covered my cheek with his free hand. I could feel the heat rise in my face with his touch. "Jules, you look like a sack of flour. I'm calling an ambulance before you pass out on me. You're probably in shock."

"Shock? I'm not in shock."

"It's not up for debate. I'm calling an ambulance."

"Can't you just take me?" I asked, looking into his eyes.

"Me?"

"Yeah, it's not far. I mean, I'm sure you have other important things to do. Forget about it."

Thomas sighed. "Jules, I have nothing more important to do than to be with you, but I don't want you to go limp on me on the way there."

"I won't. I'm better now that you're here." I was. What

did that mean? I tried to stand a little. Thomas caught my free arm and helped me to my feet.

"You're sure?" He gave me a hard look.

"I'm sure." I looped my healthy arm through his and let him walk me to the front door. For the first time in the last week I felt safe and secure. I wasn't sure if it was because of having Thomas's strong arm keeping me upright or because I knew that Marco's murderer was on his way to police headquarters.

Thomas walked me outside. Three squad cars surrounded the theater with their lights flashing and their sirens blaring. Thomas showed the backup team where to go, and helped me into his squad car. The sun was shrouded by thick, gray clouds and rain leaked from the sky.

"It's going to be a wild afternoon. They're calling for thunderstorms."

On the ship I used to sneak up to the observation deck whenever storms rolled in. I loved the sound of the rumbling sky and watching lightning strike out in the middle of the sea. The air felt heavy, like I could reach out and touch each individual particle.

This morning the rain felt refreshing as it spattered on my shoulders, like it was washing away all the events of this past week.

"You're sure you're okay?" Thomas asked, clicking my seat belt on.

"I'm fine." I braced my arm to my stomach.

Thomas drove well below the speed limit to the hospital, but even so every tiny bump or pothole in the road sent shooting pain through my arm. I clenched my jaw and held my wrist tighter.

"Can you believe it was Elliot?" I asked.

Thomas turned partway to meet my eye, keeping one hand on the wheel. "I can. But I can't believe you stood me up, and went after a killer on your own."

"Huh? Stood you up?" My head must have been woozy from the pain. Nothing was making sense.

"We had an appointment this morning, remember?"

"Uh, no."

Thomas chuckled. "Remember that suspicious note shoved under your door? You left me a message last night. We were supposed to meet at Torte."

"Oh, that." I nodded.

"Yeah, that." Thomas frowned. "So quickly you forget. Anyway, when I showed up and you weren't there, your mom said you went to the theater early. And then I got your call."

We hit a bump. I winced.

"Sorry. See, I knew I should have called an ambulance."

"No, keep going. I'm fine."

He kept his gaze on the road in front of us. "You are so stubborn, you know."

I didn't know. "It's not like you haven't told me that a thousand times." I almost reached over to sock him in the arm out of habit, but then I thought about my throbbing arm and decided against it.

"I called the Professor. He said that you may be in danger and to use any force necessary to get inside the theater." Thomas let his gaze veer from the road and looked straight at me. "You can't keep doing this to me, Juliet. When I heard you were in danger, I—I . . ."

"I'm sorry," I said, really meaning it. "I called you the minute I realized it was Elliot. I didn't go there to confront him. I went to the theater to talk to Nina, and Elliot found me there." I didn't tell him about Nina and the butter. I made a promise to her, and I intended to keep it.

Thomas shook his head. "I was confident we had the case wrapped up with Sebastian. The Professor was too. Or at least I thought he was. He told me to keep an eye on Elliot. He thought Elliot was acting suspicious."

I thought back to Stephanie and Elliot coming to Torte last night. Stephanie had seemed uncomfortable. Elliot cut her off when she tried to tell me why they were there. Had Elliot been using her to get inside the bakeshop?

"He was afraid I was trying to take his job," I said to Thomas. "That's why he killed Marco too. For a stupid show."

"What?" Thomas maneuvered the car into the hospital parking lot.

"I know. Don't ask."

He pulled in front of the emergency entrance. "Wait here. I'll be right back." He returned a couple minutes later with a wheelchair and a friendly nurse.

"I don't need a wheelchair. It's just my arm," I protested.

Thomas gave the nurse a look. She nodded and proceeded to position me in the chair. She wheeled me inside without another word.

It didn't take long to confirm that my arm was broken. The X-rays showed a fracture in two places. The doctor on call splinted my arm in a temporary cast and sent me home with pain medication and a referral to an orthopedic surgeon who would properly cast it once the swelling went down in a few days.

Thomas was waiting for me when the nurse wheeled me out to the front.

"Nice accessory you have there." He pointed to the cast.

"I hear it's the new look. What do you think? How does it look?"

"You look good in anything, Jules." He moved closer and covered my swollen fingers with his hand. "Does it feel better?"

"Much better now that it's stabilized. It's going to be a bit tricky to bake like this, but I've done it before."

"About that." He placed his hand on the small of my back and directed me to the car. "This is twice now, Juliet.

Twice since you've been home that you've gotten yourself in the middle of a murder investigation."

We walked quickly through the rain to where he'd parked the squad car. One perk of being a police officer was that he didn't have to worry about getting a ticket for parking near the front door.

I started to respond, but he cut me off.

"Nope. Not now. I'm taking you straight home and putting you to bed. That's doctor's orders. We'll talk about everything else later."

"But Torte and Mom," I said.

"Already taken care of. Your mom is going to meet us at your apartment."

"The show," I blurted out. "I'm supposed to be doing the show this morning."

"That's also going to wait. The Professor and I need to sort out a bunch of details now that we have Elliot in custody. No one is filming anything today."

I didn't have the energy to protest anymore. My bed and a handful of Advil sounded like exactly what I needed at the moment.

Chapter Thirty-five

Mom was indeed waiting for us at my apartment. She took me from Thomas like I was an injured baby bird. He left to finish his work on the case with the Professor. I don't remember much of the morning, other than Mom helping to peel off my shirt and tuck me into bed.

Despite the dull pain in my arm, I slept for close to three hours. It was lunchtime when I woke up.

I stumbled out to the living room where Mom had her feet propped up on the couch and a pot of coffee and two mugs waiting on the coffee table.

"I thought I heard you stirring," she said, sitting up and pouring both of us a cup of coffee. "How are you feeling?"

"Stiff, but okay." I took the cup with my left hand. My grasp felt shaky.

"That's to be expected."

"Mom, you didn't have to hang out here while I slept. I'm okay."

"I know you're okay, but you're also my daughter. I wanted to be here. I'm glad I could be here."

"Me too. Thank you." I sipped the coffee.

"Juliet." Mom paused and clutched her hands around her mug. "I told you I would stay out of things with you and

Carlos. Thomas is a part of this too, and I have to tell you he was distraught when he left. Absolutely distraught."

"I know."

She waited, taking a long sip of coffee.

"Mom, I'm really confused. I think I may have feelings for Thomas that I didn't know were still there. But then I wonder if that's just because I'm *here*. If I weren't here, he probably wouldn't even cross my mind. It's not like I was pining away for him on the ship. Or is it because Nina showed interest in him? Then my competitive side came out and I wanted to win, not really because of him, just because of winning."

"Have you talked to him?"

"Thomas? No. What would I even say?"

"Have you ever talked about how things ended with you two? Maybe there's something from the past that needs to be resolved."

I placed my mug on the table and examined the fingers on my broken arm. They reminded me of hot dogs sticking out of buns. "Maybe."

Mom stood and cleared our coffee mugs. She returned with a steaming bowl of chicken soup and a cornbread muffin. "I thought you might be hungry."

"You know, I hadn't even thought about it but, yes, I'm starved." I blew on the soup. It was chockful of carrots, celery, onion, garlic, corn, peas, herbs, noodles, and huge chunks of rotisserie chicken. Whenever I was sick as a kid, Mom would make a pot of her homemade chicken soup. The aroma of it boiling on the stove would waft up the stairs to my room. I remember feeling better just from the smell.

The same was true today. I let the steam invade my pores. Mom and I talked through everything that happened with Elliot. I told her about Nina and the butter and Sebastian not being French.

"For someone not actively involved in the case, you certainly learned your fair share of secrets, didn't you?" She winked. "I have to admit, I think Doug will be impressed when he hears what you pulled together in terms of clues. That doesn't mean I condone you staying involved when we all told you it was too dangerous."

"My crime-solving days are behind me, Mom. Now it's going to be back to baking." I tapped my cast. "One-handed baking."

We finished our soup and Mom returned to the bakeshop. She told me to rest for the day. They had everything covered. Stephanie was doing all the prep work for Lance's party and Andy and Sterling were running the shop. Mom hadn't broken the news that Elliot was a killer to Stephanie yet. I wondered if, once Stephanie learned the truth about Elliot, she and Sterling would start speaking to one another again.

Mom promised to stop by after she closed up the shop for the evening. She and the Professor would bring me dinner. I was reminded once again just how lucky I was to have her.

I spent the rest of the afternoon reading and half dozing on the couch. Rain lashed against the window and the wind sent leaves scattering in the sky. Watching the storm roll past was strangely calming.

Someone knocked on the door around two o'clock. I flinched for a second and then remembered that Elliot was in jail. There was nothing for me to be afraid of.

It was Thomas. He stood holding a bouquet of wildflowers tied with a simple string.

"Come in." I stepped to the side.

He handed me the bouquet and then grabbed it back.

"I guess those aren't for me."

"No, I figured I could put them in water for you, what

with your arm." He shook his raincoat off and folded it over the banister in the landing to dry.

"Thank you." I closed the door behind him.

He took the flowers to the kitchen and returned with them in a Mason jar. "Where would you like them?"

"How about on the bookcase."

After placing the flowers on the shelf, he paced around the living room.

"Would you like to sit?" I patted the spot next to me on the couch.

He stopped pacing and joined me on the couch. "Listen, Juliet I—I'm not sure how to say this. I tried earlier and it didn't come out right, so I'm just going to say it and get it out there."

I waited. He fidgeted with an imaginary string on the couch and jumped back to his feet. He started pacing again.

"When I thought you were in danger—or worse—I couldn't handle it. If something happened to you I'd be devastated. We've never talked about what happened when you left, and I guess this morning made me realize that I do need to talk about it. I need to tell you how I felt. Why I did what I did."

"Thomas, it's okay, really. It's in the past. I'm over it." I wasn't sure that was entirely true.

"But I'm not, Juliet. I never have been since the day you packed up and left. I feel like I made a big mistake back then by not coming after you."

"You didn't. It's okay. I needed to go."

He stopped near the entrance to the kitchen. "If I hadn't told you I wanted to take a break, would you have left?"

I sighed. The memory of that afternoon came flooding back. Thomas, or Tommy as I used to call him back then, and I had had plans to go to college together. We were going to stay in town and attend Southern Oregon University. He had a football scholarship, and I could work in the bake-shop and go to school at the same time.

Mom cautioned me against the idea. She thought I should have the experience of going away to school, but I pushed that thought aside. Tommy and I had been dating since our sophomore year of high school and we were inseparable. He'd been my steadfast supporter after my dad died, and I couldn't even imagine leaving Ashland and him behind.

The night of our graduation party he was acting weird. When I finally called him on it, he pulled me outside. I can still remember the way the air smelled and the sound of our classmates singing karaoke in the background.

When I asked him what was bothering him, his words floored me. "I think we should take a little break, Juliet. Give each other some space over the summer. I'm going to be training hard with football camps and stuff, and I know you want to really learn the trade from your mom."

A break? I couldn't believe he was saying those words.

I don't remember what he said after that. It was all jumbled through my tears. I do remember fleeing the party and crying all the way home.

Mom comforted me. She made me hot tea and let me cry on her shoulder, but she also said, "Maybe it's for the best, Juliet. Sometimes taking a break makes everything clearer."

Nothing was clear that night. Her words stung, but after a few weeks they began making sense. Without Thomas tying me to town, I suddenly started to wonder why I wasn't leaving. I'd daydreamed for years about going off to culinary school in New York or even overseas. I'd even applied to a few schools and been accepted, but I never told Thomas. I'd hidden the acceptance letters in my dresser.

After Thomas broke up with me, I pulled them out again. Mom and I read through them after dinner one night. She couldn't hide her delight that I'd changed my mind, and she was convinced that getting out and experiencing the world firsthand was exactly what I needed. She and Dad had set aside college money from the time I was young. Not only was I accepted to a school, but I had a way to pay for it.

The summer flew by. I did work side by side with Mom at Torte, but I also spent it packing and preparing for a new adventure. When it came time to go, I left. I didn't bother to tell Thomas I had a major change of plans. He'd had a major change of heart, so we were even.

Mom had been right. Leaving for culinary school had been one of the best decisions I ever made. And until now, I never looked back.

Chapter Thirty-six

"Juliet, I just want you to know that I'm sorry. I never thought things would end up the way they did. All my football buddies said I shouldn't start college with a girlfriend. I was eighteen and so stupid. I shouldn't have listened to them." He paused, and then said in almost a whisper, "I never thought you would leave."

"Thomas. Really, trust me. It's okay. It's one of the best things that ever happened to me."

He looked injured.

"Sorry, I didn't mean it like that. I meant leaving town. If you hadn't broken up with me I probably wouldn't have left, and I needed to go. I just didn't know it. Mom did. I think you probably did too."

"Maybe I did." He sighed and came and sat next to me. "It's just nice to have you back again, Jules."

His radio crackled. "I better get this." He stepped outside.

I wondered how Mom was so astute. How did she know that I needed to hear what Thomas had just said?

Thomas opened the door halfway. "I've gotta run. I know there's more I should say." He waited for a response.

"It's fine. Go." I pointed to his radio, which sounded again.

"You promised to come see all our old friends this weekend, and I'm holding you to it," he called as he left.

I took it easy for the remainder of the day. As to whether I would uphold my promise to Thomas, I'd see how I felt in a day or two. Mom and the Professor delivered homemade pasta, salad, and bread. We popped open a bottle of wine and had a feast around my coffee table.

The Professor gently ran his hand along my splint, as I showed them to the door. "Juliet, the bard would say, 'What wound did ever heal but by degrees.'"

"We're not talking about my arm, are we?"

Mom guided him out the door. I gave her a halfhearted promise that I wouldn't come in until late the next day.

I woke before dawn as usual. Sitting around my apartment wasn't going to make my arm feel any better, so I opted to ignore Mom's pleading and head to Torte at my usual early hour.

The rain had cleared. Stars glittered in the predawn light as I walked along Main Street. Sleepy downtown Ashland looked peaceful once again.

My arm ached and my fingers felt stiff, but considering what could have happened with Elliot yesterday, I felt pretty good.

The shop was already humming when I arrived. Mom, Nina, and Linda were all gathered around the island with coffee and scones.

"There's our hero," Linda said, giving me a hug and planting a kiss on my cheek. I could feel her lipstick on my skin. "Your mama was just giving us the recap."

Nina offered me coffee. "I feel terrible. I must have missed him on my way out." She shuddered. "To think a murderer was with us all along."

"How's the arm?" Mom asked.

I touched my cast. "Not too bad."

"Right."

"Are you sure you're gonna be up for finishing the competition?" Linda scooped two heaping teaspoons of sugar in her coffee. "Philip is flying in a new host. He's really hoping that you'll consider finishing the show."

"Of course." I held my cast in my best superhero pose. "This isn't about to stop me."

"Whew." Linda stirred her coffee. "Philip will be so relieved to hear that. Y'all want to hear a little gossip? Philip and I are dating."

I wasn't sure how to respond. Mom caught my eye. She squeezed Linda's hand. "I'm so happy for you. Isn't it wonderful to find someone at our age?"

Linda beamed. "It is, honey. It sure is."

"Before you go, can I ask you one thing that's been bugging me?" I asked.

"Of course."

"Where were you during *Othello*?"

Linda looked thoughtful for a moment. *"Othello?"*

"The play. You said you were at the play the night Marco was killed, but you never went, did you?"

"Oh, the play. That's right. I forgot all about the play. No, I am guilty as charged. Philip and I snuck out for a cocktail, I sure do miss cocktail hour like we have back at home. But I was terribly jet-lagged and had to call it an early night."

"Why didn't you just say that?"

Linda's cheeks warmed with color. "I didn't want anyone to know I was out with Philip, sugar. We ladies have to keep some secrets, don't we?

"Speaking of Philip, I'm going to go meet up with him now, I'll see y'all later."

Nina swirled her coffee cup as Linda left. "I think I'd be in a fetal position on the floor if a murderer had tried to take me out."

I wasn't sure how to respond. The truth was that I had surprised myself. I was stronger than I realized. That felt good.

"Oh, I don't know," Mom said to Nina, reading my mind. "Don't underestimate your strength—either of you." She gave me a knowing look and then explained that she needed to look through the menu for Lance's bash this evening. She went to the office to make sure we were lined up with supplies, leaving Nina and me alone in the kitchen.

"I made a new pie." Nina pointed to the counter behind me. A berry pie with a lattice crust sat in the window. "No butter. This one is all mine."

"It looks great." I studied her pie. The crust was a golden brown and looked like it would flake nicely when sliced.

"We'll see." She shrugged. "I feel good about it, though. I'm really sorry I lied. I appreciate you not saying anything to the others."

"No problem. I'm glad that you're taking the risk. Mom always says that anytime we take a risk and put ourselves out there it always pays off—even if we don't realize it at the time." I thought about my conversation with Thomas yesterday. It was true.

Nina refreshed her coffee. "By the way, we tried to salvage your pie. It's in the fridge. I scraped the whipped cream off it and stuck your caramel sauce in there too. Philip is going to explain what happened to the judges. They'll all understand that they're going to be tasting day-old pies."

"Thanks." I broke off a bite of scone and popped it into my mouth. "Who is he getting to host?" I guess I shouldn't have been surprised that Philip was pushing to wrap up the show given the intensity of the last few days, but the fact that we were filming in light of Elliot's arrest seemed bizarre. I was ready to be done with *Take the Cake* for good.

"No idea."

The next few hours passed at a smooth and easy pace. I wasn't much help in the kitchen, so I mainly oversaw production on Lance's party prep. Nina and Linda both offered their skills too. Between Stephanie and Mom and Linda and Nina, onions and garlic were chopped and sautéed, bread was rising in the oven, and rows of desserts and appetizers were lined on trays and stored in the fridge.

Stephanie watched over the Bolognese sauce. I peered over her shoulder into the bubbling pot with vibrant red tomatoes. "That smells fantastic."

"It's your recipe."

"That must be why it smells so good." I laughed.

She stirred the sauce. "Is it true what they're saying about Elliot?"

"I'm afraid so."

Stephanie stopped stirring. "I can't believe it. I thought he was a nice guy."

"I don't think anyone thought it was him."

The pot erupted, sending sauce splattering on the backsplash and stove. Stephanie stirred quickly and turned the heat down. "Sterling was right all along. He's never going to let me live this down."

"Oh, I don't know. I'd give him more credit than that."

She wiped the splattered sauce with a rag. "I've been such an idiot. He's going to throw shade my way. I know it."

"Throw shade?"

"Yeah, you know, like hate on me."

"Stephanie, trust me. He's not going to 'hate on you.' I think he was probably a little jealous. You should talk to him this morning." I sounded like I knew what I was talking about when it came to love life advice. Ha!

By the time Torte opened for customers, we had the pastry case stocked and the prep for Lance's party nearly complete. Linda, Nina, and I left for the Black Swan. They carried my pie, and fussed over me the entire way up the hill.

Philip was waiting at the front of the theater when we arrived. He kissed me on both cheeks. "Here's my TV star. Thank goodness Elliot didn't go for your face."

"He tried," I said, nodding to my cast. "That's how I broke this."

"I'm terribly sorry to hear it, but this is going to make for some incredible television. I've been on the phone for the last twenty-four hours with the lawyers at the network trying to figure out how we can spin Elliot's breakdown. I haven't figured out our angle yet, but I do have a special surprise for you all. Follow me."

We followed him to the set. My pulse picked up a bit as I stepped under the lights. It was in this very spot just yesterday that I almost met an early death.

Nina grabbed my left hand and held it tight. She must have sensed my tension. I appreciated the gesture.

"They're here," Philip hollered to the stage.

The curtains parted and out stepped a devastatingly handsome man. I'd recognize his face anywhere as he was probably the most famous living chef. Philip had definitely called in a major favor to get Chef Antonio Pacco to Ashland. The world-class chef had been commissioned to bake cakes and pastries for everyone from the British royal family to Hollywood stars at Oscar parties.

Carlos idolized the Spanish chef. He had a signed copy of Antonio's cookbook next to his side of the bed. I couldn't believe he was standing in front of me. I wanted to snap a picture on my phone and send it to Carlos, but the chef stepped down from the stage and walked directly to me.

Chapter Thirty-seven

Chef Antonio caressed my left hand. "You must be Julieta." The way he pronounced my name in Spanish sounded exactly like Carlos. His Latin skin tone and dark hair reminded me of Carlos too.

"It's an honor to meet you," I replied.

He kissed my hand. "No, no, I assure you the honor is mine."

The rest of the filming was a blur. Chef Antonio and the other judges deemed my pie the best. Tomorrow we'd wrap the show with the grand finale—wedding cakes. Nina's vegan pie came in second. Sebastian rounded out third place, and Linda's ice-cream sundae pie didn't make the cut. Nina, Sebastian, and I would be competing for the prize tomorrow.

Philip pulled me aside after we were done shooting. "We all understand that you have a hardship with your injury. The judges and I have agreed to bend the rules. You are going to be allowed one assistant. In order to make it fair, the other contestants will be offered the same option, with one catch."

"What's the catch?"

"I get to decide on the assistants. I'm assigning Richard

Lord to Sebastian and pairing Linda with Nina." He gave me a sly smile. "You're welcome to choose your own assistant."

"Thanks." I left the theater and headed down the hill. I knew that Stephanie would love to help and, even though she wouldn't admit it, would also love a chance to be on TV. Plus maybe getting to meet Chef Antonio would help ease the pain of learning that her crush was a killer.

Back at Torte I noticed that Sterling had left his post up front. Andy manned the counter and coffee. There were only a few customers in the shop. Sterling and Stephanie were deep in conversation at the stove. I didn't want to interrupt them, so I ducked into the office. Mom sat at the desk, reviewing a stack of paperwork.

"What are you up to?" I asked.

She jumped in her chair and sent the paperwork scattering all over the floor. "Oh, honey, it's you."

I bent over to help her pick up the papers. "Sorry. I didn't mean to startle you, but seriously, when are you going to break down and get yourself a pair of hearing aids?"

"I'm fine." She brushed me off, and then sighed. "I was looking over our numbers again. I hope that catering Lance's party turns out okay because if we want to upgrade we're still short." She handed me a spreadsheet.

I looked it over. She was right. Even with the extra cash we'd be getting from the Pastry Channel, we still needed more money. Business had been maintaining a steady pace, but we'd hired Sterling and me, of course. With paying out extra salaries, our income was just breaking even.

"It's going to be great," I assured her. "Have you smelled it out there? I can't wait to taste everything."

Mom placed the spreadsheet back in a file. "You're right. I shouldn't worry so much. This is going to be a fun, new challenge tonight."

"That's the spirit." I checked to see if Stephanie and

Sterling were still talking. They weren't. He'd returned to the front counter. "Now I need to get baking. I have a wedding cake to create for tomorrow."

Mom clapped her hands together. "I love weddings. Let me file this stuff away, and I'll come help."

I called Stephanie over as I sketched out a design for the cake on a piece of a paper. "Did you talk to Sterling?" I asked, making sure he couldn't hear us.

A small smile spread across her face. "I did. Thanks."

"So we're all cool around here now?"

"We're cool." She nodded.

I designed my cake over a cup of coffee and was ready to start making the batter. That was a task I could complete with one hand. Stephanie would assemble and frost the cake once it had baked and cooled. I opted for a basic yellow cake with almond flavoring. We'd make French cream frosting and secure each tier with dark chocolate and seasonal berries. I'd run over to A Rose by Any Other Name later and choose some fresh flowers to adorn the top. Simple and elegant.

I creamed butter and sugar in the mixer and watched them whip together. Baking is exactly what you need at this moment, Jules, I told myself. The batter came together quickly. I handed it off to Stephanie to pour into greased pans. Soon the smell of almond cake mingled with the scent of the sauce simmering on the stove.

We spent the remainder of the afternoon putting the finishing touches on the food for Lance's party. Philip sent Nina and Sebastian to Richard Lord's kitchen in order to give us all enough space to assemble our cakes. A little after two o'clock, Lance pranced in.

He did his usual round of greetings, like he was a celebrity. In fairness, he sort of was, at least in Ashland.

"Darling, I heard the horrific news." Lance blew me air kisses. "You should have heeded my warning."

"What warning?"

"My little note. Didn't you get it?"

"I knew it was you!" I flicked him. "You know, I lost sleep that night thanks to you."

Lance looked shocked. "That can't be true. I made it crystal—crystal-clear that it was a joke. Didn't you read between the lines?"

"In case you hadn't heard, there was an actual murderer who tried to kill me."

Lance grimaced. "I may have heard something about a real killer on the prowl, but I did warn you that we were going to have a little fun."

"Fun? That's your idea of fun?"

"Testy. Testy, aren't we?" Lance assumed a namaste position. "Breathe."

I punched him.

"That's more like it."

It was hard to stay mad at him. "What did your note even mean? 'One clue, two clues, three clues, you're through.' I don't get it."

"What's to get? It was just a little fun, a touch of whimsy, a nice little rhythm to keep you on your dainty toes." He marched toward the stove. "Now let's talk about my fete tonight."

I sighed, and followed him. Stressing about Lance's misunderstood joke wasn't going to do me any good.

Stephanie removed the lid on one of the serving dishes when Lance and I approached. "We're ready."

"Divine." Lance took in a whiff of the Bolognese sauce. "I'm heading up to the house now. See you there soon. Ta-ta." He waved with his fingers and strolled out of the kitchen.

"He's insane," Stephanie said as Lance waltzed around a customer waiting for a drink and through the front door.

"Well, what do you expect? He's the artistic director of one of the most famous theater companies on the planet."

She shrugged, unimpressed. "Should I start packing everything?" Stephanie asked, returning the lid to the pot.

"Yep. Let's do it." I paused. "Well, you guys do it. I'm going to scoot over and grab some flowers for the cake."

I told Andy and Sterling to help Stephanie box up everything for Lance's party, and I flipped the sign to CLOSED on my way out.

Large black tubs with flowers sat outside A Rose by Any Other Name. I picked a handful of pale purple roses and brought them inside. I half expected to see Thomas, but his mom stood behind the counter instead.

"Juliet!" She scooted from behind the counter and embraced me. "Thomas called me last night to tell me the news. I'm so glad you're okay." She released me and stared at my cast. "Well, you know what I mean."

"I do." I smiled. I'd always gotten along well with Thomas's parents. They treated me like one of the family.

"Good choice on the roses," she said, taking them from my hand. "Would you like them in a vase?"

"No. They're for a cake actually. Do you have any of those plastic containers? And I'm hoping for some greenery too."

Thomas's mom bustled behind the counter. "I have just the thing." She placed a box with miniature plastic tubes on the counter. "They can be filled with water and pushed into the cake. That way the flowers stay fresh and the cake stays intact and untouched by the stem."

"Perfect. Any thoughts on greenery?"

"What about some of this?" She held up a handful of dried grape vine. "It's not green but it might be interesting with those roses."

"Great idea! I'll take all of it."

"How are you baking with one arm?" she asked as she wrapped everything in glossy butcher paper.

"Help. I have lots of help." I chuckled.

She handed me the neatly tied package of flowers and box of containers. "Can you get this okay? I can walk it down for you."

"No, that's not necessary. I'm fine." I started toward the door.

"Juliet," she said softly.

I paused.

"Has Thomas spoken to you?"

"About what?"

She shook her head. "Never mind. It doesn't matter. I don't want to keep you from your work. Go ahead."

I hesitated.

"Go. Go. We can talk another time."

She smiled, but behind it there was a sadness. I wanted to ask more, but could tell that she was resigned not to say more.

Sterling and Andy were loading Mom's car when I returned. They'd blocked a space in front of Torte on Main Street with two large buckets.

"Hey, boss!" Andy stacked a tub of desserts in the back. "We're almost done. What do you want us to do next?"

"Get in!" I laughed. "How are you guys getting to Lance's? Do you need a ride?"

"Nope." Andy flipped his baseball cap backward. "I've got a sweet ride tonight. Borrowing my mom's minivan. We're all going to ride out together."

"Great. If this is everything, Mom and I can take it from here. We'll meet you out there to unload." I continued inside. Stephanie had finished frosting the cake with French buttercream. I was impressed. Her lines were smooth and seamless. I cut the stems from the roses and grape vine, filled the miniature vases with water and positioned them on each tier.

I stood back after I finished to appraise my work.

"That is truly a work of art," Mom said, coming into the kitchen with her arms full of clean Torte aprons and dish-towels.

"Not too shabby, is it?"

"Honey, I think you might win. Especially if the cake tastes as good as it looks. And I know it will."

"We'll see. Fingers crossed. That cash would be nice."

"Are you ready for our next adventure?" Mom dangled her car keys. "It's showtime!"

"Too soon, Mom. Too soon."

Chapter Thirty-eight

Lance's party was a smashing success. The evening couldn't have been more beautiful. Lance had transformed his garden into something fit for Shakespeare's stage. Tea lights hung in glass jars from the branches of trees, dotting the sky like flickering fireflies. Golden-colored twinkle lights had been strung from an arbor and three canvas tents had been erected throughout the grounds. Musicians played in one of them, which was draped with greenery and fruit as it would have been in Shakespeare's time.

Tables with giant candelabras, ornate floral displays, and bottles of wine were arranged throughout the grass. Andy, Stephanie, and Sterling circulated with trays of appetizers. Mom and I set up the dinner buffet in one tent. Lance had hired an event planner who provided all the dishes and serving trays. As a bonus they were responsible for cleanup too.

People snaked through the buffet line helping themselves to servings of our pasta, bread, and salad. Mom and I stood behind the table in our crisp Torte outfits, making sure each serving dish was constantly refilled.

Once everyone had been through the buffet, Mom and

the rest of our little team dismantled it and replaced it with a tower of desserts.

"Sounds like people are lovin' the food, Mrs. C," Andy said, sliding an empty tray under the skirted buffet table.

"I hope so." Mom beamed. "You guys are doing so great. I'm proud of all of you."

Sterling tried to wrap a tattooed arm around Stephanie's shoulder. "You're not going to believe this. Even Stephanie has been smiling out there."

Stephanie threw his arm off, but Sterling was right. She looked lighter and happier than I'd seen her in a while. She left with two carafes of coffee. I pulled Sterling aside. "Is everything okay with you two?"

He watched her walk away. "I don't know. She's been acting weird for a while." His voice cracked a little. "Love sucks, you know."

"I know," I said, placing my hand on his sleeve.

"You do, don't you?" He turned to me. His blue eyes looked especially bright.

I wanted to say more, but Lance tripped into the tent. He held a wine glass in his hand and leaned in to kiss both Mom and me on the cheeks. "Wonderful, darlings. Absolutely wonderful job. You're catering all of my events from here on out. Understood?" His words slurred slightly as he spoke.

Mom nudged me under the table. Her face gave away her joy. She practically glowed.

Lance took a sip from his empty glass. "This is no good. I'm off to find another bottle of vino. Lovely work, ladies. I'll be in touch. Ta-ta."

As soon as he was out of earshot, Mom squealed and hugged me.

"He liked it."

"I hate to say it, but I told you so."

Mom bumped my hip. "You know what this means?"

"Maybe we can save up for more ovens?"

She shook her head, untied her apron, and rested her hands on the table. "I was thinking it's going to be a lot more work to try and run the bakeshop and a catering business. I don't know about you, but I'm beat."

"More work is always a good problem to have." I tried to untie my apron with one hand. Mom finished undoing it for me. "Especially in this town."

"You're right, honey, but let's call in the kids, get this packed up and hit the road."

Mom chattered all the way to my apartment about what a success the event had been and how much fun she had being out of the shop. I hadn't thought about how tied she'd been to Torte for all these years. Getting out and doing events in the community was going to be good for both of us.

I practically fell up the stairs and was asleep the moment my head hit the pillow. The next morning I felt surprisingly refreshed and eager for the final day of *Take the Cake*.

Sterling and Andy delivered my cake to the set. Nina's and Sebastian's cakes looked equally impressive. Nina had opted for a vegan chocolate torte with a white and dark chocolate ganache. Sebastian created a tiered sponge cake with fresh berries and a simple dusting of confectioners' sugar over the top.

The theater felt cool. I wasn't sure if it was because the heat hadn't been cranked on, or because of my nerves.

Nina wrapped her arms around her chest and rubbed them. "Is it freezing in here, or is it just me?"

"It's freezing," I agreed.

Chef Antonio took a bite of my cake. I held my breath. He closed his eyes as he considered the taste. Then he took another bite. Was that a good sign? I couldn't believe how nervous I was. From the way Nina bounced her foot on the floor, I guessed she was feeling the pressure too.

The other judges deliberately took their time sampling and savoring our desserts. Sebastian sighed audibly twice. It was as if they were considering each morsel on the plate in front of them.

After they finished tasting they made marks on their score sheets for design, aesthetic appeal, and technique.

"Can they just get it over with already?" Nina chomped her fingernails. "It's like they're intentionally trying to drag this out as long as they can."

"I think that's sort of the idea," I whispered. "It makes for good television."

"But it's going to give me an ulcer." She grimaced.

Chef Antonio cleared his throat and pushed up from his chair. He had a commanding stage presence. "Ladies and gentlemen, it is with great pleasure that I am to announce the winner of *Take the Cake*."

The room went silent. The tension was palpable. Who was going to win? Honestly, I had no idea.

"We were fortunate to have three incredible pastry chefs in the final competition. The judges and I would like to applaud you for your creations." Chef Antonio clapped his hands and gave us each a small bow.

The other judges smiled and clapped politely.

"Now it is time to crown our winner." Chef Antonio gave us each one final nod and pulled a piece of paper from his chef's coat. "The winner of *Take the Cake* is . . ." He paused for dramatic effect.

My heart rate sped up.

"Nina!" Chef Antonio announced. Confetti and balloons rained from the ceiling.

Nina gave me a look of disbelief and a quick hug before jumping on stage to claim her moment in the spotlight.

I felt happy for her. I knew the money would help save her bakeshop. I hoped that now she would have confidence in her vegan pastries too.

There were hugs and laughter as we all congratulated Nina. The judges had wonderful things to say about my pastries. After a celebratory round of champagne, the crew began to break down the set.

Sebastian caught me on the way out. "Thank you for not saying anything. If you make it up to Portland, stop by. I'll make sure you're taken care of."

What a wacky week it had been. A French chef who wasn't French. A vegan chef who used butter, and then of course Marco's murder and Elliot's subsequent arrest.

I watched as Chef Antonio handed Nina a check for twenty-five thousand dollars and wrapped a *Take the Cake* winner apron around her waist. As much as I would have liked the extra cash for Torte, I was glad to see her win. After the success of Lance's party last night, I knew that we could secure many more catering gigs in the future. Plus, I wouldn't have wanted all the other things that came along with winning the show—like magazine interviews, talk shows, and most importantly having to leave Ashland to film in L.A. For the moment I was happy with my mostly quiet life in Ashland. Really happy.

Recipes

Bavarian Chocolate Cake

Ingredients:
- 1 cup butter
- 2 tablespoons butter
- 2 cups sugar
- 4 eggs
- 2½ cups flour
- 8 oz. bittersweet dark chocolate
- ½ teaspoon baking soda
- 1 teaspoon salt
- 1 cup sour cream

Frosting:
- ½ cup butter
- 1 8 oz. package cream cheese
- ½ cup Dutch processed cocoa powder
- 1 teaspoon vanilla
- 2 cups powdered sugar

Directions:
Cake
In a saucepan melt 2 tablespoons of butter and dark chocolate. Cream butter and sugar together. Add eggs, vanilla, salt, and baking soda. Alternate adding flour and sour cream until all ingredients are combined.

Pour into two 8-inch round pans and bake at 350 degrees for 30–40 minutes. Allow to cool completely. Slice cakes into 4 equal layers. Assemble with chocolate cream cheese frosting (below).

Chocolate Cream Cheese Frosting
Remove butter and cream cheese from the refrigerator and bring to room temperature. Whip together with vanilla in an electric mixer. Sift in chocolate and powdered sugar. Spread thin between layers, reserving enough frosting to cover the cake. Dust with powdered sugar, or drizzle entire cake with melted dark chocolate.

Amaretto Dream Cookies

Ingredients:
    1 cup butter
    ¾ cup granulated sugar
    ¾ cup brown sugar
    2 eggs
    1 tablespoon amaretto liqueur
    1 teaspoon Mexican vanilla
    1 teaspoon almond extract
    ½ teaspoon anise extract
    1 teaspoon baking soda
    1 teaspoon baking powder
    1 teaspoon salt
    2¼ cups flour
    ½ cup sweetened coconut flakes

2 cups dark chocolate chunks
1 cup sliced almonds

Directions:

Beat butter and sugars together until creamy. Add in eggs, amaretto, vanilla, almond, and anise. Mix together until blended. Sift dry ingredients in a separate bowl; add to butter mixture and mix on low. Stir in chocolate, coconut, and almonds by hand.

Scoop 1-inch balls onto cookie sheets. Bake at 375 degrees for 10 minutes.

Futter

Nina's vegan futter can be used as a butter substitute, and is delicious spread on toast.

Ingredients:

1 cup of coconut oil
1 tablespoon olive oil
1 tablespoon canola oil
½ teaspoon apple cider vinegar
½ teaspoon sea salt
¼ teaspoon turmeric

Directions:

Whisk all ingredients together in a glass mixing bowl. Add ice and water to a larger bowl and place the bowl with the futter mixture in it. Keep whisking the futter until it turns opaque in color. Be sure not to get any water in the mixture. Once the futter is opaque store in an airtight container. Do not refrigerate.

Torte Chili

Ingredients:

    1 pound lean ground beef
    1 pound beef cut for stew
    6 whole tomatoes
    4 stalks of celery
    1 large onion
    3 cloves garlic
    1 can black beans, drained
    1 can pinto beans, drained
    1 can kidney beans, drained
    1 6 oz. can tomato paste
    ¼ cup dark beer (Mom uses a chocolate stout)
    1 cup beef stock
    ¼ cup molasses
    2 heaping tablespoons chili powder
    2 teaspoons cumin
    A bunch of fresh cilantro
    1 teaspoon salt
    1 teaspoon pepper
    Olive oil

Directions:

Brown ground beef and stew meat. Drain fat and set aside. Bring a large pot of water to boil. Gently slice an *X* into the tomato skins and place in boiling water. Remove tomatoes from water when the skin starts to peel. The skins will easily come off. Dice and set aside.

Add a large glug of olive oil to a stockpot, and turn burner onto medium-low. Wash cilantro. Cut and dice the stalks. Reserve the cilantro leaves for later. Chop onion, celery, and garlic and sauté with the cilantro stalks until the onions become translucent. Add tomatoes, beans, and beef. Mix well, then add all remaining ingredients. Mom usually finishes off the rest of the beer while she's cooking. Cover with a lid, turn heat to low, and simmer for 3 to 4 hours.

Garnish chili with your favorite toppings. Mom usually puts out: sour cream, shredded cheese, green onions, olives, tortilla chips, peppers, salsa, and fresh cilantro.

Luscious Linda's Banana Cream Pudding

Ingredients:
   4–5 bananas
   1 cup sugar
   1 cup half-and-half
   1 cup 2 % milk
   3 eggs
   2 tablespoons cornstarch
   1 teaspoon vanilla
   Pinch of salt
   Shortbread cookies or Nilla Wafers (your choice)
   Whipping cream

Directions:
Beat eggs and sugar together. In a saucepan add milk, half-and-half, vanilla, salt, and cornstarch. Stir in eggs and sugar and whisk together. Bring to a gentle rolling boil. Stir continually until thickened (approximately 5 minutes). Remove from heat and allow to cool.

Slice bananas. Layer in a clear glass bowl starting with cookies, bananas, pudding. Repeat. Top with whipped cream.

Pork, Apple, and Fontina Sandwiches

Ingredients:
4 baguettes of your favorite bakery bread (or homemade)
1 pork roast
1 large onion
1 cup apple cider vinegar
2 cups apple cider
6 apples (Jules uses Oregon Gala apples)
Fontina cheese
Fresh arugula
Olive oil
Salt and pepper

Directions:
Prepare pulled pork in advance. Massage pork roast with olive oil, salt and pepper. Place in Crock-Pot. Wash and rough-cut 5 apples and onion, and add to Crock-Pot. Pour apple cider and apple cider vinegar over roast and cook on low for 6 to 8 hours, or until internal temperature reaches 150 degrees. Check roast to make sure it's not drying out. Add more apple cider if necessary. Shred pork once it has cooled and refrigerate overnight.

To assemble sandwiches, cut the baguettes and brush with olive oil. Peel and thinly slice apple. Layer shredded pork, apple slices, Fontina cheese, and arugula. Season with a shake of salt and pepper and serve cold.

Pumpkin Cream Latte

Andy's latest espresso mixology is the perfect accompaniment to a crisp fall morning, or can be served cold over ice.

Ingredients:
  Good quality espresso (Jules and Mom serve Stump-
    town at Torte, but are always open to trying new
    blends)
  2 % milk
  2 tablespoons fresh pumpkin purée
  1 heaping teaspoon brown sugar
  ½ teaspoon nutmeg
  ½ teaspoon cinnamon
  ¼ teaspoon cloves
  Whipping cream

Directions:
Prepare espresso and steam milk. Mix pumpkin, sugar, and
spices together in the bottom of your favorite coffee mug.
Once milk is steamed add to pumpkin purée and stir together. Pour over espresso. Top with whipping cream and
a dusting of cinnamon.

Read on for an excerpt from the next installment in
Ellie Alexander's Bakeshop mystery series

On Thin Icing

Available soon from St. Martin's Paperbacks!

Chapter One

They say that you can't go home again. I'm not sure that's true. I'd been home for almost six months, and found myself settling back into a comfortable and familiar pace.

Working at our family bakeshop, Torte, had helped ease the sting of leaving my husband and the life I'd known behind. I didn't have any answers about what was next for Carlos and me, and the longer I was home the less it seemed to matter. Ashland, Oregon, my welcoming hometown, was the perfect place to mend. Being surrounded by longtime friends and family for the past few months had made me realize that while my heart may have been a bit broken, I wasn't. It was an important distinction, and hopefully a sign that I'd made the right decision.

I'd been so consumed with baking and growing our catering business at Torte that I hadn't had much time to reflect. Now that winter had closed in and the famed Oregon Shakespeare Festival had closed its doors for the season, it was as if the entire town was shuttered in as well. I'd forgotten how quiet Ashland becomes in January—and how cold!

After spending ten years working as a pastry chef for a cruise line, I hadn't experienced a winter like this in a long time. My winters had been spent island hopping in the

Caribbean and sailing in the Mediterranean, where the sun sparkled on warm waters despite the fact that the calendar read January.

January in Ashland was a different story. The temperature had been dropping steadily since October. Fall's cool crisp mornings felt practically balmy compared to icy layers of frost that coated the ground. I'd invested in a new collection of sweaters and wool socks. Despite pulling on heavy layers before leaving my apartment, I still shivered on my short walk to Torte.

Torte is located in the heart of downtown. The bakeshop sits in the middle of the plaza, nestled between shops and restaurants and with a front-row view of the bubbling Lithia fountains across the street. It's a prime location for grabbing a pre-theater snack or a catching up on the latest gossip. Helen, my mom, had been running the bustling bakery solo since my dad died and I took off to see the world. Her delectable handcrafted pastries are legendary with locals and anyone passing through town. Not only do people find comfort in her sweet creations, they also seek her out for advice and her kind listening ear. Everyone who walks through Torte's front door is treated like family. That's the secret to Torte's longevity. Well that, and the binder of recipes passed down through generations of my family that mom keeps locked in the office.

Keeping baker's hours means that I'm always awake long before anyone else. This morning as I hurried through a biting wind to Torte, the streets felt especially dark and gloomy. I quickly unlocked the front door, flipped on the lights, and cranked on the heat.

A large chalkboard on the far wall displayed a Shakespearean quote reading: *In winter with warm tears I will melt the snow, and keep eternal spring-time on thy face.*

My dad started the tradition of a revolving quote when I was a kid. He loved everything Shakespearean, hence why he insisted on naming me Juliet. I prefer Jules. There's way too much pressure attached to having a name like Juliet. But each time I glanced at the chalkboard, I smiled at the memory of my dad's sparkling eyes and quick wit.

Torte's front windows had frosted overnight. I rubbed my hands together for friction and made my way to the kitchen. The bakeshop is divided into two sections. Customers can nosh on a pastry or linger over an espresso at one of the tables or booths in the front. A long counter and coffee bar separates the dining space from the kitchen. It gives the bakery an open feel and allows guests to watch all of the action in the back.

I grabbed an apron from the rack and tied it around my waist. Our red aprons, with blue stitching and a chocolate Torte logo in the center, are as close as it gets to a uniform around here. Everyone on staff wears one of the crisp aprons that match Torte's teal and cranberry colored walls.

My first task of the day was getting the oven up to temp. We'd been down an oven for a while. Managing with one oven was doable during the slow season, but Mom and I had been tucking cash away in hopes of upgrading our equipment before things got busy again. I turned the oven on high, and leafed through the stack of special orders waiting on the kitchen island.

On today's agenda were two birthday cakes, a pastry order for the theater, and our normal bread deliveries. The tightknit business community in Ashland diligently supported and promoted each other, especially in the off-season. Wholesaling our bread to local restaurants and shops definitely helped with cash flow.

I washed my hands with honey lavender soap and got to work on the bread. There's something so therapeutic about the breadmaking process. From watching the yeast rise to kneading the dough, I allowed my thoughts to wander as I went through the familiar steps. Some of my colleagues in culinary school complained when they had to work early shifts. I remember one aspiring chef said that she always felt lonely in an empty kitchen. Not me. I like working in a quiet space with nothing more than the hum of a mixer and the scent of sourdough bread baking around me. That's not to say that I don't enjoy a vibrant kitchen with bodies squeezing past each other and a counter chock-full of delectable treats. I guess, like so many things in life, it was finding the balance between solicitude and socialization that counted.

With the first batch of bread rising, I quickly sketched out a menu for the day. Once the team arrived everyone would have an assignment. The cold weather had our customers hungry for hearty breakfast options. I'd have Stephanie, one of the college students I'd been mentoring, bake chocolate, cinnamon, and nut muffins. Mom could handle stocking the rest of the pastry case with an assortment of sweet and savory delicacies. That would give me time to focus on the special orders.

As I finished writing the menu and task list on the whiteboard, the front door jingled and Andy walked in. He wore a puffy orange parka and knit stocking cap. His shaggy sandy hair stuck out from beneath the cap. "Morning, boss," he called, rubbing his arms. "Man, it's cold out there."

Andy had been working for Mom since he was in high school. Now he attends Southern Oregon University part-time, and runs Torte's espresso bar whenever he's not studying. He's genius when it comes to crafting coffee drinks. His creative flavor combinations have earned him a loyal following. There's always a line for one of Andy's expertly pulled shots or specialty lattes. He has an innate talent, and I've enjoyed watching him thrive.

He shrugged off his parka, stored it and his backpack behind the counter, and tied on an apron. Without missing a beat, he revved up the espresso machine. "You want to try something new?" he asked, pulling a canister of beans from underneath the bar.

"I'll love anything you want to make me," I said as I roughed out a sketch for one of the birthday cakes. The order form read: Anything chocolate. Talk about a dream client. Chocolate was wide open for interpretation. Since this was for an adult birthday, I thought it would be fun to work some childhood nostalgia ingredients into the cake. I'd make an Oreo mousse cake and slice it into four layers. Then I planned to fill each layer with chocolate mousse and fresh berries. I would top it with more berries, Oreos, and gold dust. It should give the cake a whimsical yet elegant touch.

While I whipped egg yolks and sugar in the mixer for the mousse, Andy plugged his phone into our sound system and blasted some tunes. I watched as he swirled steaming milk to the beat of the music.

Mom and Stephanie arrived a few minutes later. Stephanie had originally been hired to help at the front counter, but her more introverted personality—and the fact that she could really bake—made her a much better match for the kitchen. When I first met her, I thought she was a bit sullen. I've come to realize that there's a kind and caring young woman underneath the layers of black eyeliner, purple hair, and her standoffish attitude. Mentoring Stephanie in the bakery had been one of the highlights of the last few months. She was a quick study and had an eye for design.

"Morning, everyone," Mom yelled over the music. She really needs hearing aids. "It's already hopping in here this morning."

I signaled for Andy to turn down the music. He nodded and turned the volume down.

Mom patted Andy on the shoulder in silent thanks as she walked toward the rack of aprons.

"You know it, Mrs. C. It's Monday. That means we crank up the tunes and the grinds." Andy grinned and drizzled white chocolate sauce over a steaming latte. "Order up, boss," he said to me.

"What is it?" I asked, grabbing the coffee from the front counter.

"I'm thinking of calling it a snowflake latte." He reached under the bar and pulled out a notebook that he uses to track coffee recipes and ratios of milk to espresso. "It's an almond latte with a little touch of white chocolate and whipped cream. Give it a try. I'm hoping it's not too sweet. It's my gift to the snow gods. We need some fresh powder on Mt. Ashland. I'm dying to hit the slopes."

The coffee smelled heavenly. I caught a whiff of almond as I took a sip. The creamy latte was perfectly balanced with just the right touch of sweetness. Andy had succeeded once again. We make all of our sauces and syrups at Torte. Our white chocolate sauce is a customer favorite. It's much richer in flavor and texture than mass manufactured sauces. I'm not a fan of sugary coffee drinks. Andy knew exactly how to add a splash of sweetness without letting the sugar overpower the drink.

"This is delicious." I held the mug up in a toast. "It's like winter in a cup. I think the snow gods will love it."

"That's what I was going for, boss." His cheeks reddened. "Anyone else want to give my snowflake latte a try?"

Mom and Stephanie raised their hands in unison. Andy laughed and started steaming more milk. I knew he appreciated the praise. It was well-deserved. I could drink Andy's lattes all day. That is until I started to shake from too much caffeine intake.

"This one needs to go up on the special board today," I said, cradling the warm mug in my hands.

Stephanie tucked her hair behind her ears. "What do you want me to do first, Jules?" She normally wears her dark hair with streaks of purple, but today it was dyed in a shockingly bright violet. The look was startling.

"You changed your hair," I noted.

She shrugged. "Yeah, I was tired of the black."

"It matches your gorgeous eyes," Mom said, returning to the kitchen and handing Stephanie a snowflake latte.

"Thanks." Stephanie looked at her feet as she spoke. She was dressed in all black, quite the contrast from her cheery red apron and purple hair.

"Can you start on the muffins?" I asked, pointing to the whiteboard. "We're going to need an extra dozen of each flavor for Lance's order."

Stephanie sipped her latte and studied the board. "What are you thinking for the cinnamon muffins?"

One of the many things that I appreciated about Stephanie was her willingness to ask questions. When I worked on the cruise line one of my biggest pet peeves with apprentice chefs was that they were afraid to ask questions. How are you going to learn if you don't ask? I'd much rather have a chef-in-training ask too many questions versus doing it wrong and having to dump an entire batch of pastries in the trash.

"What do you think?" I threw it back at her. "We could do cinnamon chips or a cinnamon crumble on the top."

"I'll do both," she said.

"Works for me." I returned to the mixer.

Mom squeezed between me and the butcher block island that sits in the middle of the industrial kitchen. She's shorter than me by a few inches. I inherited my height and lean frame from my dad. Even in her clogs, she has to stand on her toes to meet my eyes. "I see you've relegated me to pastry case duty." She winked.

"That's not such a bad job, is it?" I whipped the yolks and sugar together until the mixture turned into a creamy lemon color. One of the things I've been trying to teach Stephanie is that each step matters when it comes to baking. The most common mistake novice bakers make is to dump all the ingredients in at once. For a light and airy cake, it's imperative that the egg yolks and sugar are slightly thickened before incorporating the chocolate.

Mom rolled up her sleeves. She cubed butter and measured brown sugar into a large mixing bowl. She chatted with Stephanie and Andy about their classes as she creamed cookie batter together by hand. Baking was in her DNA. Despite the fact that Torte has two industrial mixers, Mom was old-school when it came to making cookie dough. She prefers her large stainless steel bowl and wooden spoon.

"Mom, you know we have an industrial mixer, right?"

"How do you think I stay so fit?" She flexed her arm and raised the wooden spoon. "Who needs a mixer when I have muscles like these?"

I worried that years of physical labor were taking their toll on her. Her pace had started to slow a bit, but not her enthusiasm, so I let it go.

I filled the double broiler with an inch of water and placed it on the stove. Then I measured dark chocolate chunks. I would melt the chocolate on a low boil and slowly incorporate it with the eggs and sugar. Soon the entire kitchen became infused with the delightful smell of cinnamon muffins baking in the oven, steaming coffee, and chocolate. I couldn't resist swiping a taste of the warm chocolate as it turned fluid in the pan.

"Where's Sterling?" Mom asked, glancing at the clock on the wall. It was almost six. In a few minutes Torte would be bustling with locals stopping by for a coffee and pastry on their way to work.

"He said he'd be here by 7:00," I replied, wiping chocolate from my fingers. "He stayed late last night." Sterling was our newest staff member. Like me, he thought Ashland would be a temporary resting place, but had come to love our quirky small town. His piercing blue eyes, tattoos, and skater style had earned him quite the following amongst teenage girls. I wanted to tell them that they were wasting their time, while they stood in line, giggling and ordering hot chocolates. Sterling was into Stephanie. I wasn't sure where she stood. The chemistry between them was definitely palpable, but as far as I could tell that was where it ended.

Sterling and Andy made a dream team in the front. Their personalities complemented one another. Andy with his boyish all-American good looks, and knowledge of local sports, chatted up customers with easy banter. Sterling had a sexy edginess that customers responded to. He discussed indie bands and dabbled in writing poetry. He reminded me of a young Johnny Depp.

After the holidays, Sterling asked me if I'd be willing to give him cooking lessons in the evenings. He didn't think baking was his style, but he was interested in learning his way around the kitchen. It was great timing for me, since Torte's catering business had been steadily increasing. Having an extra hand to help prep would be huge.

By the time Sterling arrived, Andy had sold a dozen snowflake lattes and packaged up pastries to go for our regular clients. A handful of locals occupied the tables in the front, but we were nowhere near as busy as we are in the summer months. I arranged the theater pastry order in a large white box with the Torte logo stamped on the side. Lance, the artistic director for the Oregon Shakespeare Festival, was hosting a breakfast for some local board members and requested pastries to be delivered before eight.

Mom and Stephanie had things under control in the kitchen. My chocolate mousse was cooling on the counter, so I zipped up my coat and balanced the box of pastries. "I'm off to deliver these to Lance," I called as I pushed open the front door.

A blast of cold air assaulted my face. *Hurry, Jules,* I thought as I quickened my pace. It's freezing. Little did I know things were about to get much, much colder.

Chapter Two

The Oregon Shakespeare Festival complex is just up the hill from Torte. This morning I opted to cut through Lithia Park and take the Shakespeare stairs. The staircase leads directly from the park's expansive grounds up through the tree line to OSF's theaters.

The park sat empty. Even the birds had flown south in search of warmer skies. I took the steps two at a time, as my breath frosted in front of my face.

Although the theater was shuttered, OSF's senior staff works year round. It was odd to see "the bricks" (as locals refer to the brick plaza in front of the theater) deserted. The marquee read: Thanks For Another Stunning Season! See Us Again In February When We Open With *Three Amigos*.

I smiled to myself as I hurried past. People tend to associate OSF solely with Shakespeare. The company is known for producing the Bard's works, but it also stages a variety of modern plays and even the occasional musical. Theater lovers from around the world return season after season for OSF's offerings.

Lance's office is located in the Bowmer Theater. I knew the way. Lance and I became friends last summer. He drives me crazy with his insistence that I should be on stage. Somehow word got out—that tends to happen in Ashland—that I'd dabbled in theater when I was younger. Lance had made it his personal mission to convince me that I should return. It wasn't going to happen. I had no interest in being on stage. Pastry was my medium.

I passed the dark stage. A single lamp with a glowing yellow bulb stood like a beacon in the otherwise vacant theater. It cast a ghostly shadow on the empty stadium seats. Lance had told me the practice of leaving a light on the stage was an old theater superstition. It gave me the creeps, I hurried past and walked down the back stairs to Lance's office. Balancing the box in one arm, I knocked on his door. "Lance, it's Jules."

"Juliet, darling, *entrez. Entrez*," Lance said, waving me in with one hand and studying me through a pair of black wire-rimmed glasses that rested on the tip of his nose.

Lance's office was like a miniature museum showcasing the theater's success. Playbills and awards lined the walls. A stack of scripts sat in a pile on his desk. Against the far wall there was a couch with purple, gold and black pillows. Behind the desk, a wall of windows looked out onto the complex and the dreary winter sky.

He removed his reading glass and jumped to his feet when I came in. "Darling, let me take that." He placed the pastry box on his desk and kissed me on both cheeks. "Look at you, with nice rosy cheeks. I do believe that winter is becoming on you."

"Stop, Lance." I rolled my eyes, but my hand went to my ponytail. It's my typical style for working in the bakery. I can't stand it when hair gets in my eyes.

"What is it going to take to get it through that beautiful skull of yours that my makeup artists would die to work on your pristine palate?"

I ignored his comment.

He opened the box and waved his hands in front of his face. "As always your pastries look equally smashing."

Lance had a flair for the dramatic. He was perfectly cast as artistic director for the award-winning theater. He looked the part, too. Today he wore a pair of tapered jeans, a black turtleneck, purple scarf, and expensive shoes. "I'm so glad you stopped by," he said taking a cheese blintz from the box and returning to his seat. "I have a favor to ask."

I handed him a stack of paper napkins. "Does this involve me and one of your productions? Because you know that my answer is going to be no."

"One day, darling. One day, I'll convince you. I'm good at getting what I want." He bit into the blintz for effect. Dabbing his chin with a napkin, he continued. "But no, this favor involves your culinary prowess."

"Okay, I like the sound of that."

"Have a seat." He motioned to the empty chair in front of his desk.

I sat and waited for him to continue. His large mahogany desk looked as if it had been built to intimidate. I could imagine a new actor gulping down fear as he waited for an audience with Lance. I could also imagine Lance flashing his signature Cheshire grin and enjoying every minute of watching an aspiring actor sweat.

"You may have heard that our quarterly board meeting is coming up." Lance set the blintz on a napkin. "Usually we have it here in town, but I want to do something more extravagant this year, so I'm hosting a weekend retreat for the entire executive board at Lake of the Woods Lodge next weekend."

"Okay." I glanced out the window. It looked like it was starting to rain.

Lance rifled through a stack of scripts. He removed a file folder and slid it across the desk to me. "I want *you* to cater the weekend. The theme is 'cozy cabin.' I've rented out the lodge for the entire weekend. I'm pulling out all the stops. I want the board to feel pampered and dazzled by the food. We have a huge giving campaign that we're going to kick off next month, and I need them feeling ready to get out there and raise new funds and friends for the theater."

I opened the file folder. It contained an agenda for the board retreat which involved breakfast, lunch, dinner and snacks for forty people over the course of a three-day weekend. Wow. Even though I'd served tens, if not hundreds, of thousands of guests while working on the cruise ship, I'd specialized in pastry and I had a team of sous chefs and dishwashers. An entire weekend of meals would definitely be a new challenge.

This is what you've been hoping for, Jules, I told myself as I returned the agenda to the file folder. "Thanks for thinking of us," I said to Lance. "There's not a lot of time to prepare. Your event is in just over a week. I'll have to call our suppliers right away and make sure they have enough in stock."

He waved me off. "Darling, you're the best chef in town, you'll figure it out I'm sure. That Sunday supper last weekend was like stepping back in time or into the pages of a storybook. I know you won't disappoint."

Mom and I had started hosting Sunday suppers at Torte. For twenty dollars, diners were treated to an appetizer, entree, and a signature Torte dessert. Each course was served family-style in the dining room. We pushed tables together to make an inviting space for everyone to gather. The concept had been a hit with locals. The last two suppers had sold out.

Without asking whether or not I was going to take the job, Lance launched into a list of details. "I'll need you to coordinate with my new assistant Whitney. She'll order anything you need. I've already tasked her with ordering extra booze. I want the wine to flow freely, if you know what I mean."

I started to ask for clarification about the menu. Lance pushed to his feet. "Must run, darling." He kissed me on both cheeks. "Talk to Whitney. I'll see you at the lodge next weekend."

Before I could say anything else, he snatched the box of pastries from his desk and walked away.

I sat for a moment, lost in thought. Catering OSF's executive board retreat might push me out of my comfort zone, but it was exactly what Torte needed.

What a welcome surprise, I thought as I hurried back through an icy rain to the bakeshop. I couldn't wait to tell Mom and the rest of the team. A new corporate account would certainly give our bottom line an extra boost.

Torte was humming when I returned. The heat from the oven had significantly raised the temperature. The ice on the windows had begun to melt, and dripped down the single glass panes. I needed to remind Stephanie to wipe them down soon.

"Hey Jules, you look excited," Sterling said, as I stepped inside and shrugged off my coat. He wore a gray hoodie that matched the sky outside.

"I am." I grinned, and glanced around the bakeshop. A couple sat at one of the booths in front of the windows, and two of the bistro tables were taken. Otherwise the shop was quiet. "You two want to take a quick break, and come hear my news?" I said to Sterling and Andy.

They agreed and followed me into the kitchen. Stephanie stopped the blender, and Mom turned the sauce she was simmering on the stove to low. "Come see the gig we just landed, you guys," I said, placing Lance's agenda on the island.

Andy snagged a cinnamon muffin from the cooling rack.

He ate non-stop. Playing football for Southern Oregon University had him burning calories around the clock. *No wonder he likes working here*, I thought, as he devoured the muffin in two bites and grabbed another. Mom has always had an "eat whatever you want policy" for staff. We used to joke on the ship that you could tell who the newbie baker was by how much they ate. Once you've been around a bakeshop for a while, the lure of consuming every tasty morsel in front of you tends to dissipate. That wasn't the case for Andy.

"Lance wants us to cater an executive retreat at Lake of the Woods next weekend," I said, passing around the file.

Mom dusted her hands on her apron. Her walnut eyes lit up as she read the agenda. "This is great news, honey!" She paused and looked concerned. "But this is a big order. You can't do it yourself."

I nodded. "It's a big order. It'll mean preparing every meal for all forty guests."

"And more dough, right, boss?" Andy said through a mouthful of muffin.

"Right, and I have a plan." I turned to Sterling. He stood next to Stephanie, their arms almost touching. "I'm wondering if you want to be my sous chef for the weekend?"

Sterling took a step back. "Sure. I can do that."

"Perfect!" Mom clapped. "Andy, Stephanie and I will keep Torte in tip-top shape while you two are away."

"You better." I pointed my index finger at her.

She grabbed a dishtowel and flicked me with it. "If our fearless captain here will let us little people help, who has suggestions for the menu?"

I found a pad of paper in the top drawer by the whiteboard and started taking notes as everyone started talking at one. Mom is a genius at collaboration. I loved that she had instilled that in our young staff. It was something I tried to model too.

"Breakfast is easy," Andy said. "You guys can just do all our standard morning pastries, right?"

"Yes, but you know Lance. His exact words were that he wants us to *dazzle* the board members with our food." I mimicked Lance's dramatic speech pattern.

"But he wants comfort food?" Sterling asked. "Dazzling and comfort don't exactly go together."

Mom picked up the dishtowel again and flung it at him. "Sterling, how can you say that? Isn't dazzling comfort exactly what we make here at Torte?"

Sterling held up the towel in surrender. "You've got me there, Helen."

"I heard good things about your lasagna last weekend," Stephanie said.

"Okay," I scratched notes on the paper. "We start with morning pastries. Maybe one day we can do a warm egg dish. Lunch should be easy. We can do sandwiches on homemade bread."

"And soup," Mom said.

"Yes, and definitely soup." I made a note, as we mapped out a menu and supply list.

I spent the remainder of the morning feeling the familiar jitter of a new challenge. I hadn't been to Lake of the Woods since I was a kid. Spending the weekend at a remote high mountain lodge and putting my culinary skills to the test sounded perfect.

Only I would soon come to learn that much more than pastry was on the menu for the weekend.